ROSE BOUND

THE ROSE AND KING SERIES
BOOK ONE

J.J. MARSHALL
J.R. WALDEN

WARNING

The following story has explicit language, graphic violence and adult sexual content. Reader Discretion is advised.

To Gavin Jax.

ACKNOWLEDGMENTS

A big thank you to Jessica Boaden for being our Junior developmental editor on this gem, without her help Rose Bound wouldn't be as polished as it is today.

To our developmental editor, Maggie, from Ms. K Edits for making sure that we have provided you all with the best story possible.

To our proofreader, Morgan Maynard and to our beta readers, Mercedes Gomez, Nicola Dooley, Maria Shanklin-Fleming for being with us on this crazy ride!

And finally, thank you to Moorbooks Designs for our stunning cover!

TERMS

Fangbanger: derogatory term for vampire

Moon juice: insult to werewolf; watery diarrhea discharge that can happen when a werewolf changes during the full moon.

Moon child: Name used by vampires for werewolves; in reference to the goddess Artemis.

Bloodwhore: a term used by vampires for humans who willingly give blood with sexual favors, oftentimes these humans live in bordellos.

Ripper: a vampire that cannot control their blood lust. Oftentimes, resulting in serial killings.

New Cresshill

Farm Land

Deadpark Ruins

Forest of
Knowing

Underground Es

Lake
Diamond
atum
Daimis
Northpass
Bloodworth
Sables
Caradar Hill
tales
N
ne
E
se
S
sw
W
nw

PART I

EXORDIUM

LEGENDS

*C*eleste had been warned about the things that lurked under the cover of darkness; a time when chaos ran free and the god, Limos, had dominion over the realm. But the shadows within her sang, luring her to play with the Night.

She shared a cottage- a small cobblestone ramshack with just enough room for the three of them- with her two sisters, Artemis and Dia. It sat on the edge of the Dead Run River, far away from the Night King and his revelry.

Celeste, eldest of the three, looked to her left to where her younger sisters slept soundlessly in their shared bed. Artemis's white-blonde curls splayed out like a halo around her pillow and cold blue eyes resting, and Dia whose caramel locks fell around her face, shielding her warm complexion and cheeks flushed with sleep. Celeste released a sigh, her attention drifting to the open window and to the alluring chaos beyond its panes. Phantom kisses peppered her jawline, carried on the breeze.

Come to me, it sang. *Come and join the darkness.* And oh, how she wanted to join the darkness, nestle up with him and rule the realm. Celeste closed her eyes, relishing the cool wisps on her skin before rising from the bed and tiptoeing to the open window.

Their bedroom window wasn't high up, so the fall was mere feet to the ground, just enough to tousle her hair and wrinkle her raven-colored nightgown, but she didn't mind. She had a man to meet. A *king*. And on this particular night, Celeste knew he was going to ask her something that would forever change her world.

Before trudging off, she looked over her shoulder to the window where her sisters slept. A tinge of sadness clouded her eyes. The Forest of Knowing wasn't a far walk from her home, and soon, she'd meet Limos, the prince of destruction, and taste his sweet darkness. Her lips tingled at the thought and then, without another glance back, she set out into the night.

✦

ARTEMIS FELT THE SUDDEN ABSENCE OF HER SISTER'S warmth. She shivered, her eyelids fluttering open, only to find an empty space where Celeste should have been. The air nipped at her neck as she slowly arose, her eyes falling on the window where she watched Celeste push off the window ledge. The air froze in her lungs, choking her, sending Artemis into a coughing fit. She turned, nudging Dia from her slumber.

"Dia, sistermine, wake up!" she whispered hastily. Dia groaned, her caramel curls shifting into her face.

"I'll get up at morn's light." She yawned, pulling the duvet tighter around her.

"Nay!" Artemis growled, yanking the cover away from her sister. "Celeste has leaped from the window! She's going to see Limos and we have to go after her! We have to stop her before he brings her harm!"

"Then she got what was coming to her," Dia hissed, "We were told not to wander the darkness, but Celeste turned a deaf ear! I'm going back to sleep. If she is still gone on the morrow, then I'll set out. 'Til then, sistermine, good eve."

Artemis gnashed her teeth, set her jaw and pushed from the bed. She would bring her sister back, with or without Dia at her side. Her feet padded against the cool wooden floor toward the window, and placing her palms against the sill, she pushed herself up and over.

Come to the forest, a voice called to her. *I love you, Artemis.* She gulped.

Limos. Her heart jumped within her chest as she sucked in a breath and sighed. She was off to find her sister and to see the boy that had captured her heart.

*

Dia heard Artemis land in the grass outside the window. Her body thudded upon impact, followed by a string of curses. With a frustrated grunt, Dia sat upright in the bed, rubbing the sleep from her eyes. Artemis was right. They couldn't let Celeste roam Elirion by herself, especially at night with chaos running amuck. If something happened to either one of them... No. She couldn't think like that.

Throwing back the covers, Dia swung her legs over the

edge of the bed and placed her feet against the chill wooden floorboards. She called to the light within her, watching as golden tendrils streamed from her fingers, illuminating their bedroom enough for her to find her boots. With a flick of her finger, the light took the shape of a glowing orb, freeing her hand as it hung in midair. Dia pulled on black leather boots and slowly crept to the front door, unlatching the lock from its place, she pulled it open, her light trailing behind her. She reached out to her light, calling it back to her before cupping it gently and using it to illuminate the dirt path before her. Dia groaned inwardly and set out to seek chaos.

❦

A canopy of leaves loomed over Celeste as she walked the silent forest floor. She'd heard rumors that the trees in this particular forest knew secrets and held magic, but she'd yet to experience it.

The smell of rain permeated the air, invigorating all of her senses. She stopped, closed her eyes and just listened to the silence. Maybe then, the trees would speak to her.

"My sweet." Limos's sultry voice greeted her as he materialized from the shadows. He shimmered in her vision, dressed from head to toe in glittering black that reminded her of a liquid night.

"I came," she breathed, tensing as he took a step toward her. His raven hair curled around pointed ears beneath his black top hat, its brim casting a shadow that hid his eyes from her view. Eyes that would tell his intentions and make her privy to his secrets. She saw his lips quirk up, a sly smirk crawling across his immortal face.

"You did," he replied, taking another step forward before reaching for her hand. "Will you join me?" She gulped; her eyes wide.

"W-what?"

"In ruling the night? In bringing chaos to a forefront? Will you join me in forever?" he asked. A rustle to the right snapped Celeste's attention back to her surroundings.

"Do not fear, nothing here will hurt you," Limos said. But the truth was, she did fear. She was afraid of everything the King of the Night stood for, yet she yearned for it all the same.

"No!" A cry pierced the night, crashing footsteps in its wake. Artemis screamed, hurling herself from the trees. "You will not touch her!" A touch from the king would seal the deal, would pull the deceit and darkness inside of her, out. She would be transformed into a dark queen. Celeste needed time to think. Time to get her affairs in order and make sure that her sisters were taken care of, if she accepted his offer, that was.

"Go home, Artemis," Celeste snarled. But Artemis continued to barrel toward them. Her milky skin began to glow, shrouded in moonlight. Artemis dropped to all fours, fur springing where bare flesh had once been. Bones cracked, cloth tore. Screams ripped from her throat in agony, and then silence consumed the trio. Standing before Celeste and Limos was a wolf, whiter than the moon itself.

Celeste's hand covered her mouth, choking back the scream that threatened to erupt. The wolf's lips curled back in a snarl before she launched at the King of Chaos.

CELESTE WATCHED IN HORROR AS HER SISTER LUNGED AT Limos, baring her razor-sharp teeth, snapping at his neck. She knew that if her sister got a hold of the god, she would die. Immortals didn't die, but Artemis was very much a mortal... or was she?

Limos ducked and dodged each snap of the wolf's

teeth, keeping only a breath away, his smirk never leaving his lips.

"Come and get me, sweet puppy," the god taunted before he leaped backwards into the trees, hands still neatly tucked into his pockets. Shadows curled around Celeste.

You will be mine, they sang. *And then, you will truly die.*

Celeste gasped, mesmerized by the shadows dancing around her. She felt the familiar allure take hold, a taste of danger evolving on her tongue. Slowly, she called the darkness within her to the surface. Power coursed through her veins, faster than the speed of light. Celeste trembled, her breath leaving her lungs as her head tilted back. She opened her mouth to scream, but no sound escaped her parted lips. Every nerve in her body burned. Fangs sprang where canine teeth had once been, oozing with venom down her chin. Her heart slowed... slowed... until it hardly beat. Celeste's vision clouded, a thirst for bloodshed calling her, stronger than her infatuation for Limos, stronger than her need to breathe.

She needed to kill.

✦

SNARLS ECHOED THROUGH THE SILENCE AS DIA WALKED through the forest. A chill crept down her spine. She had the feeling she was being watched, but that didn't surprise her. She knew the stories about the Forest of Knowing, but she didn't have any secrets. She never did. That's how she stayed safe. Though she couldn't see more than a few paces ahead, Dia ventured further into the woods against the clenching feeling in her gut.

. . .

Unearthly sounds roared through the leaves as Dia's light grew brighter. She saw a boy, no older than eighteen, clad in black from head to toe, dancing with a white wolf. He was perhaps the most beautiful thing she had ever seen. Stopping, she watched for a moment before a blur of black raced toward the pair, spilling streams of crimson into the air.

Celeste, sistermine, what have ye done?

Dia knew who the boy was as soon as she saw her sister. She also knew that the wolf, a child of the moon, was her sister Artemis. Sucking in a deep breath, Dia whispered a prayer and made a decision that would forever shape time. It was the only way to stop the fighting. The only way to save Elirion from impending doom.

Her fingers danced in the air, streams of light curling and swirling on command into a singular white rose. Dia pulled the rose from where it hung and slid her thumb over the thorn-laden stem, piercing the tip until drops of scarlet welled onto the thorn. She removed her finger and slowly, she painted the petals red before whispering a spell that bound her and the prince of darkness together into an eternal prison in the pit of the sun.

1

GAVIN

*S*creams rang through the Underground as the crowd chanted to the rhythm of wolves fighting below. Werewolves, bloodied and soaked with sweat, lunged at one another with bared teeth and claws, tearing at flesh while vampires and bloodwhores filed along the railing of the poorly lit pit. Coins of gold and silver passed discreetly from palms into bony ghoul fingers, each placing their bets while the carnage continued. Above the pits, along the back wall of the establishment was a bar, and sitting at that bar, swigging back the last of his amber drink, was Gavin Sinclair.

The smell of sweat, blood, and sex hung in the air, feeding something dark within Mister Sinclair as he pushed from his stool to his feet. The room began to spin, blurring his dark brown eyes.

A good day.

A good fight.

And a goddessdamned good drink. It seemed as though nothing could sour Gavin's good mood until the bell chimed that the fight was nearing an end. Oliver Dawson, his best friend and the wolf he'd bet on, was winning until his opponent threw his shoulder into the werewolf's gut, pile-driving him onto the dirt floor. Gavin threw his crystal glass to the ground, shattering it around his feet, and stomped on the remnants before stepping toward the railing.

"Goddamn it," he cursed under his breath, watching Dawson fall.

"Sir! You'll have to pay for that!" a lowly kitchen maid scolded from behind him.

"Sod off, lady!" Gavin barked and shot a damning glare over his shoulder before returning his attention to the fallen wolf. His confidence in his betting ability had cost him the rest of his coin. Coin Gavin needed to buy a few humans their freedom from Palmer, the skeevy ghoul king. Another win meant another life saved.

A smile played on Gavin's lips as he thought of his parents' faces and wondered what they would think of their heir sitting in a slum betting house. He wondered what they would say if they knew why he'd ran. But Gavin knew that they'd never have approved of his decision or of *Daimis*. Humans were scum, it was the wayward thinking of vampires. They enslaved those that couldn't afford their freedom and sold them on the black market, known in Elirion as Bloodwhore Markets. But Gavin was different. He believed human life was worthy and began to save one soul at a time, buying their freedom from Palmer and setting them free in Daimis. There, he could ensure their safety and allow them to live happily.

Gavin sucked in a breath and pinched the bridge of his nose. Squinting his eyes shut, he willed the thoughts away. He had other things to worry about. He opened his eyes a moment later, scanning the pits as the next fighter entered the ring. A ragtag wolf in tattered, moth-eaten clothing was going up against a burly mutt twice his size. If Gavin had had any winnings, he'd place a bet on the brute, but he didn't have a goddessdamned coin to his name.

Heavy footsteps creaked up the stairs to the bar, slowing behind Gavin. He'd known who it was without having to spare him a glance.

"Gavin, you mangy bastard," a voice greeted from his right. Gavin's eyes drifted from the pit to the face of the hulking man now standing at his side. He was dressed in a white cotton shirt and weathered jeans. And with a mischievous grin on his face, he sidled up with a bar stool and took a seat next to his friend, slinging an arm around Gavin's shoulder.

"Piss off, Ollie, my coin purse is empty because of you!" Gavin snarled, exposing his fangs. Oliver smiled a toothy grin and ordered Gavin another glass of dark amber liquid. The barkeep, a slender vampire, muttered under her breath and obliged, handing the wolf two glasses moments later. Gavin wrinkled his nose as he took a whiff of the drink, smelling the sweet harsh tones.

"How am I supposed to pay for those, Dawson?" he fumed. "How am I supposed to pay for *anything*?"

"Oh, brother, don't be so sour. All you care about is coin and whores, all of which come at your best mate's expense. What would the fangbangers think if they really knew their prince?" Oliver goaded, smacking Gavin's coated arm, wrinkling it. His suit was dark, standing in stark contrast to his milky skin, and complemented Gavin's own chocolate locks.

"You've wrinkled my sleeve." Gavin glowered, reaching to smooth away the imperfections. Oliver let out a hearty laugh.

"And if the *fangbangers* knew who their prince really was, I'm sure they would be miffed to find him hanging around bloodwhores, ghouls and werewolf mutts," Gavin replied. Oliver fawned offense at his friend's hateful words. Reaching his hand into the pocket of his sports coat, Gavin fished around for something to take the edge off. Cigarillos. His fingers fumbled with the small pouch he stashed them in. Unzipping the dainty bag, he pulled out his guilty pleasures. Raising the cigarillo to his lips, Gavin flicked a match to life and lit the end. He never used to smoke, but Gavin found that amongst the turmoil both within himself and the Underground, the sweet taste of the tobacco was the only thing that helped calm his nerves.

Gavin's body tensed and he slowly removed the cigarillo, watching as the ragtag wolf dodged an attack from the bigger werewolf. "You've killed them, you know," Gavin said coolly, his voice low enough that no one around would be able to overhear them. A stream of white filtered out from the vampire's parted lips. Ollie turned to face his friend, the grin that splayed on his lips moments before, now gone.

"It's not your job to save them, mate."

"If I don't, then who will? You know damn well that Palmer and his ghouls will eat them. The vamps will only suck and fuck them, and the wolves act as though they don't exist. Someone has to help them."

"And why does that someone have to be you, Gav?" Oliver asked, a worried crease drawing his thick golden brows together. Gavin rolled his eyes at his typical wolfish logic.

"Because they have to have someone in their corner. There has to be order." Gavin's jaw clenched as he scanned the room, returning his attention back to the pits. The crowd was going wild, chanting for the hulking wolf covered in blood to snap the ragtag in two.

"There is order, Gav," Oliver replied, his gaze also fixated on the fight.

Gavin remained quiet, knowing that nothing would change his friend's mind. He was lucky Oliver was helping him at all. Maybe one day, he would open his eyes and seek justice.

"Ollie, why did you fall?" Gavin asked a moment later, changing the subject. "You were bound to win." He took another drag. The big brute of the man next to him shrugged his shoulders nonchalantly.

"Eh, didn't feel like it today, mate," he replied.

"You fucking bastard!" Gavin hissed and rounded on his friend, but Oliver only stared, as if he knew something Gavin did not, which made Gavin seethe with anger. He curled his fingers into fists and dug his nails deep into his thumbs. Oliver Case Dawson was one of the biggest were-wolves in the circuit and Gavin knew it. Hell, everyone in the Underground knew it, which was why Gavin and a handful of others had bet on him.

"I'd check how you're speaking to me, Gav." The low grumble in Oliver's voice shook the surrounding tables—a warning that the vampire should let the topic drop. Puffing out his chest, Gavin let it fall in defeat.

"Fine." He knew it was his fault in the long run. Betting had become as natural to Gavin as breathing, and despite being a vampire, Gavin did have to breathe. If he hadn't placed all of his coin on Oliver, then he wouldn't have been as fucked as he was. He'd find another way to scrounge up the coin and buy some humans from Palmer.

Gavin knew how to survive.

He knew how to play politics and games. Releasing a sigh, Gavin leaned back onto a rotting pillar.

The next fight was about to begin and the space around the pits grew in numbers. Chants and laughter rang through the air, the spectators growing rowdier with each passing moment. Bloodwhores hung on the arms of the rich, dressed in clothes that barely covered their assets, giggling and begging for a bite to quench their fix. Gavin scanned the crowd, checking for telltale signs that one of the rich would let their guard down long enough for him to pickpocket a coin purse. Or perhaps he could tap into his Ripper and use compulsion on a bloodwhore to do his dirty work. Either way, he'd figure it out.

A flash of gold to his right interrupted Gavin's thoughts. A curly head of blonde hair bobbed in and out of sweaty bodies, a beautiful sea of lush light in an otherwise colorless world.

Rosalie Coston.

Oliver elbowed Gavin in the ribs, causing the vampire to wince as a sharp pain radiated through his bones. He shot the werewolf a *'fuck you'* glance and returned his search for Rose.

"That lass is trouble with a capital T," Ollie mumbled, but his words sounded muffled in Gavin's ears as the blonde woman came into full view.

Curvy and sensual, the petite vampire pushed through the remaining men in her path to stand in front of Oliver. *What would a Coston want in the Underground?* Gavin blinked, watching as Rose stuck her hand down her low-cut shirt and retrieved a dark red coin purse that hung around her neck. She lifted the purse over top of her head, smiling as she unclasped the crushed velvet bag and checked the contents inside. Clicking it shut, she lifted her ocean blue eyes to Oliver, flashed him a pearly white grin and handed it to him. "Here, I believe I owe you this, doll," she drawled, her Elirion accent as seductive as it was authoritative.

"Why thank ya, lass. My friend 'ere was just busting my

16

chops for losing." Oliver smirked in Gavin's direction, nudging him once again. Gavin rolled his eyes, biting back the retort on his lips, fighting to keep his temper in check.

"Coston," Oliver said, a smile beaming across his wild features. "You've outdone yourself."

"The best, for the best," she replied. The woman's gaze turned to Gavin and he stared into her piercing silver-blue eyes. Her rosy lips pouted as he found himself unable to look away.

"Gavin Sinclair, do my eyes deceive me?" she purred, crossing her arms in front of her chest, pushing her bosom up until they nearly brimmed over her shirt. Gavin's nethers jolted, feeding a hunger within him. Forcing his gaze away, Gavin glanced to the floor.

A slight bout of shame washed over him. Of all the places in Elirion to find him, Rosalie had to find him here, at the bottom of the barrel scraping for scraps. Such a long fall from where she'd last laid eyes on him.

"Oh," Gavin coughed, blood rushing into his cheeks. "They call me Jagger, here," he replied sheepishly, rubbing at his perfectly manicured neck. Her eyes roamed over him like a lioness sizing up her prey.

"I see," she replied, clicking her tongue against white canines. Rose lifted to her tiptoes, pulling the werewolf's neck toward her puckered lips. A pang of jealousy nipped at Gavin as he watched Oliver lean in, allowing her to plant a swift kiss on his cheek.

He didn't understand it. He could have had any woman in the joint, hell in the *kingdom*, but this one was different. Rosalie was royalty and one of two of the highest born heiresses to Elirion. The pits, the Underground, the bloodwhores and wolves that fought for Palmer and all of the debauchery belonged to her family. Belonged to *her*.

Rose raised her hand, cupping Oliver's cheek. Her

hand lingered for a few moments more than Gavin liked, and then she whispered, "You did well, Dawson," before she flipped her hair over her right shoulder and turned on her heels, retreating back into the crowd. Oliver's face was beet red when Gavin turned to look at his friend. Another tinge of envy swept over Gavin as his gaze drifted back to the disappearing head of gold. It should have been his kiss. *His.*

When Gavin was sure Rose was far enough into the throng of gamblers not to hear him, he said, "How the fuck do you know her?" Oliver rolled with laughter, clutching at his toned belly. "And what did she pay *you* for?"

The wolf beside him sighed, his amber eyes drooping lazily as he grinned and looked to where Rosalie had disappeared, "That, there is fine enough reason to lose a lousy mutt fight, cuts and all."

"*She* paid you to lose?" Gavin gasped, feeling the bite of darkness as it crept over him. The blonde beauty had *purposely* cost him. "Why?" he snarled.

"Don't know, don't care. When something that looks like *that* asks you to do something, brother, you do it," Oliver replied, wiggling his eyebrows. Rosalie had deliberately undermined him and in that moment, Gavin knew that she was onto his plan. The humans that he'd been buying had belonged to her. A chill ran down the vampire's spine, a sensation he hadn't felt in ages. If Rosalie knew, then how many others did and would she keep quiet?

2

GAVIN

"*A*lright, you arrogant ass. You're buying food," Gavin said and grabbed the wolf by his enormous shoulders, shoving him hard in the direction of the tables in the back. Lights flickered overhead, buzzing louder and louder the further the pair went from the pits and the bar; the noise of the fights muffled enough for them to hold a conversation. Slinging into the torn leather booth, Gavin immediately felt eyes on his back. Ignoring the urge to turn around, he beckoned for the nearest waitress.

Dressed more like a harlot than anything else, with a skirt barely to her mid-thigh and a rack that caused her blouse buttons to scream, Gavin imagined the things he could do to her and the moans that would escape her lips as he plunged his fangs deep into her neck. He'd drink until he was satisfied, until they both were. *Oh she'd let me too*, he thought. She smiled and quickly scampered up to him, her dark ponytail bobbing in time with her steps.

Though his looks were no mystery to him, it often took Gavin aback by the amount of attention his dark eyes and hair got for him. Women were drawn to his sharp cheekbones and mysterious persona like moths were to a flame.

Oliver was the stark opposite of Gavin, with long unruly sandy-colored hair that was usually pulled back with a leather strap, olive skin, and dark amber eyes. Not to mention that he was double the size of Gavin, not in height, but in build. The girl barely batted an eye in Ollie's direction. To most, Oliver appeared to be nothing more than a fighter, but Gavin saw him for what he truly was.

"What can I getcha, lovely?" the waitress asked in a sultry voice, propping up on the table to poke out her chest. She glanced through dark lashes at Gavin, lust gleaming in the dark parts of her eyes. Gavin ordered another fried potatoes and whiskey with a shot of blood. "What do you want, Ollie?" Oliver was too busy looking the waitress up and down to reply right away.

"Besides looking at the backside of this one, a steak, raw. Thanks," he growled. The waitress jumped as though she was on edge and a phantom hand had grabbed her rear. Gavin was unsure if it was Oliver's tone or the betting house in general that set the eerie tone. Gavin moved his hand to her cheek, peering into the mortal woman's eyes. Her body slackened, eyes glazing over as Gavin spoke, "You're going to leave now and put in our order. And when you return, you're going to forget whatever sets you on edge. You're going to leave us to ourselves and stop making eyes at me. Do you understand?" A thin veil glimmered in her irises, a sign that his compulsion had taken hold. The mortal swallowed and blinked slowly.

"Right away," she replied, shaking her head as she cleared her throat. She turned on her heels before running off, and Gavin turned his attention back toward his friend.

"Mate," Oliver began, a disapproving look settling in across his features.

"Relax, you hulking brute, she wasn't worth bedding and you know it." Gavin slouched back in the booth, yearning for another smoke.

"That's not the point, mate. What's so alluring about yer kind anyway?" Oliver pouted and followed suit, settling into his seat.

"We're hypnotic by nature. You know this. That's why you love me," Gavin goaded. Oliver sputtered a laugh.

"I'd hardly say that." His grin was wide and sinister, and Gavin couldn't help but to return it. This was his friend. His *best* friend. The man who had picked him off the bar floor and made him presentable again after an all-night bender. He was the man who had fought off the vultures circling a newly fallen prince. He was the man who had given him a new identity. The man who risked everything to help him with his agenda. Oliver Dawson was his anchor.

They had traveled to this wasteland by horse months back, both trying to escape a past they'd rather forget. *The Pits*, as it was known, sat along the edge of Elirion. The ocean was a stone's throw away, but the only place worth a damn was the Underground bar and fight ring from which the town was named. Where the rich and the vagabonds gathered when the moon rose and the merchants slept. *Palmer's* was the spot to be to bet and bed slags, to feast on bloodwhores who willingly gave blood in exchange for sex. It was said that a vampire's bite was better than the act itself, though, Gavin supposed if it were true, more humans would live the unsavory lifestyle. Whatever you were after, you could find it here. It was exactly the place neither man should be.

The hair on the back of Gavin's neck rose on end, sending his stomach into flips. A cool sweat peppered his brow. His pulse quickened as the eyes behind him bore into the fallen prince's back. Gavin sighed and fished in his pocket for his matchbook and cigarillos. He retrieved them and lit the end of one before lifting it to his lips. A puff of grey, clove smoke eased Gavin's nerves, until the smoke was gone. When the prince could no longer bear being the phantom's spectacle, he turned around in his seat.

Across the poorly lit bar, stood a prominent shadowed figure, one that gnawed at Gavin's insides. Something in his gut told Gavin to stay put, to not even acknowledge the presence of this stranger.

Pulling the cigarillo from his lips, Gavin held the unlit end out to his friend.

"Hold my smoke," he grumbled, hardly waiting for Oliver to grasp it before taking a deep breath. Gavin let out a sigh as foreboding filled him. His instincts screamed for him to turn around and leave the cloaked being to the shadows, but Gavin ignored his internal warning and pushed forward anyway.

"Jagger!" Oliver called, but Gavin didn't stop or hesitate. His blood was pumping, rushing like a geyser, filling his ears. His heart beat faster, though most of the time it hardly pumped at all, and his fingers clenched into fists readying for a fight.

Before Gavin could reach the table, the ghost was perched behind, a bookie grabbed Gavin by the scruff of his tailored shirt, flipping him around. He stared straight into a pair of vacant, dead eyes.

"Let go of me. You're fucking up my collar," he snarled, flashing his fangs. A grin curled on the dead man's cracked lips, exposing his rotten teeth. The prince's stomach lurched as he peeled decaying fingers from his shirt and shoved the withered corpse away.

"You owe great debts here, Jagger Mcfarland," the

haunting voice replied. One of Palmer's ghouls. *Great.* Gavin grimaced.

"Piss off, mate," Oliver said, coming up behind the bookie.

"Yeah, mate." Gavin spat into the creature's sunken face.

"'Fraid I can't do that. Boss wants his coin. And his coin he shall get."

"Well, I'm afraid he'll have to be disappointed." Gavin shrugged and turned back to the figure he had originally been headed over to. All he found was an empty corner. The ghoul chortled.

"Pay you will." A deeper voice drew Gavin's attention.

"Sven," Oliver chided, rolling his yellowing eyes, a color Gavin knew to mean change.

"Dawson, Jagger," the stout older ghoulmaster greeted the pair, "I believe you know how dire the situation is if I must personally make an appearance." Sven Palmer was a full foot shorter than Gavin and a foot and a half shorter than Oliver. However, that did not mean he was a pushover or someone to take lightly. He was known to be bloodthirsty and ruthless. The leader of all things criminal. Sven Palmer was a force to be reckoned with and a profitable one at that. From bloodwhores to wolfsbane, if it was outlawed, Palmer had a hand in it. Nobody fucked with him and lived.

"Give us some more time, Palmer, you bastard," Gavin argued. His mind whirled. He knew if Palmer was there to collect that he was completely and utterly screwed. He had to think fast, but Gavin's mind drew blanks.

"I think I have been more than gracious with you, Jagger." He turned to Oliver. "You may be one of the best fighters and the best showman here, but that does not mean you can escape your debts which are racking up by the way."

Oliver snorted, folding his arms over his massive chest. This did not bode well. "My debts are paid you, greedy fuck," he snarled.

"Your debts are his debts." Palmer nodded to Gavin. "He is your sponsor, after all, and if he owes, then you owe too. Now hand me my pay, mutt," Palmer barked.

Gavin watched as Oliver thrust his hand into his pocket where the coin pouch should be, coming back short. Gavin struggled to breathe. Nerves wreaking havoc in his mind, pain splintered through his temples. He stared at his friend; there was not enough there. As hands seized them, claws threatened to break Gavin's skin as the ghoul stepped forward. "I will get my pay, gentlemen, and we'll settle this now."

"And how do you propose we do that? I could rip your head from your body. That'd be satisfying," Gavin replied coolly, a muscle in his cheek twitching. Palmer laughed, ignoring Gavin's taunt.

"I'll spare one of you. Only after a duel in the pits. Seems fitting."

"We're not fighting for our freedom," Gavin hissed.

"Ah, but you are. See, we could do this the easy way, the way I proposed, or I could just take your pet back to the cages where he belongs and end the issue *permanently*. Either way, I still get what I want."

"I swear I'll kill you, you son of a—" Palmer held his hand up, causing the rest of Gavin's reply to catch in his throat. The ghoul at Palmer's side curled his fingers into a tight fist. The air whooshed from Gavin's lungs as the dead man drove his fist deep into the prince's gut. Gavin's knees threatened to buckle and delicious pain stirred the beast that had started to awaken within.

"Gentlemen, please, remember, my house, my rules. Now, you'll each fight. The winner will be pardoned and the loser will die. I say it's a win-win." Leering through his winded haze, Gavin and Oliver both scoffed. It was hardly a win. And to fight his best friend? Was Palmer out of his goddessdamn mind?

"You've got a lot of fucking nerve," Oliver growled.

Palmer cracked a smile, exposing yellowing teeth that were in remarkable shape for a man on his way to being a corpse, before letting out another haunting cackle. "And you have the nerve to cheat me. I say I'm being fair here, boys. It's only business. Your fight starts in an hour. I'll give you enough time to bed a woman or each other, if you're keen, and then the fight commences. I look forward to watching you bleed, gentlemen. Please don't disappoint me, hmm," Palmer said, turning his back to them as he and his undead goon retreated back into the shadows. Gavin turned and made his way back toward their booth. His mind whirled as he ran his fingers through his tousled locks. He slid into the booth without another word.

The waitress crept back with their food, although Gavin's appetite had vanished by now. She kept her gaze downcast as she set the plates down in front of the prince and his wolf without muttering a single word. The meal was not as appealing as it had been when they had ordered and Gavin left his untouched, ignoring the smell that reached his nose.

Things were bad.

So incredibly bad.

Looking to his friend, Gavin silently pleaded for a solution from whatever goddess would answer a nocturnal beast like him.

"Gav, I-I'm sorry, mate," Oliver told him, lowering his head. They could barely make eye contact with one another. Escaping this horrid place would likely be impossible. Especially with Palmer on alert. Gavin knew who the victor would be, beast against beast. His blood heated his otherwise cold limbs. It was not fear he was feeling.

No.

But anguish at the prospect of battling his friend. The Prince of Blood had lain dormant for a very long time. Gavin had locked him away into the deepest facets of his mind, in hopes of redeeming himself from years of bloodshed. The human wars had brought out the truest of night beasts, but the vampires had won, vanquishing the human rebellions until they bowed down or died at the hands of immortal beings. Gavin and his king were born from the carnage of death. Humans were nothing more than slaves and meat sacks in the eyes of the vampires, but Gavin knew they were much more than that. They deserved to live amongst the realm as more.

"Gav!" Oliver's voice drew him from his dark thoughts.

"Yeah?"

"I know what you're thinking. And it won't happen, you hear me? You've come too fucking far for that horseshit."

Gavin couldn't help but laugh at Oliver's unending faith in him. "You're so optimistic in such dire times."

Oliver shrugged his massive shoulders and turned his attention away. "You keep him leashed, ya hear?" His glance shifted toward the waitress who was leaning over a nearby table, washing it clean. Her skirts hoisted, just barely covering her backside as she leaned in further, giving the boys a gracious glance at her bottom. "If this is our last hour, I'd like to get wasted and bed a woman. Perhaps bend that waitress over and—"

"She's not into you man. Don't waste your time chasing someone who doesn't want to be chased."

Oliver whirled his attention back onto Gavin, narrowing his eyes into a glare that Gavin was unaccustomed to seeing. His friend's demeanor shifted into something voracious. "I'm getting wasted and fucking. Do what you want with yours. I'll see you in the pit," Oliver snarled before pushing from the table and stalking off, leaving Gavin alone.

3

ROSE

*R*osalie Elena Coston, one of the wealthiest vampire heiresses in the realm, was tired of her lush life hidden behind the scenes. Lavish parties and suitors at the beck and call of her father, Lord Zachary Coston, no longer pleased her, as if it ever did. Now in the belly of the underworld, she sought out information on the disappearance of her older sister, Dahlia, and the sordid life that brought her family their coin.

Paying off a werewolf was just one of the things she'd done to earn favor with the snake, Sven Palmer. The fighter, Oliver Dawson, was his mark of the evening and for whatever reason, she felt the need to help the beast, if only to serve her own best interests. She had hoped that his losing the fight would relieve the spotlight placed on the wolf's head. She was wrong.

A hushed conversation she'd overheard had fueled her fire to stop this madness. Palmer was planning to pit Oliver against his friend in order to put on some grand show. There was something he needed to announce. That something he felt needed extra flair. *Blood* was that *pizazz*, and tonight there would be plenty of it. Rose let out a sigh. She would do what she could to foil Palmer's plans.

Finding Dawson was easy. He was lounging outside the brothel door awaiting a woman who caught his fancy. Treading into this part of the establishment always made her queasy. The men stared at her with hunger in their eyes and lust in their pants. It made her skin crawl. She could feel them pulling the clothes away from her body with a glance, but Rose had to ignore it. She had to get Dawson to throw the fight... again. The less remarkable he looked at the moment, the better this night may pan out for him.

As if on cue, Dawson looked up, licking his lips as he caught her gaze, a wolfish smile playing on his lips. He pushed from his spot against the wall and thrust his hands into the pockets of his pants, pushing them down and revealing the sharp ditches of his abdomen. Rose's eyes drifted to the *V*, drinking it in as the wolf approached.

His eyes raked her body, undressing and sending chills through Rose. His gaze was unlike the others. It held her respect in a way most males lacked. Despite his ruggedly handsome looks, Rose had to keep it casual, if only for a night. Nothing could stop her plan. Not even a handsome wolf.

"Hello, Trouble," Dawson purred. "What's a lass like you hanging around in a place like this?" he asked with a hint of disapproval Rose found endearing. He gestured around them with an open palm and Rose's eyes followed the movement. Red lace draped the hall lined with mahogany doors. A settee sat down at the end under a large painting of a naked woman. Moans, both male and female, chorused from the rooms. A chandelier of crystal hung above, giving off low light to the lowlifes in this part. Rose closed her eyes, her breaths coming in shallow puffs.

Her stomach twisted and flipped over on itself. She gritted her teeth and opened her eyes, feigning control.

"A brothel?" she asked. Oliver's smile disappeared and his eyes flicked to hers, taking on a serious tone.

"Yes. One might think you're up to no good," he replied, moving closer to her. "Unless you are looking for a good time?"

"Hardly," Rose replied, her tone harsh. She stifled back her annoyance, though deep down she follied for a good distraction. "You need to lose this fight, too. Palmer wants blood."

"Palmer can go fuck himself. He expects me to kill my best mate. Skeevy son of a bitch."

Rose clenched her jaw, her irritation growing by the second. "Lose this fight too, or I swear I'll come back for my coin. All of it," she nearly hissed. "The fights need to end."

"If I lose the fight, then I'll be dead and will have no use for your coin. Besides, the fights are none of your concern."

"Everything in the Underground is my concern. Lose this fight or I'll make you pay."

"Don't threaten me with a good time, lass. I like a little pain in the bedroom. Makes things a bit more exciting," he replied, flashing Rose a toothy grin.

"In your dreams, wolf boy," Rose snapped.

"Oh I assure you, in my dreams we take things to a whole new level," Oliver purred, wagging his eyebrows.

Rose rolled her eyes at the werewolf's innuendo and fished into her shirt for a second coin pouch, extracting it. Oliver looked at her, confusion masking his face. She'd defeat Palmer at his own game. Opening the purse, Rose retrieved a vial she never thought she'd need to use, a vial that if anyone saw, would get her thrown into prison for a decade or more.

"Moonchild," she crooned. "Ever sample some of the finest Wolfsbane, Elirion has to offer?" Oliver flicked his eyes away in a worried glance, surely looking to see if anyone was around to overhear the conversation.

"Rose," he began, though his voice quivered as he bit his bottom lip. "A lass like you has no business with a vial like that. The Sinclair's would have your head on a pike if they saw you with it."

Rose looked up, smiling as she gazed into the wolf's peculiar eyes. She knew exactly what and where her endeavors would lead her. Pulling the purple vial out of the shadows, she held it freely in the air, pinched between her forefingers. "They can't touch me if they can't catch me. Besides, I've put my own twist on this gem. Care for some?"

"Let's go someplace private," Oliver whispered, issuing for Rose to lead the way.

"Second door on the left," Rose replied, stopping before a dark wooden door. Turning the dark knob, Rose pushed into the room with Oliver on her heels. She nodded to the door and Oliver kicked it shut. With the click of the lock, Rose knew she had him in the palm of her hand.

"I-I have a fight soon," Oliver murmured. Rose felt the edges of her lips curl upward, a grin forming across her beautiful face. She knew the wolf would give in; no wolf could resist Wolfsbane. It was a drug like no other to their kind. From the look on Oliver's face, she knew he'd sampled it once or twice in his life. He wouldn't be able to resist the pull.

"I know," she replied, spinning the corked vial between her fingers, batting her lashes flirtatiously. "But it may be your last and maybe I am looking for a bit of fun." Rose sank to her knees as her fingers fumbled with the wolf's trousers, working the buttons free. A strong hand knotted in her hair, pulling her head up.

"Don't play with me, lass," Oliver whispered. His amber eyes begged for more.

"Take your bane, Moonchild, and ride the wave of ecstasy." Huffing a sigh, as if to say she was silently right, Oliver took the vial of purple liquid and flicked off the cork. Tilting his head back, he brought the vial to his lips and downed the entire thing.

Perfect, Rose thought as she rose from her knees and seized the glass from the mutt's fingers, watching the effects of the bane work almost immediately. Oliver's eyes drooped and his body slumped. She hoped her added twist was enough to slow his heart rate to keep him from shifting into the wolf.

"Alright, big guy," she said, releasing a stored breath. "Just relax." Her plan was shaping up nicely. Oliver would be safe for a while longer and then it was up to him.

✿

ROSE COULD HEAR PALMER'S RANCID VOICE COMING FROM above and she knew it was about time for the gates to open. His magnified tone echoed through the pits and dining booths, making the floor beneath her shake.

"Shit," she cursed under her breath, looking back to the now snoring wolf. Crouching down, Rose was nose to nose with the beast as she raised her hand. *What doesn't kill him, makes him stronger, right?*

Crack!

Her hand smashed against his cheek. Pain strung along her fingers. Rose winced, a cry escaping from parted lips as she caressed her reddening hand with the other. Her eyes darted to Oliver's cheek, watching as a red handprint formed there. The werewolf jolted to life. A snarl erupted from Oliver's lips, as the beast within him threatened to transition.

"Get up," Rose hissed. She hoped Gavin would stall, not wanting the evening's events to proceed faster than necessary. She knew Gavin well enough to know that her plan would not work if he knew Oliver was impaired. He'd hold back. Rose needed Palmer to think that he had succeeded in breaking Gavin. She needed him to think that he had succeeded in whatever he was planning with these two. Oliver squinted his yellowing, beastly eyes in her direction, fanning a snarl. "Fucking bit-," he muttered, cutting off the last word before pushing to his wobbly legs. *Good boy*, Rose thought.

"Hey now! I'm still a lady, you overgrown man child." Rose gritted her teeth, biting back the words she desperately wanted to say. She needed him to fight and lose. Palmer needed the rug pulled out from under him, but she wanted to do it as gracefully as possible. Why he wanted to destroy this nightwalker was beyond her. All Rose knew was that the slimy son of a bitch wanted blood and she needed to find out within that hate where her sister lay.

4

GAVIN

*G*avin felt the beast rumbling within, begging to be released as he stood in his six by six holding cell, shirtless and waiting for his name to be called. His clothes sat in a neatly discarded pile on the floor, a shame really for such expensive fibers to sit in. The smell of blood, sweat, and piss drenched the air, choking Gavin's vampire senses, silencing his Ripper demon. A demon that relished in destruction, death and blood lust. Oftentimes, born from tragedy itself. That was the case for Gavin when he was forced to fight against the human rebellion.

COOL RAIN RAN DOWN GAVIN'S FACE AS HE SCANNED THE woods surrounding him. The midnight sky was crying in protest to the betrayal brought down upon Elirion. For five hundred years, the vampires had ruled, placing themselves on a pedestal. They treated the humans like garbage. On Hallows Eve, the rebellion struck back against the capitol of Tatum. Blood painted the streets and stained the soil from one end of the realm to the next and Gavin's regiment was tasked with mopping it up.

A creak.

A snap meant that an enemy was close by. And though Gavin knew that the Forest of Knowing took pleasure in taunting his kind, he also knew he could never be too careful. Ghosts came in all different forms. Gavin's heart thudded wildly in his chest. His ears twitched at the snap of a branch. As the prince turned, a silver-tipped arrow whistled past his right ear, sinking feathers deep, into the bark of a nearby tree. His hand bolted to the hilt of his sword as he searched the trees for his assailant. A silver-tipped arrow to the heart would end him, permanently. Death, true and immediate, was in the vicinity, especially if the enemy had silver weapons. Every fiber of Gavin's body stood on end.

"Come out and fight me, you bastard!" he howled into the night. But only rain answered, running down his face, soaking him to the bone. He sucked in a breath, sending out a prayer to whatever goddess would listen and pulled his blade from its resting place.

Shadows flit above in between the branches, catching in the corner of his eye. Screams ricocheted through the trees as friend and foe dropped, and death enveloped his troops.

The hair on Gavin's neck rose. A shuffle to his left had him turning and steel against steel rang through the night. A two against one attack. Gavin's feet danced against the scarlet earth, dodging and deflecting blows. Arrows whizzed through the branches, landing in the sodden ground around him. His second assailant was a poor shot, something he was thankful for.

"Fuck," he hissed, as his first attacker lunged the tip of his blade toward Gavin's ribs, marring his skin.

"Serves you right, fanger," a male voice broke from the tree. Gavin's eyes flicked to the branches.

A mistake.

His attacker lunged again, driving his weapon home in Gavin's gut. Pain seared through the prince, doubling him over. Hot, sticky blood poured from the wound, drenching his tunic. Stars swam in the vampire's eyes and a chill set about his bones—a shivering

35

embrace as death neared, calling him home to her side. He breathed in a ragged breath, wincing as the pain turned to numbing blindness and then something dark took hold of him. Gavin suspected what it was but had no way of stopping the killer that laid dormant within.

His lips curled into a sinister grin as he gripped at the blade and thrust it deeper into himself. His attacker lurched forward, fear etched in his eyes.

"You thought you could bring me down?" Gavin sneered, slicing his palms open. "You thought you were burning down the Sinclair empire? You're nothing and you'll die as nothing." Fangs bared, Gavin hurled forward and tore the man's throat from his neck, awakening the darkness within.

Survival.

It was all about survival.

Strength flooded his broken body, bringing with it a blood lust so insatiable Gavin feared he would never overcome it. Flesh still wedged between his teeth, Gavin felt sick, guilt plummeting to his stomach in droves. But the Ripper born in that moment was not done. It needed more.

Wrenching the sword from his abdomen, Gavin's eyes flashed red in the moonlight. Turning eerily slowly to face his second attacker who was frozen in shock, Gavin's face pulled into a feral snarl of its own accord.

"You've created a Prince of Blood."

Blood sprayed the trees behind the assailant, forever marking them as the birthplace of the Sinclair Coven's greatest tragedy.

GAVIN WINCED, THE MEMORY OF HIS FIRST KILL FLOODING through him. How harsh he had been during that time, the day his Ripper was born. But the humans deserved better. They'd been right to revolt. And every day since, Gavin had been buying their freedom. But blood didn't wash easily from his hands. He'd killed and he'd do it again before the day's end.

Chants from the pit echoed through the tunnel as Palmer riled the crowd above. Gavin sighed, tearing his discarded shirt into strips before tossing the rest of it into a heap on the dirty ground. Quietly, he used the shreds of fabric to wrap his wrists and began preparing for what felt like the beginning of the end. And maybe it was.

He knew Ollie, his every swing, every jab, and every dodge. He'd trained with the wolf, learning and sparring to hone his reflexes, which made this fight one for the books. On the other hand, Oliver didn't know *his* strategies, didn't know his dirty little tricks and secrets. Although Gavin wished he'd spent his time bedding a woman or drinking her blood, he'd known that the sleepy stupor would give his opponent an edge.

Oliver was a hulking brute, one of the best damn fighters Gavin had ever seen, but *he* was better. He'd cheated death once and embraced her with open arms, drinking in her darkness.

"Ladies and Gentlemen," Palmer's ghoulish voice rang. "From the hand that gives to the hand that takes, I expect payments to be made in full. Each and every one of you betting this evening knows the rules. You know *my* rules. Come up empty and your debt will only be forgiven... at a cost. This evening, two of our very own have decided to learn that lesson the hard way.

"I have a treat for all of you. A debt must be repaid. So, without further ado, from the pits of Elirion, to the whore houses, to your hearts and wallets, I give you Dawson!" The crowd erupted into applause and cheers as the gates on the other side of the pit opened to reveal Ollie, glistening from head to toe in sweat, clothed in nothing more than his undershorts while his hair was knotted in his typical bun. Ollie stalked into the pit, kicking the sand up behind him. He looked up to the rails, howling at the crowd and waving his hands in the air. If Gavin wasn't on the other end, he would have been smiling, laughing even at his friend's attempt to win bets. But he was on the other side. Soon there would be bloodshed and one of them would be left a corpse.

"And last but not least, the man of the hour, the man that takes what he does not have. A fallen prince, if you will. Ladies and gentlemen, I give you Jagger!"

Gavin's heart thumped wildly against his ribcage, threatening to break free. Just the word prince, so trivial, was enough to shake him. Sucking in a breath, Gavin clenched his fists at his sides and walked from the tunnels into the pit opposite of Ollie. The crowd fell silent. The eerie quiet where one could hear a pin drop.

He was *not* what they were expecting, and he couldn't blame them for their shocked expressions. It was unheard of for a vampire to battle a werewolf this unceremoniously. This kind of fight warranted grandeur that was not present today. No, today was not grand, but rather, a spur of the moment event. One Sven Palmer had likely been dreaming of since the two started frequenting his establishments. But now, Gavin would have to kill his best friend. And for what? A pouch full of coin and Palmer's entertainment?

Ollie deserved better.

"Ah, two friends on opposite ends of the pit. What will the outcome be, folks? Place your bets! But remember! If you don't want to end up like these two, pay up!" Palmer's voice chilled Gavin to his core. He was teaching his betters and bookies a lesson. He was *not* to be crossed.

Pawns. That is what he and Ollie had been reduced to. Anger welled anew in Gavin's chest, spilling into his eyes, changing their chocolaty color to something more sinister. They would rival that of even Limos.

Across the pit, Oliver's face was made of stone. A spark of sadness in his eyes, the only sign that this was anything other than a regular match for the brawler. Gavin doubted wholeheartedly that Oliver would transform during their confrontation, but there was always the instinctual change that was uncontrollable. Gavin hoped, for Oliver's sake, that neither change would occur.

To either one of them.

Briefly, Gavin wondered what Palmer's slimy ass would do if they both just stood there. What would he do if they refused him in front of his spectators?

A blonde head caught his attention in the stands above, tearing him from his thoughts. *Rose.*

Her presence made all of this so much worse. She was about to see the worst in both of them. What would she think of him? A murderous bastard who would bring down his own friend?

It wasn't confidence that made Gavin fear he would be victorious. It was what lay *within* him. He feared his Ripper would be the end of Ollie. Bloodthirsty and cruel, Gavin's instincts began to take hold as the werewolf started to move toward him. At first, it was a hesitant waltz between the two. One stepped one way, the other stepped another. Back and forth they danced, throwing jabs that they refused to land. Gavin ducked to the right as Ollie's fist swung to the left. He circled his friend, crossing his feet as he took steps, ever the agile predator.

"Alright ladies, enough fiddling around!" Palmer thundered, magnifying his voice with only a thought. Gavin took a deep breath and shook his head.

This was it.

✿

OLLIE

KNOTS CURLED IN OLLIE'S STOMACH, COURSING GUILT through his veins. Anguish spread across his face as his heart pounded in Ollie's chest, threatening to burst free of his ribcage. This was the man he'd sworn to follow until he was seated on the throne. And now, he was about to tear him to pieces. Or try to.

Oliver knew his strength was nothing compared to that of the Blood Prince. A legendary murderer in a life long past, the prince was a ripper if there had ever been one. He waited for the first glimpse of red to appear in his friend's glassy eyes, knowing the sleeping beast within him was simmering beneath the surface, yearning to break free. The knowledge that *it* would take over and what that would mean for Oliver weighed in his chest like lead.

Ollie didn't want to watch this unfold, but he would put up as much of a fight as he could. He feared who would change first, and one of them would surely transition. Ollie lunged, rearing his fist back before swinging at Gavin's jaw. Gavin sidestepped, dodging Oliver. A smile crept across Gavin's face.

"Cute, Ollie. But I expected more from a regular brawler." The air buzzed with life around Ollie before Gavin curled his fingers into a fist and swung. Ollie pushed back, feet digging into the dirt, barely dodging his friend's attack.

Damn it! Ollie thought. He was still incoherent from the bane little- miss-trickster gave him, though he knew he was also at fault. His own demons were already aching for more.

With Gavin's god-like speed, he reappeared behind

40

Ollie. Oliver turned, coming face-to-face with the vampire, catching a glimpse of what he could have sworn was impossible for the immortal prince. A single tear slid down his stony alabaster face, dropping from the tip of his nose. Ollie could see it clear as day. The werewolf swallowed down the lump of emotions that formed in his throat and refocused. He had to lose the fight, but to lose meant death. Was he ready to die?

No, his mind screamed. Ollie never imagined dying at the ripe age of twenty-four. He always assumed he would pass, surrounded by his pack and their pups, not like this and not at his best friend's hand. He had to give it his all. And if he perished, at least then he knew he had gone down with all that he'd had.

The sluggishness of the bane had not dissolved enough for him to control his emotions. Chemical reactions told the wolf he should be enraged. Oliver allowed anger to emanate from him. Anger at being imprisoned for so long. Anger at Palmer for inciting this brawl with him and Gavin at center stage. Anger for all the hate he received for just being who he was.

A werewolf.

A dog.

A *monster*.

Ollie attacked again and this time he made contact. Pain erupted through his knuckles like fire. A horrid *crunch* resonated from Gavin's jaw as blood sprayed through the air. Gavin's eyes widened, his body frozen in place as Ollie delivered a kick to the vampire's gut. Ollie knew that he'd fractured a rib as Gavin hurled through the air, sailing back into the rock walls of the pit. The crowd roared. Gavin staggered to his feet. With a sickening crack, he reset his jaw and spit blood into the sand before lunging forward.

First blood.

🍄

GAVIN

AGONY RIPPLED THROUGH GAVIN LIKE SCALDING WHITE fire as the monster within stirred. Red flashed in his eyes as hot, sticky liquid poured from the gash in the back of his head down his shoulders. Gavin's fangs clipped his lower lip, dripping with venom as he shot Ollie a devilish grin. He felt the change almost immediately. He had battled up until this point, but with blood came the overwhelming *need* to spill more.

"Bad move," he snarled, bolting toward Oliver with immortal speed, driving his shoulder into the wolf's belly. The pair fell to the ground and Gavin was atop his friend in seconds.

He reached out, his fingers curling around Ollie's neck, forcing the air from his windpipe. The vampire pushed to his feet lifting the beast with him, his arm screamed beneath the wolf's weight. The Ripper within Gavin didn't seem to mind the strain. Ollie's yellow eyes widened, fear gripping his features as he feverishly dug at Gavin's unyielding hand.

"I'm sorry, brother, I win," he said, his grip tightening on the wolf's throat. Ollie's eyes bulged, his complexion growing purple. Gavin looked up at him, his arm trembling. "I'm so fucking sorry," Gavin whispered, breaking through the Ripper's grasp on him momentarily. His voice broke as he swallowed and the Ripper tore back into Gavin's consciousness. Releasing Oliver from his grip, he slammed the wolf onto the ground.

. . .

DUST PEPPERED THE AIR IN A CLOUDY HAZE. THE GROUND shook, cascading debris from the ceiling in a steady stream. Gavin flexed his jaw, fangs aching from the kill, wanting the tang of blood on his tongue.

Shaking the high off, Gavin's heart sank. He had done exactly what Oliver had told him would not happen. He had let the Blood Prince out to play. Caging the beast within came easier than usual with the sobering view of his dead friend, lying in a lifeless heap in front of him. Something about this seemed too easy. Oliver shouldn't have fallen so effortlessly, even for the Ripper. Ollie should not have fallen so quickly.

Gavin took tentative steps toward the body. He stared down into Ollie's paling face before falling to his knees. The wolf before him ceased to move but the urge to kill still ran rampant through the Prince of Blood. The cage Gavin had built seconds earlier shattered at the sight of Oliver's blood, but a part of him remained, allowing Gavin to feel the weight of what he had done.

"Ladies and Gentlemen." Palmer's voice boomed from the sidelines, tearing Gavin's attention away from Ollie's broken body. "It seems we have a winner and a very dead loser. Such a pity. Dawson was a good fighter, one of the best." Palmer turned his attention toward Gavin, his gaze cold and hard as if studying the vampire prince, but Gavin refused to budge. He would kill Palmer and release all of his fighters of their debts. Steeling himself, Gavin chose to focus on the roaring crowd above and raised both fists into the air before letting out a victorious howl of his own. He could play along if that's what Palmer wanted. For *now*.

"The *King* of Blood, ladies and gentlemen. I give to you the new King of Tatum!" Palmer's voice reverberated through the betting house, striking a chord in Gavin's chest.

His eyes widened as he pulled in another breath, trying to steady himself. What did he mean by *king*? Palmer turned, a smug look gliding across his undead features as his squad of ghouls picked up the body lying in the dirt. Grunting, they hoisted Ollie into the air, seizing his arms and legs as they crept back into the tunnels. The crowd erupted with cheers once more, but Gavin's blood ran cold as ice through his veins. Something was very wrong.

"Your parents," Palmer said, jumping down from his precarious perch and coming close enough to Gavin that he could smell his rancid, hot breath, "are dead." It came out as a deathly whisper just for him. Denial rang in Gavin's ears, finally and truly sobering him. Palmer was a vial trickster, surely this was just another way to play with his head? And yet, he knew who he really was. His true identity.

Gavin blinked before his anger and grief consumed him. Ollie and his parents were dead because of him. Everyone he held dear suffered.

Something inside him shattered, forcing Gavin back to reality. He moved at immortal speed, fleeing the pits and down the tunnel, snatching his torn shirt from the ground. He raced through the underground betting house toward the door that led out into Elirion. He needed to get back to his coven before the realm fell into the wrong hands.

His mind swam with thousands of thoughts as his body propelled him forward into the night. But the pain, he would not let it in. Not now. He, nor his kingdom, could afford for him to fall short if Palmer's declaration was true.

Gavin's legs burned, begging for him to slow his pace, but he pushed onward. The trees blurred around him as he passed, each one holding their own secrets. Gavin had always hated the Forest of Knowing, had always dreaded going through it on his way home to Tatum. Hallucinations lured all his demons to the surface, and although he should have been used to seeing the Blood Prince's victims by now, Gavin still couldn't stomach his crimes. Each vacant face drenched in scarlet blood with a gaping hole in their neck where their windpipe should be.

So many ghosts to haunt him, all brought to life by the magic of these trees.

"Enough," he hissed. "The dead will stay dead. Do not follow me, demons of the night. I'm protected by the goddess's blood!" Slowing, Gavin fell into an easy step, attempting to catch his breath. He'd invoked his grand-mother, Celeste, goddess of the Night, to shield him from the hauntings. Her Darkness shrouded the prince, warding off his phantoms, and the Forest of Knowing remained eerily silent.

A rustle of leaves stirred in the breeze that kissed his cheeks. Crows cawed overhead, their silhouettes taking shape against the moonlit sky as the tip of a knife pressed into Gavin's back. He stiffened as blood began to ooze beneath his tattered shirt. Every nerve throughout his body screamed to unleash his Ripper, begging to tear out his attacker's throat. Gavin inhaled sharply, breathing in the scents of cedar and lilac as his attacker spoke.

"The dead will always speak from their graves, but will you?" the assailant asked in a confident female tone. Exhaling, Gavin whirled around, allowing the knife's point to drag against his muscled torso before he wrapped his hands around her blade. Blackened blood began to seep from his palms, but he ignored the stinging pain.

"How many of you are there?" he asked, keeping his voice low so that only the girl could hear. She, to her credit, remained firm, smirking as her eyes locked onto Gavin's.

"Enough to kill you and your coven." Twigs snapped as more bodies came into view, engulfed in the shadows of the trees. Gavin's nostrils flared, his jaw set. He ground his teeth as he fought against the call for blood. They were women. Every last one of them. Gavin shook his head, not knowing whether to laugh at the notion of a gang of women bandits or at the fact that they were trying to jump him.

"Ladies," he said, casting his gaze around the forest, willing his eyes to adjust to the darkness. "Surely, there is enough of me to go around." He thought of Ollie. That was what his dearly departed friend would say. A scoff sounded from the girl in front of him.

"Fucking disgusting, your kind," she hissed as the blade cut deeper into Gavin's hand.

"Tora," one of the women called. The bandit turned toward the voice. It would be enough for him to escape and Gavin knew it, but he continued to hold firm on the blade. Letting the pain smother some of his bloodthirsty thoughts. Letting his scent squander that of the women around him.

"Let him go. The Black Widows have no reason to bid war with him. He is clearly distraught already."

"Silence," Tora snapped. "Don't ever question your queen!" Gavin heard whispered responses slither all around him.

The woman who had spoken coughed, as she emerged from the throng of bandit women. "Tora Belle. I am still your mother regardless of whatever self-proclaimed title you have thrown on yourself. Now, kindly remove the knife from this man's flesh."

Tora huffed a loud rough breath and pulled her dagger up, slicing deeper into Gavin's hand before wiping the black goo on her tanned pant leg, smearing it with pride. Her eyes shone deviously, but she remained silent as the older woman's words choked her own away. Women in pants were a new sight for Gavin. The ladies back in Tatum wore only the finest dresses and skirts, well, except for Lorelei.

When he took a step as if to leave, Tora whipped around, slinging her long black braids around her shoulders. "Where do you think you're going, bloodsucker?"

"Well, ya' see ma'am," Gavin drawled before his voice deadened, taking on a harsher tone, "I was hoping to leave." As if these woods weren't creepy enough, now Gavin had to deal with a mini band of bandit women. He rolled his eyes, setting his jaw as his tongue flicked over his fangs in frustration. He had to bite back his words. Something about these women rang death. Power given only by those that had killed. A power Gavin knew all too well.

"Is that judgment I see in your eyes, vamp?" Tora waved the blade around in the air, juggling it from finger to finger as she spoke.

"Judgment? Hardly." Gavin was growing more and more agitated the longer he was confined in this estrogen circle. "Let me go."

"Why should we do that?" Tora snapped.

"Tora," her mother chided. Tora shot her a 'wither and die' look before turning back to Gavin.

"Give me one good reason why? You seem to be on the run, which means there's probably a hefty bounty on that chocolate head of yours?" A sly smile curved the corners of her caramel lips.

"Speaking of delectable candies, your skin is the perfect shade of deep imported toffee. M'lady, why if you were to tame that unladylike spirit, you could be the belle of the ball." Gavin placed his uninjured hand to his chest. The Bandit Queen scowled and rolled her eyes.

"If I ever see you in my forest again," Tora hissed, coming within inches of Gavin's face, "I'll fucking gut you and string your innards from the trees as a warning to all those who cross the Black Widows." Gavin bit back the retort that played on his lips, having wasted too much time already. He waited for the Widow to make her final word.

"Oh, and one more thing," the Bandit Queen added. "Those spirits you see will never rest until you join them." With that, she turned and disappeared into the trees with the gang of women in tow. Gavin puffed out a breath. Sure, he could have used compulsion to free himself of the bandit, but he had more important things on his mind. The women disappeared almost as quickly as they came, leaving Gavin alone once more with the Prince of Blood breathing down his neck.

5

ROSE

*R*ose crept silently through the musty darkness, running her fingers along the rusty cages beneath the pits. "Ollie!" she hissed, venturing further in. She still could not find the big bastard. The wolfsbane she'd given him contained a tad of magic and a dash of hope that it would keep him alive and only *appear* to be dead. Rose knew the latter had worked. What worried her was the former.

"Oliver!" she snarled, growing frustrated, hoping beyond hope that he would hear her. Her hem was saturated with goddess knew what, and the stench in the air was potent enough to make even a mortal gag, never mind her sensitive immortal nose. Her nostrils burned, making her eyes water as she forced herself to continue searching for the wolf.

A soft moan echoed from one of the body carts in the far corner of the dungeon. The shadows grew stronger, creating a blanket of darkness so thick that Rose's vampire eyes couldn't see through it. Her anxiety intensified with each passing second as she fished in her skirts for a candle she'd been saving. Her trembling fingers curled around the wax and she was quick to bring it to her lips, whispering a spell. A spark was soon followed by a small flame engulfing the wick. Orange light flooded the block as Rose's gaze fell on a small cart.

Oliver Dawson was sprawled out atop it, lying on a heap of rotting corpses, bloodied and bruised. His throat no longer looked mangled, due to the concoction she had given him before the fight. She knew he would likely be furious, but she didn't care. He was *alive*.

"Ollie!" Rose gasped. Stepping lightly, Rose moved like the shadows until she was next to the wolf. His right eyelid was shades of purple and blue, swelling shut, and scarlet blood dried on his lips and matted his brows. Rose's eyes softened as she took his head gently in her hands. "Dawson, you big ass. Come on. Wake up!" Tears pricked at the corners of the heiress's eyes, threatening to spring free. There was so much riding on him living. If he died now, after everything, what would it all be for? Only part of Palmer's plans had been foiled. Rose realized she shouldn't have placed so much faith in her magic or the wolf, but seeing him lie there because of her...

Goddess save him, she silently prayed to the Night Queen.

Voices slithered through the darkness, catching Rose's ears, halting her breaths. Her heart thundered in her chest and her muscles tensed. If she was caught, it would be the end of her. It was one thing to be rooting around upstairs, but to be in the dungeons, saving a 'dead' wolf, was another.

"Sorry," she muttered quickly to an unconscious Ollie before turning and snuffing out her flame. Darkness descended all around her and her eyes blinked rapidly, trying to adjust to her new surroundings. The voices echoed closer as their footsteps reverberated through the tunnels. Rose moved silently, trying to listen. If they had information, she wanted it.

"You blithering idiot! How could you let him disappear!" a familiar voice hissed.

Palmer.

"S-sorry boss! He went into the Forest of Knowing…" A henchman squirmed. Rose smirked. Of course, Jagger had gone into the forest. A good ploy, but a dangerous one. Rose knew of the magic that lay hidden within the trees. The tricks that Limos played on vampires, turning their hunger and bloodlust into an unquenchable ache. The victims one would see… Rose only hoped that the goddess was with Gavin, protecting him from such debauchery.

"And what exactly do you have to fear in there? You're dead, you fool! If you weren't, you would be now!" Rose could hear things being tossed around on the other side of the wall. Glass shattered and the familiar smell of tonic wafted through the air. She imagined what expensive gin had just been wasted. The smell of it bloomed along the halls, mixing like toxin with the smell of rot.

Rose fidgeted in her spot, clasping her fingers as she craned her neck to hear more. A door creaked in the distance, cracking a sliver of yellow light onto the floor. The echo of footsteps grew faint and an eerie silence took hold of the dungeon. She sucked in a deep breath and inched closer to the door, rounding the corner of the block. Slipping closer so that she could see through a large crack in the partially closed door, Rose kept her breathing even and shallow.

Palmer was shaking his head, making ugly red curls sling about. "He was meant to break, not escape. What the flying *fuck* are we going to do now?" Palmer bellowed, deep and throaty, to the room of idiots around him. His short legs waddled, his feet hitting the stone with a dull *thud* before stopping. "Son of a bitch!" he shouted, tossing another brass tray, likely one of his own heirlooms, into the air. It hit the floor with a furious clatter. Rose winced, her muscles tensing as she eased in closer.

"Boss?" a man stepped forward, his voice tentative. It was raspy, and the ghoul was uncharacteristically clean. Grey skin clung to his bones, sinking into areas where organs once were. A mess of dirty brown hair sat atop his head. His eyes were clouded over, sunken into his skull. Brown trousers hung from his hips, a size too large for his skeletal frame. He was a wretched sight, and Rose wondered why her father entertained himself with such creatures. Slowing her breathing until it halted, Rose turned to take in the rest of the ghoul. She didn't care what his name was, that was irrelevant, but if he knew where her sister was...

"What?" Palmer snapped.

Recoiling in on himself, the ghoul fidgeted with the bones of his fingers. "What if we use the wolf?" the ghoul boy asked. Palmer whirled to face the bookie, arching a brow.

"What the actual hell are you talking about?" He eyed the creature, taking a step closer.

"The w-wolf and prince were friends, right? Wh-what if we taunted Jagger into coming back?" The look Palmer gave the ghoul made him shrink back into the shadow of the others.

"Hmm," Palmer stroked his double chin thoughtfully, "maybe something can be done with that. Bring me the body!"

No!

Rose turned on her heel and scurried back to Oliver. "Ollie!" she whispered, but the wolf remained motionless. "Oliver Dawson! If you don't move your ass, we're both gonna be in deep shit, now come on!" Ollie's eyes cracked open, searching her face.

"Whaaa...?" Oliver moaned as he began to stir. Sluggishly, he brought his hand to his forehead. Rose noted its coloring, watching as the wolf winced. Purples, blues, and blacks painted his knuckles as hues of pinks and reds swirled in a swollen mass to the rest of his hand. He must have broken it on Gavin's cheek.

"Fucking 'ay," he slurred, pushing himself upright. Silent but quickly, Rose moved to his side with ease and slung an arm around the fighter's naked torso, helping him to his feet. He was much heavier than she'd anticipated, though Rose didn't know why she expected the wolf to be anything but difficult. He was a full-grown brawler, an alpha. Tight, corded muscles tensed beneath the his bronzed skin as Ollie staggered, leaning into the vampire. The bane's effects had done a number on him, but moreover, they'd saved his hide. Rose turned to look at the wolf, watching cautiously as the last of the bane wore off and Oliver Dawson grew more aware of his surroundings.

"Where are we?" he whispered, looking around.

"Shut up!" Rose hissed. "I need to get you out of here." Ollie opened his mouth to speak but quickly shut it. *Good*, Rose thought. They needed to move quietly if they wanted to make it out. Despite her questions for the evil Palmer, Rose needed to get Ollie to safety. She would not have him hurt because of her actions.

"Taking me to your bedroom, eh?" Ollie asked, wagging his eyebrows at the vampire. Rose glowered, flicking her tongue over the tip of her fang as she kept silent. "I see you've come around to shagging me, eh?"

Nausea swept over Rose, bile lurching up her throat as she thought about Ollie's touch. He was a dog and yet, there was something alluring about him. She let out a sigh, scrunched her nose, and replied, "If we get out of here safely, I'll give you a night you won't forget."

"Lass, I intend on taking you up on that," Ollie drawled, before bending down to scoop her up with both arms. She wanted to object, given his recent run-in with death, and if circumstances had been normal, Rose would have swatted the wolf for touching her without permission. But with Palmer and his goon squad on their way, she left it alone. As long as they made it out of the tunnels safely.

"Move along the wall, toward the door," Rose whispered. "I'll call upon the goddess to shadow us. But those goonies are on their way to get your corpse and I don't want to be here when they come up empty-handed."

"Which goddess?" Ollie asked.

"Celeste." Ollie's brows furrowed, his eyes narrowed and jaw set, and nodded in silent agreement. Rose knew she'd struck a chord, calling on the vampire goddess in the presence of a Moonchild, but with danger quickly approaching, she knew she needed to act fast. She'd apologize later. She'd pray to Celeste for guidance and to Artemis for forgiveness.

Rose whispered under her breath, feeling the cold creep along her skin, the hair rising on her arms and the icy nip at her neck as cloaks of black shrouded them. Ollie's eyes widened at the devilry, but again, kept silent. They would be able to see, but their enemies would never know they were there.

The door to Palmer's office screeched open and a series of footsteps clambered down the corridor, echoing off the stones. The smell of rot choked the air from her lungs. Rose's ears picked up their racing pace.

"Hang on tight," Ollie whispered, his lips grazing her ear, sending shivers down Rose's spine. With no further warning, the wolf ran. Rose held on, her hair whipping in the air behind them. She nestled against the wolf's chest, whispering directions, watching as he followed each one until they were inches from the exit. Ollie slowed his pace to a stop and set Rose to her feet.

"Go," she whispered, turning to face the wolf and placing her palm to his olive cheek. "I'll fend them off." Heat greeted her palm as the slightest hue of pink crept across his features, mixing with the blues and purples. His darkened eyes widened as they stared into her own.

"Come with me." It wasn't a question, but a plea. Rose shook her head.

"I'll meet you in town, Oliver Dawson. Until then," she fished for her change purse, pulling it from her neck, handing it out to the hulking man, "Take my coin and lay low." The footsteps behind them grew louder. "I'll hold off the ghouls," she said, pushing to her tiptoes, planting a soft kiss on the wolf's cheek. His eyes softened, wavering under her touch.

"I can't just leave ya 'ere, lass."

"Please," she choked out, wrapping her arms around his torso. Rose heard his heart thumping wildly in his chest. She didn't know why, but she wanted to *feel* for this man. She gulped down the lump of anxiety forming in her throat when something within her cracked. Whether it was her hard exterior or the walls she'd placed to protect herself, Rose didn't know. Now was not the time to be weak. Her breathing staggered as she tried to compose herself before she pushed from Dawson.

"Go," she whispered, turning back to face the tunnels, but she knew the wolf was still behind her. Casting a look over her shoulder, Rose sucked in a deep breath and snarled, "Go!"

"Come back to me," he whispered.

Rose froze, the air ripping from her lungs. She could

feel her walls crumbling. She felt so exposed, so—*vulnerable.* That's when she knew that the wolf beside her would be her *downfall.*

"I will," she said, before disappearing back into the darkness. She had questions for Palmer and she would get her damn answers.

❦

LEAVING DAWSON'S SIDE WAS PERHAPS THE STUPIDEST thing she could have done. Rose knew it and yet, she had left him. Darkness swallowed her once again, shrouding her into the shadows of the tunnels as the rancid smell gripped at her senses. What she had to do was not going to be fun. Facing the ghouls was one thing, and though Palmer was short in stature, she was sure the rumors held some truth. He was not gracious, even to women.

Dahlia was close, Rose could feel it in her bones. She could always tell when her sister was near. Like a twintuition, though her sister was a few years older. Rose's inner radar had been going haywire since she'd set foot on the property. She had never planned on assisting either Gavin or Oliver, but her intuition was screaming to do something. That in doing so, they'd be helpful in finding Dahlia.

Palmer was the face of all things illegal, her father's shield against Elirion's judgment. Zachary Coston worked behind the scenes on the Pits, delivering the finest wolfsbane, pleasure houses and bets the realm had to offer. And if there was one ghoul that knew his family's dirty secrets, it was Sven Palmer. Which meant he must've had some clue as to where Rose could start her search.

The smell of decay infiltrated the heiress's nose again as she went deeper into the tunnel leading to the underground dungeon Palmer kept his skeletons in. A twist here, a turn there, had left the heiress enough time to adjust to the change in light. Rose scratched at her golden locks as she poured through the labyrinth in her mind, her eyes off in the distant facets of her brain, ears deaf to footsteps that approached.

Air whooshed from Rose's lungs as she fell backward. Her ass cracked hard against the stone floor, her spine screaming with blinding pain. Something large had rammed into her torso. Rose blinked as stars swarmed her vision and clutched at her head.

"What the fuck?" she cursed, blinking several times and looking up, her heart nearly stopped. Malicious black eyes peered down at the heiress, raking over her body. She felt every muscle within her cringe. Rose clawed at the cool stone under her and pushed up to her feet. Her muscles groaned in protest.

"Rosalie Coston," Palmer's slithery voice hissed. Rose smiled, exposing her ivory fangs.

"Sven," she greeted, dipping her head and giving the kingpin a courteous bow.

"Such a treat to find you here in the Pits."

"It's a treat to be in these parts," Rose replied as she took a step toward the ghoul, walking a circle around him like a lion sizing up her prey. Her hips swayed seductively as she reached out, tracing her index finger along Sven's fat neck. The ghoul mob boss gulped.

"Why are you in my tunnels?" he asked, straight to the point as always. Her time spent with Sven had always been business, and only with her father. Rose licked at her fangs, aching with venom. She straightened her shoulders and met the kingpin's gaze. His dark, dead eyes bore no secrets, making him extraordinarily good at his job.

She leaned in, smelling his awful breath and whispered, "Where is my sister? Where is Dahlia?"

The kingpin chuckled, taking a step away from her and clasped his hands behind his back. He began to pace, creeping in and out of the dungeon shadows. "You Coston ladies have always been the sultry type," he stated matter-of-factly. Men were always begging for their hands in marriage. Whether it was for land, power, or both. "Men like sultry little things like you," he crooned. "Which explains why your sister's little plum head earned the most coin in the Bloodwhore Markets."

No.

"You're lying," Rose snarled, curling her fingers into fists. There was no way Palmer had sold her sister, there couldn't be. Dahlia was his boss, after all, and yet, she had the sinking feeling that Palmer had just told the truth.

"Am I, though?" He smiled as if he could read her thoughts, flashing his green teeth. His lips curled into a grin. Rose's fists furled and unfurled, her dagger-like nails pressing into her palms.

"You fucking lie!" she accused again, tears pricking at the corners of her lapis lazuli eyes. Her thoughts clouded. She could see only red. She would make Palmer pay for his misdeeds.

She would make him pay for what he did to Dahlia.

Dahlia.

Rose's legs moved faster than her thoughts as she lunged forward with immortal speed, grasping at the ghoul. Cold flesh swam under her fingers as she curled her vice-like grip around Palmer's white collar and lifted him into the air. Palmer's legs dangled as he struggled to find his breath, kicking furiously at the vampire heiress. Rose paid no mind to him, seeking only vengeance. She hauled him up further and with a quick shove, Palmer's back was against the cool stone wall. Cracks echoed through the tunnels, the wall splintering as dirt and debris rained from the ceiling, showering them both.

"Where is my sister?" she roared.

"Don't you worry, love," Palmer rasped. "You'll be with your bloodwhore sister soon enough." Hands gripped at Rose. Bones and nails and weapons wielded at her spine, pressing into her skin.

"Put him down," a voice commanded, neither male nor female, only dead. Slowly, Rose weighed her options— she could crush the kingpin and allow him to take his answers to the grave, she could fight back, or she could go willingly with the chance that her sister was safe. Palmer smiled as his henchmen dragged Rose to the ground, pinning her arms and legs.

Looking at his men, he said, "Take her away. Tomorrow she faces the same fate as Dahlia."

6

OLLIE

Thump.
Thump.
Thump.

Ollie's heart beat rapidly in his chest. His head was light, buzzing with Rose's words. *'If we get out of here alive, I'll show you a night you won't forget.'* He couldn't believe his ears. *Bloodsuckers, vampires, fangbangers* never gave him the time of day and here he was about to win big! His lips spread into a wide grin across his face, one that made him look stupid, but he didn't give a damn. Artemis could strike him dead for the thoughts crossing his mind, but there was something about the lass he couldn't let go of. She was different, and if Ollie didn't know better, he would say he was falling in something short of love for the lady. She was finer than any woman in his pack, sure, but she was a *vampire.*

His eyes scrunched together, closing as he sucked in a deep breath before exhaling slowly. His mind was running a mile a minute, his finger steepled at his lips, tapping them to the rhythm of his thoughts. Rose had saved his life. But *why?* Furthermore, she'd made him a promise, and Ollie fully intended on holding her to it.

Ollie's stomach fluttered at the mere thought of Rose. She was troublesome, and his gut told him to run for the hills, but his legs refused to move.

He couldn't leave *without* her.

Oliver stood there as Rose retreated back into the crumbling tunnels. *Why… why… why?* His head was finally clear from the effects of the bane and the last thing he remembered was drawing Gavin's blood with one well-planted blow to the face. He remembered savoring the moment, giving Gavin a good wallop to his smug, little face. But Gavin didn't deserve to think he'd killed his best friend. He remembered the Prince of Blood gripping his throat, the fuzziness in his brain. He remembered the gasping, the dark circles encroaching on his vision, right before he plunged into the dirt and the world before him turned black. But, Rose, the beautiful deviant, had saved him. Though he didn't understand how, he knew that whatever she'd placed in the bane had spared his life.

Sweat beaded on the werewolf's brow as he looked at the tunnel, the sun dipping below the horizon, his breath still thick in the air. He was eternally grateful. She had not only saved him, but Oliver was sure that she had saved his best friend from a lifetime of pain and regret.

The trickstress now left him out here, assuming he would just leave her behind. Oliver may have been a lot of things in this life, but being a decent man was something he'd still held onto. Leaving a young woman alone, with Palmer, was anything but decent, no matter how capable the woman was of taking care of herself.

Taking in a deep, steadying breath, Ollie stepped back into the darkness after his golden-haired savior.

❦

GAVIN

GAVIN SIGHED AS HIS PACE SLOWED. THE FIGHT'S adrenaline began to wane, leaving him more than a little weary. It had been years since he'd returned home to Tatum. Truth be told, he wished he would never have to set foot in the kingdom again. He'd hoped that his younger brother, Declan, would have taken the throne with his parents' blessing, leaving Gavin alone with his gambling, fights, and booze. But Gavin knew that if his parents were truly dead, there would be no blessing ceremony for Declan and the throne would pass to the eldest living Sinclair heir.

Him.

Gavin sucked in another deep breath. His pulse thrummed in his veins. He reached to pinch the bridge of his nose, slowly exhaling. A Rose Bound ceremony would commence after the death of the ruling King and Queen when one full moon passed. Gavin had no idea how much time had elapsed since his parent's death. Murder was the only viable explanation for a royal blood vampires death, especially a bound pair. If one of his parents perished, both would. The Rose Bound ceremony ensured that, having tethered the two life forces together, binding their souls.

Gavin knew his choices were—*radical*—that he had cast his family into the light by buying humans and saving their lives. But he had never thought anyone would retaliate like this. Nothing in a way so… dirty. If someone had a problem with Gavin, then they needed to come face him. Gavin set his jaw, biting back the Ripper that begged to be released again, fighting against the wave of anger that threatened to consume him. He would let his Ripper out to play when he found the creature responsible for his pain. And then, he would punish them.

He clenched his eyes shut and focused on his breathing, pushing the negative thoughts from his mind. His fingers curled, nails digging into his stinging thumb. Skin broken, blood oozing, Gavin held onto one thought.

If that monster touched my siblings, the streets of Tatum would run red.

7

OLLIE

*O*llie's vision adjusted instantly, his wolf instincts kicking in. The smell of decay, the moisture in the air, everything was amplified. Ollie pushed himself into the transformation, yearning for his most dangerous form. Fire consumed his body, his bones cracked, and his spine curved. He bit his tongue, swallowing his screams. Tears sprang from his amber eyes, running silently down his olive cheeks. He couldn't howl, not if he wanted to find Rose alive. Fur sprang from his skin where clothes had once been. His nails grew into claws and Ollie hunched over onto all four legs. Piercing screams echoed off the tunnel walls, ringing in his werewolf ears, leading him to push his legs to move faster than they'd ever moved before.

Rose.

Ollie's breaths quickened at the sound of another bloodcurdling scream ripping through the air. His wolf wanted revenge. His wolf wanted to make someone pay. Those screams told him she was being handled in an unruly way. A lass, whether royal or common, never deserved a man's unwanted touch. Gavin had taught him that. Ollie prayed that he would reach her in time and that his wolf would cause her no harm, but nothing was guaranteed in this form.

There was something special about Rose, something he couldn't place his claws on, something which made him protective over her. He hadn't bonded with her, at least not yet, but Ollie wondered briefly if this instinctive protective role was what it felt like to imprint. As he rounded a bend in the cell block, he spotted four ghouls, each in different stages of decay, carrying Rose as she kicked and fought against them.

"Let me go, you ruddy stinking bastards!" she snarled, thrashing in their arms. Her eyes locked onto Ollie's and Rose stilled.

"Finally," one of the four croaked. "The bonnie lass has run out of steam, eh?"

Rose remained silent, her eyes wide as she took in the silent wolf. Ollie's teeth curled back from his maw and a growl tore from his throat. The ghouls stopped, dropping Rose to the floor below as they craned to look at him.

"Who let the fuckin' dog out?" the one closest to Ollie asked.

"Not I," the other three answered in unison.

"'Tis a jolly shame then, eh?" the leader replied before unhinging his rotting jaw, snarling black teeth at the wolf. The three others followed suit. Jaws hung open, exposing rotted teeth.

Rose skittered backward, muttering under her breath as she disappeared behind a wall of shadows. Ollie stared in her direction for a split second before his gaze flickered back to the four. He let out a snarl and then, he lunged.

Darkness, blacker than black, shielded the young woman from his view. He didn't know what happened in that moment as his wolf form took over, blocking out his memory. Teeth tore into dead flesh and black painted the walls. It was only moments of horror. Moments of pure blackout before the beast ceased its killing, and Ollie shifted back. Body parts littered the floor, and the stench of death consumed the air. Ollie's eyes widened.

He had done this.

His wolf had done *this*.

Vomit crept up his throat, emptying the contents of his stomach into the blackened mess that was the floor. His vision swam, tunneling along the edges as his head grew light. He should have been used to the gore. He was a goddessdamned champion in the Underground. Ollie reached out, holding himself upright against the stone wall. He leaned his head against the cool grey stone, trying to steady his breathing. Sweat peppered his brow, gore coated his flesh. He smelled worse than he ever had. Ollie's nose wrinkled as another bout of bile rose up his throat, painting the wall before him.

"Fuckin' aye," he hissed. He needed a moment to gather himself before finding Rose. If she were smart, she would have vacated after seeing the demon wolf he could be.

But Rose was not easily frightened. The layer of darkness dissipated, revealing the heiress where she sat. She moved to his side in a flash.

"Did you have to puke and add to the stank down here? As if it weren't unbearable enough," she chided, tossing a golden lock over her shoulder. Oliver snorted at her in response. This game between them was the last thing on his mind.

"Where's Palmer's prick ass?" Oliver asked, as he pushed himself away from the vomit-covered stone. He wiped the corners of his full lips.

"Well…" Rose trailed off.

"You don't know, do you?" Rose shook her head.

"No," she admitted and Oliver couldn't help but notice the red blush on her cheeks. Shit, she was beautiful.

"We have to get outta 'ere, lass." There was no discussion about it. No snarky comment on Rose's lips as she nodded.

"Okay, let's go."

"Oh, but the party has just begun." Palmer's rancid voice cut from behind Rose. Shadows moved in the corner of Ollie's eye. *More ghouls,* he realized. The air around them chilled. The hair on Ollie's arms stood on end as the undead crept in around Rose. His eyes flickered back to Palmer, a grin etched across the kingpin's decaying face. Sounds of a fight perked in the background. Ollie knew Rose was in battle. Flames erupted to his left, nearly singing his skin, biting back the eerie cool that descended around the shadow creatures. Ollie remained statuesque. He wouldn't give Palmer the opportunity to strike. Not when he already played dirty.

"What's the matter, Dawson?" Palmer crooned. "Don't you wanna help the bonnie lass?" Palmer was trying to goad him.

"Fuck you," he hissed between clenched teeth. His fingers furled and unfurled at his naked sides. He wanted to move, wanted to help the heiress, but moving meant giving the slime boss before him an opening. *What to do? Fuck! What to fucking do...*

More grunts, bone crunching against bone as punches flew. The shadows crept closer. Rose was being overpowered, and he, he was doing nothing...

Ollie's jaw gnashed harder, his muscles feathering. His wolf was surfacing. *Shit.* Ollie sucked in a breath and waited for the inevitable, soul-crushing pain to come back. He'd transitioned once today without the moon, a thing only alphas were capable of. But was he strong enough to do it again?

Ollie closed his eyes for no more than a blink, no more than a split second, opening them as Rose flew through the air, crashing into an empty body cart on the other side of him. Her body slumped, chin to chest, unmoving. Ollie felt the prickle of the beast within. His vision flashed red, then blurred and he felt what was coming. *Transition*, the wolf whispered within, urging him to lose control. Ollie's breath hitched in his chest.

"You bastard!" he seethed, feeling the pull of the wolf. The transition had begun. Ollie's face began to contort, taking on the wolf's snout, and thick globs of saliva seeped from his jaws. The grey-skinned ghoul beside Palmer smiled wickedly and turned to his boss.

"Erving has arrived, my lord," he croaked. A new set of footsteps echoed along the stone walls of the tunnel and Ollie's ears perked as they approached. His eyes flickered over to where the sounds came from and took in a smaller being. Erving was dark and young, no more than twenty years of age, with skin that clung to his bones, accentuating his skeletal figure. He stepped between the kingpin and his lackey before nodding to the unconscious Rose on the cart.

"She smells ripe for the taking, Boss." His voice was weak, nasally. Oliver had never seen this man before. Palmer's goons usually consisted of the undead, but this man was very much alive and lusting after what Oliver wanted.

"Touch her, you fucking cockroach, and you won't have a prick left to plow a billy goat." Oliver spat the last word, his voice not his own in this form.

Erving's smile grew across his skinny, horse-like face as he said, "Fucking try me, bitch," and took a step toward Rose.

Ollie saw red and released a guttural roar from his core and let go.

※

Blood.

Screams.

Chaos.

Ollie heard them all but registered them in the back of his mind. His wolf had taken over and with it came a massacre. Both lackeys lay dead and torn apart at his feet and yet, somehow, during the ordeal, Palmer's slimy ass had slipped through the cracks and disappeared.

No matter, Ollie thought. He would get the skeezeball and reunite him with his pals soon enough. A moan sounded from the corner as Ollie whirled back, a snarl erupting from his throat as his hair stood on end.

Rose clutched at her head, blinking several times before looking around the chamber, confused. There would be time later to explain the bloodshed, but first, he had to get her to safety. He couldn't understand what had made her turn back. They'd been free and yet, she put herself right back into danger's clutches. Ollie willed himself to turn back. He fought against his primal instincts, pushing the wolf down to take control. He could feel his fingers burn as his claws pulled back into nails. His skeleton snapped and a howl erupted from his maw. Bones broke before resetting themselves as Ollie shifted. Sweat poured from him, running in streams down his face, dripping into his amber eyes and down his nose. Tears welled as he fought the sting of his emotions. *It would be done soon,* he reminded himself. It would all be over soon.

Rose's beautiful eyes swept over the blood-soaked room. They widened a fraction when they rested on Oliver, yet, fear was not what Oliver detected in their depths. In an instant, she sprang forward, throwing her arms around his gore-coated neck. Oliver stumbled backward into the vomit-covered wall, his feet struggling for traction before stone pressed into the brute's back, cool and hard. Ollie wrapped his arms around the lassie's petite waist, taking in the sweet aroma of her hair. Rose pulled back and studied his face, which was plastered in ink-black ghouls blood. Her forehead creased as she studied him for a few moments more and then relaxed.

"Thank you," she breathed, wrapping her arms back around his neck.

"No thanks necessary, love." Rose pulled away from Ollie and gave his arm a light shove as she inspected her dress.

"You've made my clothes all bloody," Rose huffed, looking down at the inked splotches on her blouse. She made a disapproving sound, but she was alive. Ollie would take her wrath any day of the week because she was *alive*. Ollie's lips curled into a smirk.

"I think it's an improvement," Ollie replied, flashing a toothy smile. There was a light in her eyes that he had not noticed before. "What do ya say we get outta here now, lass?" Ollie asked as he dragged a hand over his matted hair. He was utterly confused by her lack of concern about the bodies that littered the floor.

"I think that's a wonderful plan, Moonchild. You need a bath." Rose pinched her nose. "You stink."

"Ah, love, is that an invitation?"

"In your dreams, mutt!" she scoffed. Ollie chuckled. The vampiress would certainly keep him on his toes and their little game of cat and mouse amused him. Rose turned from the wolf and started trekking through the bodies toward the exit. Ollie laughed again as he watched her stumble before she hurried forward. "Coming, wolf boy?" she asked, peering over her shoulder.

"Wherever 'tis you go, I shall follow," Ollie replied.

What scared him the most, is that he really felt like he meant it.

8

GAVIN

*G*avin had traveled night and day, despite the discomfort he was in when the sun was high in the sky. His legs burned and begged for him to stop, but he pushed forward. Rolling green hills and powder blue skies flooded his vision ahead, a narrow loam trail and the smells of a town, leading the way. Birds chirped from the forest trees behind him, the sounds of twitter patter in the air as spring approached. If only they knew the forest's secrets. Gavin shrugged, a small smile playing on his lips. It was silly to think birds would know the secrets of the lands any more than the trees would. It had been ages since Gavin had seen spring, spending most of his time in a brothel with bloodwhores or gambling his coin away on fights in the Underground.

His grumbling stomach ripped his thoughts back to the present and his current predicament. He would need to eat. *Soon.* Gavin struggled to divert his hunger pangs, breathing deep. He wanted blood and a good romp in the sack. If he didn't find a bloodwhore soon, the Ripper would rampage and kill the entire town.

Gavin closed his eyes and took a moment to gather himself, focusing on the things that didn't make him want to kill everything in sight. The feel of his body in the sunlight, the bogged down heaviness it left his immortal form. The crisp morning air, gently nipping at his skin, raising small pebbles, the thundering of his heart. He drew in a breath, slowly exhaling, grounding himself before opening his eyes. He was *not* his Ripper. *He* was *not* his Ripper. Ever so slowly, Gavin peeled open his eyes and set his track into the village. Tatum was another few days' travel, and he needed to find a place to sleep for the evening and rest his weary feet. He shuffled along the dirt road, kicking dust into the air as he came to a small worn sign made of wood, held together by rusted nails, it read, *Northpass.* Gavin assumed the town had sprung up after his departure from Tatum. He had never been to such a place, never ventured through such a town but shrugged his shoulders and moved onward.

✤

NORTHPASS, A LITTLE SHIT STAIN OF A TOWN, A BLIP ON THE map that sat on the lands ruled in Tatum, Elirion, came into Gavin's view as he trekked up the loam-covered trail. Townspeople flooded the streets, speaking a tongue that the young prince could barely understand. Music filled his ears, dancing out of open tavern doors as drunkards and bloodwhores wobbled onto the cobblestone streets, laughing and clinging to one another. Gavin's lip curled in disgust. As much as he supported the humans having rights, he despised the pigheaded decisions the lowly made. It reminded him of the Pits.

Oh three goddesses, the Pits... He'd killed Ollie. Pain lanced in Gavin's stomach, his eyes narrowing into a wince as his hands clasped at his belly through tattered cloth. Gavin clenched his jaw, closed his eyes and whispered a prayer to Celeste for guidance. Guidance for his soul. Guidance for his departed friend into the realm beyond.

A crash sounded in the tavern to Gavin's right, some yelling rose over the music, pulling Gavin from his self-loathing. His eyes flew open despite the aching pangs in his stomach as the young prince's gaze flitted around him. He took in cloaked figures dressed in darker fabrics, bobbing in and out of street shops. Vendors that lined either side of the cobbled road sold everything from meats to clothing to flowers. Behind the shops were small stone buildings, each likely a home to some poor family just trying to make ends meet.

Home.

Gavin missed this so much. He'd missed so much. If he'd have been there, would this have happened? Would his parents have met their untimely end? Gavin swallowed, a lump forming in his throat as his mind continued hurri-caning questions. He wondered how Aurora would be when he saw her. Would her little eyes be filled with anger? Or would they be delighted to see her eldest brother? Would she even know him? He remembered her springy brown curls, her dark hazel eyes that reminded him so much of his own, the way her chubby toddler legs tottered as she tried to walk, and he remembered the look of confu-sion on her face when he left. He remembered that day like no other, as it was his last day in the castle before his inner demons drove him astray.

"Gavin!" his mother yelled across the mile-long dining table. "This insolent behavior has to stop!" His mother rarely lost her temper, oh, but when she did, hell seemed a better alternative. Amara

Sinclair was a force to be reckoned with. There was no doubt she won the crown and the hearts of her people in one swoop during the weeks leading up to their Rose Bound ceremony. Gavin snorted in response, doubting any answer he would give her would be enough to rectify what she had caught him doing.

"Mother, it was just a game of cards."

"Cards do not result in the loss of so much family coin!" she hissed. Gavin's father piped in from his shadowed chair in the corner. "Yes, Gavin, so where did the money really go?" But Gavin remained silent. His father, Valerio, was a mysterious, quiet ruler. One that most used to fear, yet not since Aurora was born. He had taken a back seat to the violence that ran deep within his veins and subdued his unrighteous dealings, especially those concerning women. The coven was not accommodating with their ruler's new stance.

"It's not like I squandered away the entire fortune," Gavin said loosely, twiddling his thumbs in front of him. Gambling had become a nightly routine for the young princeling. It was a way for him to vanish into the shadows. He detested being in the spotlight and being a royal vampire put him there more often than he liked.

Amara growled deep within her throat, a sound Gavin had only heard on rare occasions and never directed at him. "Gavin Jagger Sinclair, gambling is not a way a prince should spend his time or his coin!" She slammed her hands down on the table, scattering papers into the air. "I did not raise a heathen child!"

Gavin rolled his eyes, such a shitty thing to do for a teenager, but he was just that. A teenager. No one could tell him otherwise. He wanted to live. To play on the wild side of the law, of his father. He wanted to gamble and drink and fuck. He wanted nothing more than to melt away into nothingness. Gavin stood from his chair, the screech of wood against stone breaking the heavy silence that loomed in the air. "I'm leaving," he slurred out. "Now, Mother." And with that, he stumbled on drunken legs out of the dining hall. The hum of alcohol still buzzing in his head.

. . .

REGRET STABBED HIS CHEST. SIX YEARS. HE'D BE GONE SIX whole years. If only he could hear her ranting once more, he would apologize and beg her for forgiveness. Had he been a better son, his parents may not have been murdered. Had he been home with them, things would have turned out very differently, and Gavin knew it.

No.

Tears welled in his eyes, spilling silent streams down alabaster cheeks. He tried to swallow again, choking on the memory. He couldn't let the past haunt him, despite the all too real, pain. The memories flooded him, pushing against his waking thoughts like tidal waves to a dinghy, feeding the Ripper that stole away in his body, waiting until he let his guard down. Gavin wiped his cheeks with the back of his hands, balling them into fists. The Prince of Blood was vulnerable, weak, despicable, and his enemies, whomever they were, were always watching. Movement to his left brought Gavin's instincts to high alert, as shadows caught his eye. Gavin spun in the grass slick beneath his boots, tearing roots from the earth.

Nothing.

Dread crept up his throat. His fangs pricked his bottom lip as they emerged at the sense of danger.

"M-mister!" a child's voice rang out. Gavin's face whipped from side to side, searching for the phantom that visited him.

No one.

"M-m-mister," it chimed again, pulling on his hand. Gavin looked down; his eyes widened as he peered into a pair of strikingly familiar hazel eyes.

Aurora?

Gavin's eyes grew frantic with realization. She couldn't be here. The castle was still miles off. Declan would never allow her to wander. Gavin shook his head and the illusion dissipated, leaving a little girl with bright red hair and blue eyes, her image a far stretch from that of his baby sister's. The girl's face was dirty and frightened. His heart roared in his ears, each thump like a clap of thunder. At his changed expression, the girl turned and ran away, just as Aurora would have. Anger reared its ugly head deep within his core. Had he allowed himself to fall so far from grace that he was ashamed of who he would be in his sister's eyes? Contrary to popular lore, vampires were ruled by their emotions. A vampire with a loose handle on his was a dangerous thing, making him one of the most dangerous.

Blood trickled from his lip where his fangs pierced his skin. The taste of it awakening a carnal need for more. Eyes blazing red, Gavin shot after the little girl who had reminded him of his shame. Reminded him of his broken heart.

He had struck down his best friend. The only man to fully stand by him no matter who he decided to become. Tears stung his eyes at the thought. He would never see his golden-headed friend again. He would never hear his witty comebacks and failed attempts at flirting his way into a woman's bed.

Gavin's vision blurred as his Ripper took hold, catching the girl in his clutches. Her screams were distant but blood-curdling enough to keep him in the present. Lurching forward, Gavin plunged his fangs deep within the little girl's throat. A hint of a whimper played in his ears as he tore into her, relishing her delectable blood as it poured down his throat. He could feel her growing limp; her body slackening as she leaned into his torso. Her life force was divine and Gavin drank until he could taste no life left within. His Ripper tossed the lifeless body aside as a hunger for death lingered in the air. He needed more.

Gavin was accustomed to his Ripper's needs. He hated

losing control, hated being a monster, but his Ripper, he loved the horror. Loved the bloodshed and chaos. His lips perked at the thought of death, at what he did. Moving faster than Gavin had ever had, Gavin's Ripper tore through the town, unleashing a bloodbath in his wake.

9

GAVIN

Blood oozed down Gavin's chin, cooling, coagulating, as he released his last victim. Life force coursed through his veins and oh goddess, was it wonderful. He loved the high of a massacre, the fear that permeated the air as he took an innocent and drained them. They didn't call him the Prince of Blood without reason. Unclenching his fist, he dropped the dead to the street like a sack of potatoes and closed his eyes. His tongue flicked out in a serpentine manner, licking his lips as he relished the tangy taste.

Gavin peeled open an eyelid and raised his arm to his mouth, smearing away the remnants of his meal and looked to the horizon. He'd spent the entire day murdering and now, the sun had retired for the evening and his insatiable hunger was quenched. He huffed out a breath, feeling his skin burn under the last of Dia's rays, delighted in the fact that her warmth would retreat for the night, back into her prison with Limos in a never-ending battle. Despite his discomfort, The Prince of Blood felt *invincible*.

Go away! Gavin's thoughts screamed at the Ripper, but the demon curled his lips upwards.

"You can't take me away that easily," he whispered.

Yes, I can.

Ah, the fight has returned. Where was it when these people needed their prince?

Gavin slammed his eyes shut, willing the beast to his cage. He had wrought enough destruction for one day, and Gavin had unlocked the door, his unraveling emotions opening the floor for bloodshed and mayhem. *Back in your cage!* Gavin thought. *Leave me to my misery.*

I'll go, for now, but I am never far, princeling, the Ripper replied, leaving Gavin alone to stand in the bloody aftermath. Relief swept over the prince as he felt the beast slither back into the depths of his mind. Regret soon followed, filling him until there was nothing left.

Dusk turned into darkness, chilling the air, curling tendrils of visible breath around Gavin. Tears pricked at the prince's eyes as he blinked, taking in the wreckage. He ran a blood-crusted hand through his hair and turned in place.

"Fuckin' aye," he whispered. "What the fuck have I done?"

Gavin's heart shuddered at the sight around him. What had he allowed his demon to do? A whole town decimated because he couldn't keep a lid on his emotions. These people had lives, and he had snuffed them out in one fell swoop. He couldn't leave these people here like this. They deserved so much better. They deserved better than him.

He would bury them. Each and every soul he had taken would have a resting place to call their own. If Gavin had to stay here all night, he would make sure of it. With a heavy heart, Gavin walked over to the closest body to him. A man, slight and covered in soot, probably a smithy. His chest ached as he lifted the lifeless man with ease and carried him to the town's edge that faced the mountain side.

With each and every body, he did the same, trying to piece together who might have been closest to who. Gavin laid them out ceremoniously before the mountain. Dirt and blood be damned, Gavin began to dig the first grave.

"Goddess, I beg of you. Guide these people to a brighter, happier place. Restore the peace that I so shamelessly stole from them. Celeste, I ask this from the bottom of my blackened heart for I had sworn to lock the monster away and I have failed. Twice now." A hiccup caught in the prince's throat. He hoped beyond reason that the goddess would comfort them. With each handful of dirt, his vampiric muscles throbbed.

Filth coated his skin and clung in his hair, and yet Gavin so usually clean and proper, did not mind. His nails tore with the effort but soon he had one grave completed. He took his time, refusing to use the speed with which he had used to kill these innocents.

Hopping up to the surface, Gavin heard howls echo through the night, a sound that told the prince a pack of werewolves were near. The creatures had never been fond of vampires, except Ollie, and a large enough pack would spell trouble for the rogue princeling. Gavin looked down at the man at his feet, the one he had first carried here to rest. "Goddess forgive me." He drew in a breath and marched toward the only place he knew he'd be safe for the evening knowing he hadn't enough time to bury them now.

Daimis.

❦

THE CRESCENT MOON HUNG HIGH IN THE SKY BY THE TIME Gavin approached the Sanctuary of Daimis, where all of his freed humans lived. The small village sat in the hills just south of Tatum, alongside Dead Run River, a place Gavin knew would keep them safe from surrounding vampiric cities. It was true, vampires couldn't cross running bodies of water, but neither could undead beings, which was why Gavin had covertly purchased the lot. These humans had had a hard-enough life, and Gavin knew they needed peace—every single one of them. The villagers fished for sustenance and lived off the land, keeping away from Tatum, the Pits, and those that would re-enslave them.

Paper lanterns hung from posts outside yurts, illuminating a small, worn path for Gavin to follow. The tiny flames burst with light, splaying it throughout Gavin's vision, an effect Dia had on darkness. Ever since his Ripper had awakened, light always played with him. His ears picked up sleeping breaths and the rush of the water to his left. The prince knew this area well and there was one person in particular that Gavin was anxious to see.

Rocks crunched beneath his dirty boots as he followed the path from between the tents up to the largest hill where a single home sat, overlooking the town's gardens and the stone quarry beyond. Gavin had designed this layout himself and warded it to the sanctuary's elder and leader, Imogen. Gavin's heart thumped a little faster in his chest as he picked up his pace. Auntie Mo was the closest he'd had to a grandmother—an actual grandparent that cared for him—one that was alive and never judged or brought darkness upon him. The elder held a special place in his decrepit heart.

Gavin's lips split into a grin as he spied the brightest lantern burning outside on the post. Flames danced with the evening air, lighting up the small circular hut and it's lean-to add-ons as Gavin approached. Dew glistened on the tanned canvas, soaking the outside, running in tiny streams down the curtains. Gavin knew that the inside would be untouched as he pulled back the canvas and ducked under the doorway. He stood in the entrance, allowing his eyes to adjust before finding his voice.

"Imogen!" he called into the empty room. Imogen tottered from a connecting room with a lantern in hand. Its flames licked at the glass, stretching for Gavin, and cast an orange glow throughout the room. The old woman's features illuminated, showing her long white hair that was expertly braided down her back, caramel skin that was rough with age and blank white eyes. Gavin smiled. Nothing had changed since he'd last visited. The yurt still smelled of cinnamon and vanilla, and small cushions formed a circle around a fire that poured smoke up to the opening in the roof.

"Aye, my boy," the withered woman bid. "Is that my Gavin?"

"Yes, Auntie," Gavin replied, walking toward the elder. He took the lantern from her feeble fingers and set it on the ground before scooping her up into a hug. His face nestled in the crook of her neck as he closed his eyes. Goddess, did he miss her. Waves of comfort crept over the prince, cradling him in its embrace. Gavin placed a kiss on Mo's worn cheek and then, he set her down.

"Such a surprise!" the elder cooed, smoothing her dress.

"I've done something terrible," Gavin admitted as guilt gnawed at his insides, building a cool, hard knot in the pit of his belly.

"Oh posh," Mo replied, wobbling toward the firepit. Despite her milky eyes, the woman knew her home inside and out. She lowered down onto a cushion, crossing her old legs beneath her. "Come, sit by my hearth and tell Auntie Mo and the spirits about your indiscretion."

"You know how I feel about all your spirits," Gavin grumbled, following the elder. He picked up a long stick and stoked the fire before sinking onto a cushion next to the woman.

"You ought to believe, my boy. They see all."

"Can they see that I've killed, Mo? That I've committed heinous acts and that I've enjoyed them?" Gavin's voice cracked.

"Oh my sweet, Gavin. *You* did not kill. The Ripper inside of you did."

"I am the Ripper."

"Nay, you're but a vessel it travels within. Gavin, you're a child of the night. It is in your nature to destroy. And you will, you have, and will continue to do so. But you're allowed to make mistakes."

"I-" Gavin started, choking on the words, on the lump forming in his throat. He coughed, attempting to clear his anguish away. "I slaughtered an entire village."

"Nay. The Prince of Blood did, who is apart from Gavin. You, you're a good boy. Why just look around, look at what you've created, what you've given us. Gavin you saved us all. You gave us a place to call our own." A tear slid from Gavin's eye, silently making its way down his cheek.

"Daimis," he croaked, clearing the phlegm from his throat, "cannot wash the blood from my hands, Imogen." Imogen reached out, placing a withered hand atop his. Her warm, wrinkled fingers curled around his blood-crusted ones, giving them a squeeze.

"Aye, but Gavin, if you never fell, you wouldn't know when to rise. We all make mistakes, my sweet, but it's what you learn from them that defines you."

"And what if I never learn? What if I can't control this demon?"

"You will," Imogen replied as she squeezed his hand again, before her blank eyes flicked to something Gavin couldn't see.

Spirits.

"Is all well, here?" Gavin asked, changing the subject. A chill crept down his spine, pebbling his skin as he watched the elder. Silence loomed between them before Mo's shoulders slumped, and she released a sigh.

"There have been some attacks in the village."

"Attacks?"

"Aye. Wolves taking people, biting them, trying to grow their numbers. The men have started fighting back," Imogen replied, unfurling her legs as she pushed to stand up.

"Imogen."

"Stay the night, sweet boy, and never forget that when you think all is lost, there is someone there to help you find your way back to grace," Mo said. "We can talk more about the attacks on the morrow. This old woman is tired as of now."

"I want to talk about them now," Gavin said coolly, his words coming out harsher than intended. The elderly woman flinched before waving off his words. Gavin knew the discussion was done. If Mo didn't want to talk, then he'd have to wait. He watched as she tottered off to bed and flicked his gaze back to the roaring blaze in the hearth. He was far from grace, far indeed.

As soon as Imogen's breaths became easy and sleep took her, Gavin rose from his cushion and snuffed out the embers, leaving the yurt in darkness. He yawned, thinking about how he should take up Mo's offer. Diamis needed his help. Hell, Elirion needed his help. Gavin closed his tired eyes and rubbed at his temples. What to do? Goddess, help him, and he let out a ragged breath before opening his eyes. Tatum was still a day's journey, at best, and that was only if he traveled at top speed. Pushing the canvas curtain aside, Gavin stepped into the night.

❋

STARS PEPPERED THE NIGHT SKY, GLITTERING ABOVE GAVIN like tiny beacons of hope. Nearly eighteen days remained before the full moon. Eighteen days before a coronation had to occur lest the kingdom be thrown into chaos and Limos wreaked havoc upon all of Elirion. Eighteen days to ensure Tatum's safety. Eighteen days... *fuck*...

Gavin slowed his pace as the dark shadow of the Sinclair castle loomed in the distance and beyond that, mountains. He loosened a breath, raked his fingers through his messy locks and let out a curse before starting toward the place that had once been his home.

Time was not on his side.

THE COBBLESTONE STAIRS LEADING UP TO THE CASTLE doors wore on Gavin's body. Blood was caked on his skin and under his fingernails, and Gavin felt like death. He'd traveled a day in order to get to Tatum. Pain raked his limbs and all he wanted to do was fall where he stood and stay there indefinitely. He didn't deserve to live. He didn't deserve anything after what he'd done at Northpass.

Slate grey walls covered in ivy rose up before him. Towers loomed on his left and right. A wrought iron balcony hung above the entrance and servants' door; black and steel embossed double doors was all that separated Gavin from his family. From the outside, the castle had an ominous air about it, but Gavin knew that his mother's impeccable taste softened the interior.

As if on cue, a steward rushed from the servant's door beneath the balcony. Pure fear slashed across the man's already pale face. The prince was covered head to toe in human blood. His tailored pants and white linen shirt soaked with it. Dark eyes locked with the servant's but the man did not flee.

Gavin was home, and he wished he were anywhere else. If only Oliver could be there to lighten the tension with his never-ending humor. Steel groaned before the double doors swung open, and without hesitation, Gavin took the last steps and entered the castle.

"Well, well, well, if it isn't the prodigal son, himself. Returned home to a kingdom that doesn't want him." Declan's voice sneered from the halls of the stone castle. Gavin had once called this place *home*, but now as he stood, it all felt foreign and cold. Turning on his heel, he met his brother's angry gaze.

Declan, a head shorter than Gavin, stood clad in royal blue robes, a color their mother said offset his dark eyes and mussed up hair, at the foyer's balcony. He moved slowly, deliberately, down the dark grand staircase, stopping before the prince. Gavin's nose wrinkled from the heavy scent of aftershave wafting from his brother. His eyes flicked toward the red tapestry that hung on the wall. His name had been etched out. He was unwanted, indeed. With arms folded across his broad chest, Declan smiled wickedly.

"Oh, I know all about you, Jagger," he hissed. "The stories reign from the slums to the lords."

"Oh, do you now?" Gavin quipped, arching a brow.

"You know, *Jagger* rhymes with *dagger* and a silver

dagger was found in Father's back. I know it was your sympathy for the humans that got him murdered."

"Declan——" Gavin stammered. Declan held up a hand, slicing the words from his tongue.

"Fuck you, I'm not finished," he snarled. "Do you think that you can just show up here and everything would be grand?" Gavin opened his mouth to speak, but Declan continued, "No. You only think of yourself. You didn't have to lie awake and console Aurora as she cried night after night for our mother. You didn't have to rule a kingdom in our parent's wake, I did! I deserve the crown... I deserve the Rose Bound ceremony. Not you! The Throne of Blood you so desperately wanted nothing to do with, it belongs to me!"

"It's my birthright," Gavin replied through clenched teeth, feeling every stab his brother threw his way.

"You gave up your birthright when you sided with the bloodwhores and ghouls! You severed the tether to Mother's lifeline! Your choices got Father killed. You deserve nothing, you worthless piece of shit!" Declan shot glares at Gavin and if looks could kill a vampire, Gavin was sure that he'd die a thousand deaths. He closed his eyes, fighting against the surge of rage his Ripper induced, and opened them to meet his brother's steely gaze.

"I could say I'm sorry to you until my last breath leaves my body, but we both know they would be wasted words."

"Fuck you!" Declan repeated. "Fuck you until the end of time. Fuck you and your descendants. Fuck the lot of you! I'm fucking done! Done with you, your shit, and cleaning up your messes! So piss off!"

"Dec..." Gavin's heart wretched at the pain in Declan's face. "I can't change the past, but I'm here now and I can change the future."

"Fuck. *You*," Declan snarled, enunciating on the last word slowly. Gavin raised a brow.

"So you've said."

Declan's face was made of stone, cold and angry once more. His brown eyes, a shade lighter than Gavin's, held nothing but pure hatred as he took a step toward Gavin.

"You're covered in blood and yet, you say you're here to change the future. Seems to me you're here to make sure no one but you has one!" Declan's words stung, hitting Gavin deep, another jab at his already bleeding soul.

"Mind your tongue," Gavin snarled, whirling his head to the side. Footsteps echoed in the foyer behind Declan as a little voice sounded from around the corner. "Our sister can hear us."

"Did I hear brother?" a little voice mused, pulling on Gavin's heart, unraveling the stitches that held it together. "I did!" Aurora squealed as she appeared, dragging a nursemaid by the apron into the castle atrium. Her hazel eyes locked with Gavin's own and she flew toward him. Navy blue skirts fluttered as Aurora ran, her small legs heaving, blond curls bobbing, as she lunged with all her tiny body's might into Gavin's soiled arms.

"Brother!" she breathed, nestling her face into Gavin's chest. As her arms enclosed his bloody neck, warmth radiated through the Prince of Blood for the first time in years. Love. It was a love he'd missed—an unconditional love that only a sister could have for her brother. As Gavin nestled his face into her curls, inhaling the lavender soap his mother bathed them in, he felt at peace. For a split moment in the universe, nothing could change the ease he felt until his sister pulled away, shattering the dream. Even covered in blood and in tattered clothes, she adored him unconditionally.

"I missed you, bigger brother!" Aurora's eyes filled with

tears and she hugged him tighter with her little arms. She had grown so much since he had last held her, but Gavin picked her up and held her to his chest. Burying his face in her curls.

"I missed you too, Little Dove." Gavin inhaled her scent, determined to memorize this moment. Tears pricked at his eyes, blurring his vision before silently falling down his face. A lump formed in his throat, choking, suffocating him. Gavin swallowed, an attempt to control his emotions as they washed through him like a tidal wave. Somewhere in the distance, he heard Declan cough, but Gavin continued to hug his sister. Aurora twisted in Gavin's arms to face their brother. "You, stop it!" she pointed angrily.

"Aurora, leave him be," Declan grumbled, his tone cool and clipped. It was clearer than daylight that Declan did not want him there. Aurora pushed against Gavin's chest as he placed her down. She had all the spirit their mother had, and now it sizzled to the surface. Aurora stomped toward her middle brother, shoulders squared.

"You leave him alone, Dec!"

"Aurora please…" Declan sighed, raising his hands up in front of his chest in submission. Gavin's lips perked as he imagined his brother scared of their little spitfire sister. Scared of upsetting her, of disappointing her.

"No! He has been gone for so long! Let him be home again! If you had been there for him, maybe he wouldn't have needed to leave!" Aurora hissed.

Gavin's body stiffened, each muscle tensing as a chill crept down his spine. Gavin felt like he had been punched in the gut by his baby sister's words. A child had picked up on his need long before he had himself. Long before anyone else had cared to.

Declan's face sobered. "If he had been the heir we *needed*, he would have been there."

Aurora's angry face grew more hostile. "That's not family! That's not what Mother taught us. She said family is forever. Family is love. If you had loved him, he would have been better. If you had been kind, he never would have left!" She tossed her hair over her shoulder, brushing Declan's belt.

Her words had hit home.

Family is forever.

But was his family even *his* anymore?

Turning on her heels, Aurora spun to face Gavin and reached up for him to pick her up again. Letting out a resolved sigh, Gavin obliged. Blood had gotten on her frilly dress but she paid it no mind.

Declan snorted. "We're not done," he said before retreating down a side hallway.

"Indeed we are not," Gavin replied quietly.

GAVIN'S HEAD POUNDED, THRUMMING PAIN THROUGH HIS temple as he laid in his plush bed. It was almost *too* soft. He'd grown accustomed to the Underground brothel beds or the dank cots in The Pits' taverns, the stench of sweat and blood and lust filling his nostrils as he slept. On the nights when he and Ollie had lost all their coin, they made do while sleeping in haystacks on the outer rim near the farms. But now, he felt as if he was suspended in the air rather than trying to sleep in an expensive bed. Tossing and turning, Gavin slowly closed his eyes, beckoning sleep to take him.

THE PITTER-PATTER OF RAIN RUSTLED GAVIN AWAKE IN THE wee hours of the morning. The prince's room was still dark; the outline of his belongings casting haunting shadows throughout his room, but nothing his vampire eyes wouldn't quickly adjust to. He huffed out a sigh and tried to fall back asleep but to no avail. After senseless minutes of fighting his thoughts, Gavin sat upright. He turned and placed the pads of his feet against the cool, dark floor and leaned forward. His fingers fumbled as he searched for the matchbook he knew sat atop of his nightstand a few steps away.

Sharp, pointed corners pricked at his thumb and forefinger as he pinched the matchbook and wordlessly withdrew a match, flicking it to life. A single gold flame singed the tip, reaching up toward Gavin as if to burn away his sins and cleanse him of his misdeeds, but there would be no cleansing for the lives his Ripper had stolen. There would be no redemption to save his lost soul. He had Celeste to thank for that.

Gavin lowered the flame to the candelabra that sat to his right and watched as they roared with light, flashing a show of shadows upon his walls. He reached for a torn picture that sat in the drawer of his nightstand and withdrew it. A single tear slid down the prince's cheek as he gazed into his family's eyes.

His mother smiled, her elongated fangs nearly nicking her bottom lip, painted red from the finest makeup Tatum had to offer. Her eyes crinkled, showing signs of her slow aging, though she was as beautiful as ever. Her dark brown hair, the same shade as Gavin's, was nestled neatly atop of her head. She bore no crown, not this day. He could remember how his mother had fussed about them looking like an ordinary family, just this once, in the comfort of their own home. His mother's hands rested on a young Declan's shoulder, her swollen belly nearly days away from giving birth to sweet Aurora. His brother grimaced, at the ripe age where everything irritated the youngster, and to Declan's left was Gavin, dressed to the nines with a shit-eating grin on his smug lips. If only young Gavin knew what he knew now. His eyes flicked to the man who stood above him, a hand resting on his left shoulder. His father. The king stood strong and proud of his family, his white fangs shimmering in the lighting as his hazel eyes wrinkled from his smile.

Another tear washed down Gavin's face.

He would never see those smiles again.

Something within Gavin broke. Pain plummeted through his body, shaking it to the core. Tears flowed freely down his cheeks, dripping salty drops onto the photo. His vision blurred and his nose stuffed up. He needed to feel, needed to feel every ounce of pain that he'd caused. He wept for his parents, who had loved him despite his treacherous ways, despite the demon living within him. He wept for smiling faces that would never show Tatum the kindness it deserved. For Ollie, his closest friend, a brother who was gone because of him. He wept for Declan and the hatred his young heart carried. He sobbed for the innocent lives he'd taken and as his tears stained his face and his cries escaped his parted lips, Gavin wept for the kid in the photo, for what his life would become.

Grief seized the prince entirely as his body trembled from the pain. He felt his heart breaking over and over again; tears saturated his photograph, smearing the ink and his family's image, but Gavin continued to weep until his body could take no more and sleep once again reclaimed him.

10

ROSE

*S*he had let her guard down and it had nearly gotten her killed. *Stupid*, she thought as she and Ollie ducked into a nearby alley. Night had taken the city, bringing out the vagrants and thieves. Bloodwhores flanked the streets, looking to make coin from rich vampires that passed through, anything that would get them into the Underground, working for the likes of Palmer and his crew, for her father. Shutters were drawn in all of the shops and the good and kind folk were tucked away in their beds.

Sweat beaded Rose's forehead as she slowed her pace. Her breath was ragged, slicing into her lungs. She hadn't run like that in ages. Her muscles ached, and although Dawson had offered to carry her several times, she couldn't let him.

He was a dog.

A mutt.

He was her *savior*.

No. Damn it! Rose held a hand to her chest, feeling her heart tighten. As much as she wanted to fight it, she couldn't. She had feelings for Oliver Dawson. He made

94

her smile and laugh and his incessant flirtation was...
charming, in that annoying way of his. But she couldn't
ignore the feeling he gave her, that warm fluttery sensation
in the pit of her belly every time he glanced at her. The
way his face lit up while talking to her. No one had ever
looked at her the way he did... well, no one since... No.
She couldn't think about *him*, not without trudging up the
hurt after he'd chosen Lorelei. The bad outweighed the
good and Rose didn't want him to tarnish the feelings she
had for the wolf.

They'd been traveling for a few days now, scrounging
up whatever coin they had left to buy a room for the
nights, but now they were out of money and with Palmer
looking for them, there was no way they could stay in the
city.

Lights loomed in the distance behind them, but Rose
knew they were miles away from the Pits. She returned her
attention to the clearing before her, taking in the Forest
that materialized before them.

"Lass, I think we ought to settle for the night," Ollie
whispered, his voice so low that only her vampire hearing
could pick it up. Rose stiffened. It had been hours since
she'd heard him speak. Her eyes widened as she gave him a
curt nod.

Still covered and caked in black blood, Ollie was a
frightening sight to behold. The ends of his golden hair
hung in dark strands. Smears of black blood painted his
arms and chest and the stench that wafted her way curdled
her stomach. Rose gulped and shook her head as images of
the tunnels came flooding back. Tears pricked at her eyes.
How could she have been so stupid and reckless? Dahlia
would have told her not to waste her life on her, but Rose
needed her sister.

Ollie put a grimy hand on her shoulder, giving it a

squeeze before pulling her into his arms. He let out a whine that reminded Rose that despite the man before her, there was a beast roaming deep within him. Rose swallowed, trying to dislodge a hard lump that had formed in her throat.

"Let it out, lassie," Ollie crooned, petting her hair. "Let it all out." Rose wept.

"Everything will be okay."

Would it? Would everything be okay? Rose felt her heart break anew, feeling as if the shards of it were protruding through her skin to rip apart her very flesh. Her sister was gone. The one she'd known all her life, the one who had been by her side through thick and thin, was no more. Deep in her gut, Rose knew the truth but her head refused to register it as fact. Not yet.

Long moments passed before her breathing steadied. She'd let it all out, every wail and snotty blubber in front Ollie. He'd cooed and whispered reassurances into her ear, petting her head until she stopped shaking and the last tear had been shed. She'd been open and raw and it felt... *amazing*. Like a weight had been lifted from her shoulders. After Rose had pulled herself together, the pair moved with the shadows of the night until the town fell to a pinprick in their vision. Rose grimaced at the muck that caked her alabaster skin. The skin that had been touched by Ollie. A flutter of emotion raced through her. This attraction was growing, but to what Rose hadn't decided.

Trees and darkness flanked them as the pair crossed through a dry field with itchy tall grass lapping at their legs. Stars blazed in the night sky. Rose looked up and stifled a sigh. Crickets and bullfrogs sounded around them and the brisk air smelled of wild lavender, momentarily reminding her of *him*. Rough fingers wove with hers as Ollie stopped at her side. She didn't flinch or pull away but instead gave them the tiniest squeeze.

My savior, she thought. *Thank you.*

Ollie squeezed back and looked up into the sky.

"I imagine," he said, clearing the rasp from his throat, "that somewhere, your sister and my best mate are looking at the stars too. Thinking about us." A breath hitched in Rose's throat as Ollie continued, "I was always an outcast, ya know. A joke of my pack. A boy set to be alpha but never good enough. I was small." He shrugged. "I know, looking at me now you'd never suspect it, but I lacked the strength and the speed the other boys had. I couldn't keep up during our hunts. It..." he began to trail off, sniffing the air. "It used to tear me up inside, so, one day, I decided that I wouldn't be the laughingstock anymore. I'd make the pack proud, grow into the alpha they expected me to be. I began training, building up my strength and endurance and hope. Before I knew it, I was larger and faster than anyone in my pack. Of course, my ego grew with my newfound muscles and I thought I was better than them because I had become bigger and stronger on my own. I thought that I could lead them because I knew what it was like to work hard to gain what one desires.

"My head swelled." Ollie paused, squeezed Rose's hand and took a deep breath. Rose looked up at the wolf who continued staring into the sky.

"But then my pops passed, and my world came screeching to a halt. It is believed among certain wolves that when one passes, they become a star in the heavens, forever to run with their pack. When he became one of those stars looking down on us now, I lost a part of myself. I broke off from the pack and started working the rings in the Underground. It was quick money and easy fame. I never worried about having full balls or a bed to sleep in. They usually came hand in hand."

"Brothels?" Rose asked quietly. Ollie nodded. Rose stifled her snort of disapproval.

"Aye. That's when I met Gavin and boy, was he in some rough shape. A high-end vamp in a low-end town. We sort of clicked, ya know? And we've been friends ever since."

"Was there a point to this story, Dawson?" Rose asked quietly.

"The last thing Palmer said before Gavin left was that Gav's parents were dead. I know my best mate and the monster that lives within him. We need to find him before the towns and hills run red all around us."

A chill ran down the heiress's spine. She knew what lived within Gavin. All the covens did, and she knew just how bloody his warpath could be. Rose lowered her gaze. Oliver Dawson was her partner now, whatever that meant.

"Then we find him," she whispered and squeezed his hand. "For better or worse, we'll find Gavin." Her eyes lifted to see the wolf's sheepish grin. Rose's heart thudded and her mind whirled when Oliver pulled her to his chest. Ollie tilted her head up toward him with his index finger and leaned in, grazing his lips against hers. Butterflies curled into fire, lighting the pit of her belly with need. She wanted the wolf. She *needed* him. She wanted to taste him, to feel his tongue dance with her own, but the moment was fleeting as Ollie pulled away.

"Thank you," he whispered, before turning back to gaze at the stars. A lump formed in the heiress's throat and she wondered if the wolf was thanking her for the encouraging words, the stolen kiss or simply just being there to listen. Rose bit at her lip as she raised a hand to her mouth.

"We should make it to the tree line before setting up camp," Rose mumbled, lost in her thoughts.

✿

GAVIN

A CLOUD OF SMOKE SLITHERED THROUGH GAVIN'S PARTED lips as he pulled a lit cigarillo from between them. He'd never been a smoker before Ollie, but feeling the burn in his lungs and the taste of tobacco on his tongue brought a sense of calm to the Prince of Blood. He remembered the first time he took a drag and the sensation that swept over him… *ahhh yes*, he'd been hooked ever since. Now, after finding Oliver's favorite blend in a small shop he'd plundered after his Ripper had devoured the townspeople, he found it brought him closer to his late friend. *Calm* was something he needed now more than ever. Even if it was forced.

The four royal covens were coming together to decide his fate, or so Gavin had been told in between drunken stupors. A week had passed and keeping to his chambers, Gavin spent days indulging in dark liquors and blood-whores from Tatum's slums. With his many hungers sated, Gavin's head was clear. His heart hurt, but was not utterly broken, not for the moment.

The covens were set to arrive later today, laying a sense foreboding thick in the air around the prince and he realized just what all that entailed for him.

Lorelei. A Bloodworth fully befitting her family name, and his former fiancée. She had caught him secretly releasing blood slaves in the middle of the Winter Commons, a holiday spent dressed to the gills, where vampires danced the night away with blood spilling from their victims and chalices. A shiver ran down Gavin's spine at the memory. His Ripper was absolutely delighted in the bloody celebration. Gavin sucked in a breath. He had run

99

shortly after the next Winter Commons, unable to face his parents, unable to face anyone after his kills.

Just as his thoughts were taking a darker turn, the pitter-patter of young feet caught his attention. A small rap on his door had Gavin lurching for the handle and yanking it open.

"Gavie!" Aurora sprang up and into his arms. He plastered a smile on his lips and looked down into his sister's face, much like his mother's—so young and wise. Negative thoughts dug their claws into his mind as Gavin struggled to think of happier times. He picked at his smooth lower lip, nicking it with his fang. Gavin could feel the air changing into something sinister. Sweat peppered his brow as his breath came in short puffs. Something was amiss, lurking, just waiting for him to slip.

Gavin struggled to breathe, his chest tightened. What the fuck? What the fuck!

Give in, little vampire, his Ripper crooned. *Give in like you did during Winter Commons. Make the halls run red.*

No! Never again! Gavin fought to focus on Aurora, squeezing her a little harder than he should have.

You disgust me.

"Gavie, you're cr-crushing me!" Aurora squeaked, tearing Gavin from his internal battle. After days of numbing the pain in his heart, he needed to be with his family.

He had missed so much of Aurora's young life, and in a few short years, her fangs would grow in and her thirst for blood would take over. Darkness would pull on her like it did to him. *Would she wield a Ripper?* So much had happened in her tragic life... Gavin shook the thought from his mind and stared into his younger sister's eyes.

"What're you doing here, Little Dove?" he asked and patted her hair.

"Declan was mean and Gavie locked himself away for a long time. Sissy wanted to check on bigger brother. Wanted to make sure he was okay." Aurora giggled, pushing her index finger into his nose. Gavin's lips quirked into a smirk as he leaned in to whisper in his sister's ear. "I escaped the maid and came straight here!" That explained the lack of supervision. Gavin smiled at the thought of his sister sneaking out of her chambers and tiptoeing down the halls to his.

"Don't you worry about a thing, Little Dove. Gavie has everything he could ever need right here." Aurora let out another giggle. "Besides, that was days ago. Gavie is fine." Gavin watched as the tension on Aurora's face relaxed.

"I love you, Gavin," she said. "Please don't leave again. Don't let mean Declan take you away from me again." Gavin's heart lurched as his sister caught him off guard. What could he say to her? Surely, he couldn't promise her that. If things went south and the covens banished him, then what would he be?

An oath breaker.

A *liar*.

And that was not something he could be. Not something he *would* be. Aurora had lost just as much as Gavin and Declan and a little more. She'd lost a childhood full of innocence and heartbreak, lost memories that would never come to pass.

Her future was forever changed because of him.

Ruined because of him.

But Gavin couldn't help feeling the way he did. He couldn't help freeing the humans from their slaved posts. Part of him knew that he would have done it tenfold, regardless of the outcome. He would change Tatum, chosen by the covens or not. No Rose Bound ceremony would change his thoughts. If not for himself, for Aurora. He would give her a better world, a freer world.

The castle shook, vibrating from the force of hundred winged beasts flapping their wings. The chandeliers overhead swung, each crystal clinking against the next. One by one, hooves pounded the stones outside, sending a shiver down the prince's spine. He didn't need to see who it was or rather what, they were. He already knew.

The Bloodworth clan had arrived.

Gavin knew that his sister had never witnessed such an affair, had never seen the regal black Pegasi descend in formation. Without hesitation, Gavin shifted his sister in his arms and bolted down the hall and staircase leading to the grand foyer.

The castle rumbled beneath the force of the beasts outside, their flapping wings deafening as Gavin pulled open the door and stepped outside.

The cool evening breeze bit at their exposed skin; dusk set in along the horizon. Gavin turned to Aurora and watched her gaze fill with awe and wonder as the beasts landed. Ten, twenty, fifty, a hundred and then as the last of the Bloodworth's descended, his sister let out a squeal.

"That one!" She pointed up into the darkening sky, her voice barely audible amongst the chaos. "It's white!" Gavin felt his stomach twist and curl in on itself, a knot forming deep within his gut. Gavin knew the owner of that beast all too well. A flash of black hair whipped from the side of the beast's neck as the Pegasus dipped and descended. Aurora let out another squeal, clapping her hands. Her eyes followed the beast's every move. Atop of the massive white beast sat Lorelei, dressed head to toe in brown fur and black leathers.

Her raven hair glistened, holding a shine that stumped

Gavin. He remembered the feel of her silky tresses, the feel of her lips on his skin, trailing down as they enveloped—

Lorelei's dark almond-shaped eyes slid to Gavin and narrowed. Her lips, as though she'd eaten something sour, curled into a sneer as though she knew the prince's treacherous thoughts. She slid from her saddle and handed the reins over to her servant before turning back to her Pegasus.

"Be a good boy for them, Demetrius," she cooed while stroking the gelding's nose. The Pegasus snorted in response and Aurora clapped her hands again. Wriggling free of Gavin's grasp, she slid down his legs and ran to the beast. Lorelei smiled and scooped the princess into her arms.

Gavin watched his ex-fiancée grin, as she turned back to Demetrius. The two spoke in low voices, cooing to the beast and scratching his nose. Gavin flicked his tongue over his fang and clenched his jaw. He fucking hated this so much. He sucked in a deep breath and then he approached.

"Well, if it isn't the Prince of Blood, ladies, and gentlemen," Lorelei snarled out to no one in particular. She turned, lowering Aurora to the ground and faced Gavin. A smile pressed her lips. "Come to escort me to court?" she asked, her tone taking on a note of innocence. But Gavin knew she was far from innocence and grace. He balked and narrowed his gaze. *Hardly*, he wanted to say. But to give Lorelei the satisfaction gritted against the prince like sandpaper.

"Such a broody little prince," Lorelei sneered and took a step forward. "Is this how you greet a long-lost friend? A princess?" Gavin choked on his laugh. *Friend, hardly. Evil bitch from hell, maybe.*

"I need a goddessdamned cigarillo if I'm to deal with

you for the next week," he hissed quietly. He wanted nothing to do with Lorelei or her conniving little schemes.

"A cigarillo?" she asked, arching a thin brow. "Since when do you smoke? Such a dirty little habit. But then again, you did whore yourself around in the Pits for well over six years. Did one of your bloodwhores give you a taste? Or did you pick up the habit to cope with your rotten choices? Need to numb the pain?"

"That's enough," Gavin snapped through clenched teeth. Lorelei's smirk grew wider, spreading across her face. "You will behave in front of the princess, Lore."

"Oh, you're right. Demetrius needs to be fed. Speaking of pets, where is Oliver? I heard he was a beautiful little snack?" Lorelei winked. "Did your Ripper have fun with him, Jagger?" she whispered, pushing into Gavin's personal space. Bile lurched in Gavin's throat as his vision grew dim. His Ripper pushed against him like a force of nature begging to be released. Gavin flicked his tongue over his fangs, slicing it and tasting the familiar tinge of blood pooled into his mouth, but his anger grew, his veins throbbing to throttle the heiress where she stood.

"Don't you *fucking* talk about him!"

"Awe, did I hit a nerve?" Lorelei replied, mirthlessly. A whimper sounded from Aurora below as she cowered closer to the beast, but Gavin's attention remained locked on Lorelei. He *wanted* to kill her. Wanted to spill her blood in front of her clan and then decimate them too. *Fuck you all*, he thought, giving into his darkness. The Ripper grinned within. He wanted to hear their screams and see their blood and—

"Gavin," Declan hissed from behind him, clasping his shoulder. Gavin's thunderous thoughts halted. He loosened a growl before turning to face his brother.

"Leave us," he commanded.

"No. You're making a scene. The entire Bloodworth clan is here. Pull yourself together." His brother's words were gentle but commanding.

"Fuck. You," Gavin snarled, taking in the clan blooming around Lorelei. Her lips curled again. She'd won. She'd gotten under his skin. Before he could do something he would come to regret, Gavin turned on his heels and strode back into the castle.

"Yeah and this is the hot temper you want to rule us with," he heard Declan reply, before Gavin slammed the door.

OLLIE

*T*rees towered around Ollie as he set up camp. He
hated the forest and its magical nonsense. Always
knowing, always watching, always haunting. The Forest of
Knowing was a brutal place to find oneself, as if he needed
to be reminded of his past. Rose laid asleep nearby on the
dew-covered grass, the sound of her gentle snores catching
on his wolf ears. Ollie smiled. Artemis, did he like this
lassie. Everything about her warmed him. Remaining alert,
Ollie continued to gather sticks. Rose had chosen a
dangerous location for camp, just on the outskirts of a
bigger town, all too close to Palmer and his goons.

He knew they could have traveled with immortal
speed, but with her lack of feeding and Ollie's injuries, the
rush would simply impair them further. He did not want to
hurry his time with her any more than he had to. Ollie
kneeled down to grab another twig for his bundle as his
mind drifted to Gavin.

Gavin was a wild card when grieving. He had seen the
aftermath of Lorelei's betrayal, and how she'd taken her
sweet time with it. He saw how Gavin had been in the

pubs and tavernas in the Pits. The amount of blood that coated his suit when he'd finally slump onto the bar. His deep-rooted need for blood was usually well contained. The Ripper tore at him when he was at his lowest, Ollie knew this. But what he didn't know was if Gavin thought he had successfully killed him or if he had fled to get to his siblings. Either way, the war raging within him was sure to wreak havoc on those that crossed his path. Oliver shuddered at the thought. Though he loved his friend, there were places in his mind even he did not dare tarry.

The trees of this place recorded time, emotion, and history. Whether it was blood or sweat spilled, the roots of the trees drank up the emotions and actions that transpired beneath their branches. Before the Wars, this place was farmland, lush and green, abundant with the sustenance of life, or so Ollie had been told. Then Limos plagued the Night, spilling the essence of innocent life into the soil. From it, grew haunting trees that trapped souls and the memories of those who perished here. If Gavin had passed through, Oliver was sure a breakdown would follow.

His friend was strong in will and body, but his heart was another entity altogether. As Oliver looked over at the sleeping vampire noble, his own heart leaped. Rose shifted in her restless sleep, making a strand of golden hair fall across her face. Oliver longed to reach over and tuck it away. But voices pricked his wolfish ears, stopping him from doing just that. He turned abruptly to the right. Females were close by. Oliver glanced again at Rose before he moved quietly, swiftly, back to the camp and lowered the bundle to the ground. He grabbed for one of the heiress's unstrapped daggers and stole away into the night with one of her knives in hand.

❧

"MOTHER! WHY MUST YOU ALWAYS INTERVENE? WE should have killed him!" a female voice chimed. Ollie approached a clearing where the lack of bloodshed failed to nourish the trees. The clearing was absent from all life, aside from a group of women. Most were young, of varying descents, except for one that was older and greying. Each woman of the clan was dressed in tanned leathers and furs, with berries juices painting their sun-kissed skin.

"Darling, in time you will see that murder is not always the correct answer. You cannot simply kill off all of your problems," the aging female said. Ollie turned, hiding behind a nearby tree and watched the group.

"I can try," the younger one responded, eager for blood. *She must be the leader.*

Ollie shifted forward to get a better look at the women, paying close mind to the position of his feet. One wrong move, one twig snapping, and the group would know his location.

"My sweet Tora, have you not an ounce of your humanity left?" the old woman asked, reaching out and placing a hand on the younger woman's shoulder.

Tora shrugged off the tender touch and turned toward her elder. Now facing Oliver, he could see her exotic beauty. His eyes scanned over her, slowly drinking her in. She'd be any man's fantasy. Her eyes were the perfect shade of cognac. She had curves in all the right places and her midnight hair braided back in five braids, cascading until they melded into the rest of her curls. Purple paint streaked along her high cheekbones. On her back was a bow and quiver, and dual daggers were strapped to her hips.

She was a warrior.

A *goddess.*

"It has been a few days and still its stench lingers here," Tora replied. Oliver inhaled deeply, trying to catch what she was referring to, but he was downwind and the only thing he could smell was a woman who was ovulating. His carnal need to procreate was surfacing.

"They must pay for what they did to me. To all of us." Tora's voice was now a whisper.

Who is 'they'?

"The beasts who enslaved us will pay for their crimes, Mother. I can assure you of that."

"My dear girl, but someone was benevolent. We were released."

Tora's eye's flickered to the older woman, her face twisting into something much darker. "Does that excuse their monstrous behavior? We were blood bags with vaginas and they used us however they wanted!" Murmurs rattled through the group of bandit women, some in agreement with the young leader.

"It does not excuse their actions, but their actions define them in the eyes of our Maker. Our actions define us. Letting that boy go was the right choice, you will see," her mother replied. Her voice wavered, drowned out by the group once more. Oliver leaned in closer, resting his hand on a tree and craned his neck.

He wanted to know more.

Needed to.

"Don't move," a young voice commanded from behind him.

Ollie turned despite the warning and came face-to-face with an arrow. His eyes focused on the point. Ollie gulped. *Fuck...* He knew he could break the arrow, but the silver tip, well, one touch of that to his flesh and he would be down for days.

A shiver ran down his spine. He imagined the horrid

night sweats, the vivid fever-induced dreams that would follow blistering flesh. He knew he did not want to experience that again, not any time soon.

"I told you not to move, wolf," the girl hissed again. Her Cajun skin had been disguised within the shadows of the trees, but here, now, he could make out her every feature. Young, likely still adolescent, but worn like that of a warrior, he knew that this girl had witnessed awful things, perhaps even done them to survive. Her hair fell in a sheet of black down her back and crushed red raspberries painted her cheeks in war-paint smears.

Oliver raised his hands in front of him, exposing his palms to the girl. "I'm not here to hurt you," he replied quietly.

"Then why are you spying like a mongrel in the shadows?"

Ollie remained silent, ignoring the ever-present canine insults relentlessly tossed his way. No answer he gave would be accepted by the warrior. Keeping his mouth shut would equally save him as it would serve as his impending doom.

"Tora!" the girl barked.

A rustle from behind him told Oliver that the leader had shifted her position and was approaching the pair. The cool prick of metal bit into his back as Ollie's muscles tensed, confirming his suspicions. It took all that the wolf had not to turn and overpower the woman behind him. *No.* That would only complicate his situation and create an enemy he did not want nor need.

"Lass, I'm just trying to pass through," Ollie said, his breath coming out in a rush.

"Looks like you chose the wrong way home," Tora snarled.

The hairs on Ollie's neck stood on end as his skin prickled. A flush brightened his cheeks. Was it being caught or her voice so close to his ear that brought the blood rushing to unwanted places?

Tora pressed her blade harder into the fabric of his shirt, the tip tearing the fabric, pushing against his flesh. Fiery pain erupted through his back. Silver. Fucking goddess-be-damned silver. Ollie winced. If he couldn't get the bandit to remove the silver, the horrible side effects would begin and he would be rendered useless. He didn't have that kind of time.

"Lassie, kindly remove your spike from my back and let me be. The hours wane and I have other more pleasurable things to do than stand here." His patience was wearing thin. Gavin was close. He could scent him now with the shifting wind.

"He had a weapon," the girl before him gritted out, arrow still poised to strike.

"Drop your weapons, puppy dog," Tora issued with a nod. Ollie silently cursed himself. He had foolishly sheathed Rose's dagger while eavesdropping, the very thing they were accusing him of. Something he had not yet denied. *Rose… Shit.* If she woke before he got back, she'd come looking for him, and her vibrant spirit would stir the shit-pot he currently found himself in.

"Where exactly were you headed?" Tora's voice was again in his ear. *Almost too close.*

"Searching for a bit of privacy. Nothing else. Now, will ya please remove the damned dagger and let me go?" Oliver stifled the annoyance that was growing in his own voice. If there was to be a blade to part of his body, this woman was *not* the one he wanted holding it there. A flash of blonde hair and steel paraded through his mind like a lucky reminder of what he could not have.

Tora inhaled deeply. "I smell a woman on you. Where

might she be?" she pushed. Ollie's heart beat faster. Had Rose's perfume rubbed off on him somehow?

"I don't see how it concerns ye, lass." He kept his voice clipped.

"Aye, you're right. However, you're in my here trees now, mutt, and that means your business is no longer your own." Tora circled around him, trailing her silver blade across his ribs. Pain seared red-hot in his side, bubbling and burning the flesh, leaving a bloodied path in its wake. Still, Ollie remained motionless, unfazed by her tactics. He'd been tortured before. Hell, before Gavin rescued his arse and took over as his manager in the Pits, Palmer had tortured him for every fight lost. This? This was child's play. As long as she kept the blade shallow, his wolf could battle the silver.

"Speak, dog!" the huntress harped.

Ollie's lips perked upwards as a grin pulled onto his face. He shrugged nonchalantly and said, "Ya know, this would be kinkier in a bed. Or perhaps you'd like to strap me up? Mix a little pain with some pleasure, eh?" Tora scoffed at the remark and buried her blade between Ollie's ribs. *Fuck, she did it.*

He let out a howl. The pain scorched at him from within. Stars danced before Ollie's eyes and hot sticky blood poured from him. He could feel his bones crack and shift before he could react, trying to mend the wound from his other form. His fur would staunch the blood. Ollie knew that he needed to shift, but doing so, would leave a bloody aftermath in his wake.

Ollie's cuticles tore as his nails turned to claws. His back popped and hunched, bringing him down to his knees. The shift would be quick and painless. Sandy fur sprung around his arms, torso, and legs. His vision blurred and then everything went red.

112

ROSE

ose jolted awake as screams tore through the silence. The hairs on the back of her neck stood and the spot where Ollie had been was vacant. A knot formed deep within her gut, twisting in on itself tenfold. Rose sat up and rubbed the crust from her eyes before scanning the surrounding area, searching, nay, *praying*, for any sign of the wolf she was falling head over heels for. *Nothing.* The vampiress pushed to her feet and turned in place. There were trees as far as her eyes could see.

"Ollie!" she called out, her voice echoing in the air until it was lost and silence greeted her. "Dawson?" A slow panic grew in her chest as the screams became more distinct, more discernible.

"Shit," she hissed, grabbing for her twin daggers, strapping them to her hip. She didn't bother with the bed roll before she trudged into the trees. *He had better have a good explanation for this!*

Leaves crunched quietly beneath her feet as Rose neared the commotion, paying close attention to the placement of her boots. A snap of a twig, and her location would be given away. She slowed her pace and inched forward cautiously. Shadows shifted before her and it took Rose's vampire eyes a moment to adjust to the darkness that had set in on the forest. She stood on a hill, hidden within the brush, looking down into a hollow. Rose gasped sharply as an enormous sandy-colored wolf backed into trees not far from where she stood.

Ollie...

Rose rested her hand on a nearby trunk and scanned the area, searching for the cause of Ollie's change. Not far from where she stood was a group of female bandits circling and closing in on Ollie. They moved, pushing him farther into the tree line. Blood seeped down his flanks, staining his shiny coat. Rose's breath caught. They'd hurt her wolf.

A woman with dark braids down her back prowled toward the wolf, blade out, ready to strike. She twirled the dagger between her fingers and took another step toward the giant wolf. Ollie backed into a tree, surrounded, and bared his teeth.

Rose's fingers grasped at her twin blades, unsheathing them. The cool leather hilt of her knives greeted her and without thinking, she flung one of her blades toward the woman advancing on Ollie. It skimmed her cheek and lodged into the bark above Ollie's shoulder. The wolf's eyes shot to her, recognition flaring in their depths. He snarled before focusing his attention back on the bandits.

The woman turned slowly. A crimson line ran down her cheek, stark against her dark skin. Rose sauntered down the embankment before stopping short of the group and placed her hands on her hips.

"I believe you're fucking with the wrong wolf, ladies. That one's taken." Though the woman was much taller than Rose, fear did not cross the heiress's mind. She'd fought against tougher opponents in more dangerous situations back in the Pits.

Ollie was panting hard in the background, fighting to change back and regain control. His torn clothes at his paws told her that his change was suddenly sparked. Anger tore through her. No doubt he had transitioned in hopes of keeping this threat from her.

Rose flicked her tongue over her fangs and smirked. She took out her other blade and twirled it in her hand, mocking the way the braided woman had moments before. "I'd suggest you step away, now. He doesn't take kindly to being berated by women. And I fill that quota on the regular, so…" Steel glinted and Rose casually turned her head to the left, narrowly missing the knife. Her heart sped up but she did not let on. A snarl ripped from Ollie's throat as Rose held up a hand toward him.

"I've got this," she said. Ollie pawed impatiently at the ground, leaving long tracks in the soft earth. "Now, that was not very nice," Rose pouted, dramatically poking out her bottom lip.

"I never said I was nice, fangbanger. Just who the fuck are you?" the woman demanded, her shoulders rising and falling more quickly now.

"I don't see how that is any of your business." A grin played at the heiress's lips as she twirled her second dagger between her fingers. "But since you asked so nicely," she said, piling on the sarcasm, "I'm Rose and that's Ollie, and we really need to leave now."

"I'm Tora and these are my Black Widows, and you're not going anywhere."

Dark eyes met hers but no recognition lit them, only sinister curiosity. Ollie shuddered behind her, a growl on his maw. Rose huffed a breath. "Please," she added, rolling her eyes. She hated to beg. She hated to bow to these women, but Rose knew the change was painful and the sooner Ollie was back in his hunky form, the better.

A wicked smile crossed the dark girl's face. "I rather like this sick game. A vamp hoity-toity bitch gallantly defending her pet. How precious is this, girls?" Silence crept through the trees. There were no murmured agreements.

Ollie rounded, moving faster than Rose had ever seen in the ring. His teeth snapped around the closest bandit's neck, tearing out her throat. Blood splayed through the air, painting the trees with gore. It spouted from his maw as he lunged for his next victim, leaving the previous one to collapse to the ground in a heap of shredded carnage. His eyes glinted red with fever.

Rose's mind whirled.

She needed to stop Ollie before he came for her next, and before he tore through every being here, leaving him to wake filled with guilt.

"Out of my way, bitch," Rose hissed. Bolstering her blade, she took in a nervous breath and shoved past the woman in front of her. She stood before Ollie and the girl. Ollie bared his teeth; no recollection of her peppering his features, not anymore. He was on the attack and she only prayed that her next move wouldn't be her last. Ollie snapped in her direction but she put her hands out in front of her in a show of submission.

"Ollie, it's me. Look at me." Rose's breath hitched, her heart hammering against her ribcage as the wolf lunged forward again. Rose dodged to the right.

"Dawson, you fuck!" Pushing her legs into overdrive, she watched Ollie barrel toward the bandit again, scraping a canine against Rose's shoulder.

"Shit," she cursed under her breath. Hot liquid pooled from her shoulder, running a slow stream down her arm.

"Damnit, Ollie, I loved this shirt!" She hoped that a spark of her personality would jar something in him; quail the beast with familiarity.

Rose leaped into action, her legs screaming as she moved with immortal speed and lunged at the girl, tackling her to the ground. Air whooshed from her lungs as each girl gasped for breaths. Rose's lungs screamed, and she shut her eyes. They were safe for the moment. Peeling her lids open, Rose pushed to her feet, pulling the bandit with her.

"Get. Up!" She ordered. Tora doubled over, resting her hands upon her knees as she struggled to breathe.

Ollie showed no hesitation as he whirled toward her again. He truly was unrecognizable in this form. Rose's throat tightened, a lump catching within it. She feared she wouldn't be able to shift him back, and if the girl left in tatters was any indication, this was not going to end well.

"Hey, beastie boy!" the bandit shouted. Rose watched Ollie advert his attention, a grunt huffing through his nose as he whirled on her. The leader drew her own pair of twin daggers holstered at her hips and twirled them before catching them at the hilt.

"This is going to be so much fun," Tora muttered under her breath. "Does the puppy want to play? Catch me if you can." Murder flared within Ollie's eyes before he barreled toward her, flanks heaving.

Tora smiled, her wicked grin widening across her face as she reeled back, releasing a dagger into the air. Rose heard the blade whiz by, burying itself into the trunk of a nearby tree, just inches from Ollie's head. Anger bubbled within her chest. If this bitch hurt Ollie again, then Rose was going to hurt a bitch.

Ollie continued forward, never faltering. He was in it for the kill. Tora rolled to the side seconds before Ollie was in her spot. Dirt flecked her hair and leathers, but the bandit didn't seem to care.

"Is that all you've got there, doggy?" she taunted. Ollie whirled again, snapping his teeth. Tora rolled, leaving a massive oak tree in her wake and Ollie hadn't anticipated her dodge. His head made a sickening crack against the trunk, reverberating through the forest around them.

Rose cringed, her heart skipping a beat as bile lurched its way up her throat. She raised a hand to her lips and closed her eyes. Sour liquid filled her mouth as she fought to push her nausea down.

"Aww, puppy doesn't want to play," Tora snickered, sauntering toward the fallen beast. Rose's eyes widened. Her breath hitched and mouth fell agape.

Anger faded from Ollie's eyes. Rose stood there, staring at Ollie as he started to change back into his human form.

Naked, purely and wholly naked as the day he was born. Rose shifted her attention to Tora, who met her stare with a shrug. Her fingers danced with the dagger unsheathed in her hand. Tora turned, raking her eyes up and down Ollie's body, a smile playing on her lips as she took in his manhood. She paused, and turning her back to Rose, said, "Get him out of here before he kills another one of my sisters."

Her gait was slow as she walked away from the pair. Rose watched in silence, unsure of whether she should count her blessings and flee with the wolf or stay and help bury the young woman.

"Condolences on your sister. I, myself, am missing a sister. And it is no pain I would wish on anyone." Rose rang her hands in front of her.

Tora simply nodded, a solemn expression overtaking her beautiful face.

13

GAVIN

Gavin retreated to his chamber, not wanting to be around the halls in case Lorelei was lurking about. He'd had enough of her and she'd just arrived. His chamber was dark, the scent of his last cigarillo lingered in the air. Gavin fished his hand into his pocket and pulled out his matchbook and pack. Pulling a smoke, he lifted it to his lips. The taste of clove filled his mouth as he flicked a match to life and lit the end. Smoke invigorated his senses, calming Gavin's nerves. He closed his eyes and sucked in a drag, slowly releasing it, before crossing his room to the hearth. He relished the drag, fumbling around with wood as he worked on stoking a fire. Flames licked at the timber, crackling in no time.

Then, thrusting his hands into the pockets of his trousers, he paced and waited for a knock on his door. He'd asked the servants to bring him a bloodwhore, someone to quench his thirst and his carnal needs, but she was yet to be seen. His fangs ached, and his balls throbbed. He stopped, his fingers trailing down to his pants button as they slipped it from his loop. He reached his hand down, as a knock sounded at the door.

Just in time. He needed release and relief. Crossing the room, Gavin's hand clasped the cool metal knob and he yanked the door open, revealing a young redheaded woman with freckles peppering her nose and cheeks. She wore a white dress, an uncommon color for bloodwhores to wear. Something that distinguished her from the rest, he supposed and smiled.

"My name is Kail," she replied. "I was sent from Madam Juniper's Bordello." Gavin remained silent, issuing her in. He knew the bordello well. Located in East Tatum, Madam Juniper's was a high-end house for royals to frequent as they pleased. The Madam's girls were always young and beautiful and taught how to please their guests in all manners.

She walked with a swing in her hips that told Gavin that he was not the first royal she'd serviced and he'd hardly be the last. He closed the door behind her and turned on his heel. Heat rushed into his cheeks and nethers as his heart thrummed faster within his chest.

An orange glow permeated the room, dancing and casting shadows upon the cold stone walls. Firelight flickered in the woman's eyes and across her milky chest. The sound of crackling wood played low in the background, setting the mood. Gavin swallowed and motioned for Kail to take a seat on the crushed velvet loveseat before the fire. She obliged and Gavin took up next to her.

There would be no formalities.

No discussion.

Just *business.*

He leaned in, closing the space and nuzzled his face into her neck. He inhaled, noting the lavender soap that clung to her skin and trailed kisses up to her lips. He grazed his fangs across her bottom lip, nicking the skin enough for blood to pool along the creases. His tongue slowly lapped up the delicious liquid, noting the tangy taste, before he pressed his lips against hers.

Lips met his with equal hunger, moving in rhythm with his own. Blood, delicious blood, trickled into Gavin's mouth, shuddering his body with a primal response. Gavin's fingers knotted into auburn locks as his tongue explored her mouth. A moan escaped her lips and she moved into Gavin's lap, spreading her legs, straddling him as she wrapped her arms around his neck. Gavin's hands roamed her body. The sheer material of her dress was doing little to hide her curves. Gavin's hands explored greedily.

Gavin moved from her mouth, the need within him surging. He kissed her neck, trailing his tongue in small circles as he made his way down to her breasts. His shaft leaped, hard and needy with excitement against her soft body.

Oh fuck…

Her skin pebbled, her nipple hardening as Gavin took it into his mouth. She moaned again. He made work out of tugging and sucking and teasing her. His fingers pulled at her skirt, lifting it above her thighs until his hand slipped beneath.

Her skin was smooth and warm against his touch, and Gavin smirked as his hands rested on her waist, noting the lack of underwear.

Goddess, fuck. He smirked before grabbing a handful of ass.

"You're so focused," Kail mused. Gavin stopped again and lifted his face from her body.

"No talking. I don't like talking when I'm—"

"Trying to fuck your meal?"

121

"Trying to let off some steam," Gavin growled. Her body shook with laughter as she pulled his face back to hers. Their lips grazed before Gavin tilted her head to the side exposing her carotid artery to him. His member leaped again, the anticipation killing him. "May I?" Gavin's voice was husky with want.

"You may," she said, surprised by the question.

Gavin sighed, plunging his fangs into her exposed neck. Delicious blood leaked down from her wound to stain the fabric of her shift, tangy and sweet and oh, goddess, was it good. Gavin's eyes closed, his hands ridding her of clothing as he drank. His head spun, his erection throbbing as he pulled back.

"Stand up," he whispered, watching her push off of him. He marveled at her unscathed body, the softness of it. Most bloodwhores in Elirion were not so lucky.

He stood slowly, peeling off his finely pressed shirt and laid it on the arm of the loveseat. Wistful eyes watched him, her chest heaving, breaths ragged. Slowly, Gavin released his trousers and stepped out of them before placing them next to his shirt. He took her gently by the hand, kissing the pulse point on her wrist. Cutting his eyes up at her, he silently asked for access to her veins.

She gulped and nodded her head. A quiet cry escaped her lips as fangs pierced her wrist, her body writhed. Gavin's tongue lapped at the blood pooling into his mouth. He groaned, pleasure filling his body. His knees quaked, giving out beneath him, collapsing the pair onto the couch. Gavin pulled her between his knees and stopped drinking. He looked up at the halo of red hair that cascaded around them in a veil and peered into eager eyes.

"Do you want me?" he purred. Kail's pupils dilated.

"Yes," she whispered.

Gavin flashed a toothy smile, his gaze flicking to the

blood oozing from his bite mark. He licked his lips and released his member without taking his eyes off her. The bloodwhore smiled and lowered herself onto his shaft, riding Gavin as he fed.

Ecstasy wracked his body, sending Gavin into overdrive as Kail increased her pace. Her moans echoed through the room like music to his ears. Pleasure built as Gavin's muscles began tensing.

Harder.

Deeper.

Gavin licked and sucked at Kail's wrist, growing heady with blood, the need within him about to release when a knock at the door halted them both.

Kail hissed her disapproval as Gavin tried to retract himself in more ways than one. She gripped his shoulders, urging him to ignore it. His eyes turned cloudy as he thrusted up, drawing a deep moan from her. Reluctantly, he picked her up as he stood and lightly tossed her onto the bed a few paces away.

"Don't move," he said. Leaving her pouting, he stood gloriously naked and strode for the door.

"What?" he rasped, voice thick with blood. Clearing his throat, he tried again more forcefully, "What?"

Before Gavin could stop it, the door flew open and there stood Lorelei in all her wickedly beautiful splendor. She clucked her tongue, eyeing him up and down, taking in his form. *All* of his form. Then her gaze traveled to the blood-soaked woman stark naked on the bed. Her lips pulled into a devilish grin and her eyes flashed with a mischievous look Gavin knew well. This was not going to end well for him.

"I see you're having fun," she sneered, her accent hanging heavy between them. Flashes of her splayed before him, peppering his vision. Gavin shook them away quickly.

"What do you want, Lore?" he asked, reining in his temper. The veins in his temple pulsed. She was already on his last nerve.

"*Tsk, tsk,* my love. If you were needy, you should have called a real woman to your service." Lorelei poked out her lip, tapping it with her pointer finger. Gavin rolled his red-rimmed eyes.

"And what woman would that be?" He leaned into her, letting Kail's blood slip from his mouth to land on her shoulder. Lorelei, to her credit, did not so much as flinch.

"Oh posh, you're so fun to fuck with when you're horny," she purred.

"Now, are you gonna tell me why you're interrupting?" Gavin asked, shifting his voice into a gravelly whisper.

Lorelei's face paled even more, if that were possible, and met his gaze. "Uh, of course. Daddy wants to see you," she replied, her voice faltering at the lust still in his eyes. "*Now,*" she amended and stepped around him to leave the room. "Oh, and Gavin, she likes the tiniest nibbles, just here." She made an "*x*" shape just below her billowing breasts where the curve started. She winked at Kail before disappearing down the hall. Gavin stared after her for a moment, perplexed. Then it occurred to him that Kail had probably visited Lorelei at some point.

She had brought it to his attention in the hopes that it would deter him. Or perhaps turn him on further. Little did she know, he didn't care with whom she fucked. He turned back to the delectable redhead and grinned.

"Now, where were we?" he asked and closed the door.

✽

124

GAVIN SMOOTHED THE VELVET OF HIS DOUBLET AND TOOK A deep breath before pushing the large wooden doors to the council room open. This wasn't going to be pleasant. For him, or anyone. After fully sating himself, his mind was clearer than it had been in a while. He could do this.

He'd take his throne and then set to finding the bastard that murdered his parents. That was his plan. Concrete or not, it was what he needed at that moment. His parents' deaths were why he was here, after all.

The council room remained just as Gavin remembered it. Tapestries of red velvet hung from the cool slate walls, painting his family lineage in golden thread, ending with Aurora. Gavin's breath hitched as he took in the long, smooth, mahogany table his father had custom made for the room, big enough to fit all the council members and then some. The surface glistened in the flickering candle-light, reflecting back images above. Maps and drawings of the realm lay scattered at one end, where the male council members stood, peering over each other as they talked in rapid low voices.

"Haunting, isn't it?" Declan said from beside Gavin, tearing his attention away from his thoughts. Gavin turned and narrowed his gaze as he took in his younger brother.

"You have *no* idea."

He steadied his breath and slowly walked to his father's chair nestled at the end where the council stood. The voices around him died as all eyes were on him. Each member moved to their prospective seats, bowing their head as he passed—a sign of respect that he did not deserve.

"You smell like you were having fun, my lord," Zachary Coston, head of the Coston coven, noted aloud and shot Gavin a wink. *Ah yes, there it was, the shit he'd expected.* Gavin remained silent as he looked the lord up and down.

Zachary's hair rivaled that of his daughters as it shone in the brazier light. Piercing blue eyes held Gavin to the floor. His sharp features and clean face gave him the aloof appearance that his name demanded. Business and pleasure. Two things that Gavin knew he'd likely experienced in his home deep within the Pits.

"He smells like sex," a stern baritone voice cut in, sounding mildly irritated. Gavin looked to his right, into the dark eyes of Tobias Bloodworth, Lorelei's father. His hair was much longer since the last time Gavin had seen him, grazing his chin in a sheet of black. His eyes were the same cat-like eyes that his daughter had, ones that knew secrets. Ones that held lies.

"Well, I should certainly hope so," Lorelei purred as she waltzed into the meeting room. Still clad in her riding leathers, Lorelei looked as strong as she sounded.

"He was balls deep and practically mid-thrust when I walked in on him and—" She stopped there, a wicked grin etched on her lips. "Oh, but never mind that," she played, tossing her hand as though his sexual experiences were of no consequence. Gavin could feel his head about to explode. His sexual exploits were on display and it was making him rather uncomfortable. Gritting his teeth, Gavin licked at his fangs as he attempted to keep his anger at bay.

"Next on the agenda," he growled. Lorelei's satisfied expression made him wish he could take the words back, but they were in the past, like much of his regrets.

"Yes, there is a particular matter up for discussion," Tobias Bloodworth said, lounging in his chair, thrumming his fingertips before him. He leaned back and crossed his ankles as he propped his leather boots up on the table.

Gavin reluctantly shifted his gaze to the man. "And

126

what might that be?" he asked, ignoring the blatant insolence.

"Your betrothal." His voice was clipped and short, something that told Gavin that the matter was not up for debate. His betrothal... betrothal? No. Just no. Gavin's stomach churned at the thought, twisting and knotting on itself. He wasn't ready to marry. Fuck, he wasn't ready for any of this. Kail's scent still hung on him and the covens wanted to talk about marriage?

"Next," Gavin grunted.

"I should say not, Sinclair. The king and queen are dead. The realm is at risk and per our bylaws an heir is to take the throne. *You*, being that *heir*. And should you take the throne, a queen is to rule at your side. Hence, a Rose Bound ceremony must ensue in order to seal the deal."

"I thought the Rose Bound ceremony served two purposes?" Lorelei inquired.

"Indeed," Tobias replied. "An heir must undergo the ceremony in order to strengthen the magic used to hold Limos in prison. And dare I say, I know just the right candidate for queen."

Zachary laughed lightly. "You honestly believe a Bloodworth is going to mate with a Sinclair, Tobias?" Gavin could hear blood boiling in the room. He could feel the tension coat them. "Dahlia is the next to bed a royal after your daughter fumbled her chance."

"However, she is mysteriously missing," Tobias countered. Zachary Coston clicked his long nails on the wooden table and crossed an ankle on his knee.

"Rose would be the next reasonable alternative," he replied. Murmurs echoed through the room as Gavin stilled. Not Rose. Not the blonde minx that had paid Ollie to throw his fight.

"Lord Coston, I think the covenants my father made,

died with him. So again, next order of business," Gavin said, clearing his throat.

"Your father did not make the bylaws, boy," Zachary grumbled. "Your father was not above the laws set in place by the goddess and neither are you."

"Oh, Gav, you need a mate," Declan replied, leaning against the wall not far from where he sat. "If I remember correctly, since you snubbed the lovely Lady Lorelei, I highly advise you to take Lord Coston up on his offer. Dahlia is a fucking fox. Rose can't be far behind."

Lorelei clucked her tongue disapprovingly. "What do those bitches have that I don't, Declan?"

"Last I remember," Declan continued, as a sly grin forming on his lips, "sweet little Rose had a nice mouth and it sure did the trick on my cock." Gavin moved before Declan could gather what happened. His fingers curled into fist and reeled back, colliding into Declan's jaw before he could finish. He felt his Ripper surfacing, begging to be released.

Kill him.

"Shut your fucking face, Declan. Before I break it," he growled. Declan flew backwards, his body hitting the wall with an explosive impact. The wall cracked and dust flew into the air, floating lazily in the candlelight. Declan stood and rubbed his chin before spitting blood onto the mahogany table. The room fell silent.

"Oh then, you've already had a taste?" Declan sneered. His eyes grew wicked, challenging Gavin.

Kill him.

Gavin's face heated as adrenaline pumped through his veins, threatening to overcome his better judgment. The monster within him roiled in the deepest recesses of his mind, growing closer to the surface. He would not let

Declan speak ill of Rose or Dahlia or any other woman for that matter. He'd beat the living shit out of him.

Kill him!

Lorelei's hand rested on his shoulder, trailing down his arm as she sauntered over toward Declan. She leaned in, whispering in his ear before flicking her tongue out to lick at his earlobe. Lorelei eyed Gavin over her shoulder, baiting him. But he wouldn't give in.

They wanted to sabotage Gavin and turn the council against him. *Again.* Gavin's lip curled upwards as he let out a snicker, shaking his chocolate locks into his eyes.

"Lorelei, get a room if you must. Bed whom you'd like. It makes no difference to me. But this is a place for the men to work. If you want to look pretty, then do it silently. If you want to moan, then leave." She scowled back at him, pressing her full chest into Declan's side. If jealousy was what she wanted, she would be miserably mistaken. "Oh, and you can take him with you." Gavin made a shooing motion with his hand. Her answering scowl was all too delightful.

"The Coven doctrine demands a binding ceremony before a leader can take their throne, your Lordship." Lord Linden Barclay spoke for the first time, looking wide-eyed and half crazed. "You must choose a ceremonial bride. After that, bed more if you must. But, sire, a royal babe must be born to secure the family line."

Gavin sputtered, "A-a babe?"

"Well, yes. The line must continue," Linden replied.

"I think we can safely skip that for now. Moving on." Gavin steepled his fingers and focused his gaze on their tips.

"But, sire…"

"I said drop it!" Gavin roared.

Linden froze, mouth agape. Gavin shifted his gaze around the table, eyeing each coven leader up and down.

"Is my daughter not good enough for you, *sire*?" Lord Coston replied. "Is she so beneath you that you cannot fathom the idea of her carrying your spawn?"

"It's not that, I can assure you." Gavin allowed images of Rose to flood his mind, bringing up memories long since forgotten and grinned.

"Then is it your sympathies with the humans that prevent you from accepting the betrothal? Surely, you wouldn't think we would agree to let them live freely? After all, we do need to eat and fuck."

Gavin remained silent. If he answered wrong, he was screwed.

"No, but—"

"Then, it's settled. Gavin accepts the betrothal and we can begin preparations for the ceremony at once," Lord Coston replied before pushing from his seat. "Gentlemen, if you'll excuse me, business calls."

"Sit back down, Zachary. The boy has yet to decide upon his bride," Linden hissed, cutting a lethal look in the noble's direction.

"Rose," Gavin replied, releasing a heavy sigh. "I choose Rosalie." And for the first time in years, he felt he'd truly damned her.

LIGHT

*S*omething was wrong. The air thrummed with life, movement, where none had been for centuries. She rubbed at her eyes and blinked. The light separating her from Darkness flickered, exposing his prison to her only for a moment.

"Your magic is running out, Sorceress," a sultry male voice crooned, taking a step forward. His hands rested on the white bars of his cell. It was impossible though, a Rose ceremony had commenced not long ago, unless... unless a pair of rulers had died.

"Oh, hush up! Your yammering bores me. Besides, light still holds you captive." But the light around them flickered again. A handsome lip curled into a grin.

"What wickedness shall I reap upon the world tonight, my demon of light? For it is my time to reign."

14

ROSE

*R*ose averted her eyes from Ollie's deliciously bare body and left the gang of bandits in the woods. Dawn approached on the purple-grey sky as the sun's rays crept through the treetops onto the forest floor. Dew glistened on green leaves, and twigs snapped beneath her boots as a slight morning breeze filtered through the air carrying hints of wild jasmine and honeysuckle to their keen noses.

With a hammering heart, Rose focused on calming her body. She was sure Ollie heard it. Tucking her chin low to her bosom, she stole a side-glance at the wolf. He wore a sleepy grin on his lips, biting at his lower one.

Rose's eyes traveled down from his face, watching the sweat bead down his tanned skin. Watching as it rolled down his solid pectorals into a valley of chiseled blood-covered abs. Rose licked at her lips, noting the parched feeling in her mouth. She wanted this wolf with every fiber of her being. But, how had it gotten to this? How had she landed herself in the company of a werewolf? How had she begun to feel things she knew she shouldn't? Things that defied the laws of nature?

Rose huffed out a sigh. She knew the answer. She remembered meeting him. She remembered the flex of every muscle and scent of his sweat in the Underground air.

Her breath hitched and blood roared within her ears.

She couldn't let herself go down that road. The one where she fell head over heels for some guy. No, she'd done that once before and gotten burned. She couldn't give in to her emotions. Because if she did, there was no telling what she might do. Shaking the thoughts from her mind, Rose focused on her surroundings. Her breath staggered as she fought to get a grip on her feelings. Her legs trembled and stopped as the trees around them opened up to their camp in the meadow. She rolled her shoulders, feeling the tension in her body ease up and sighed again, but it wasn't enough.

"You could have warned me," she snarled, breaking the silence that hung in the air between them. She headed out into the clearing before she could hear Ollie's reply. She didn't care what it was. She could have lost him. And the thought of losing him unsettled her.

The sun peeked over the horizon casting the sky in deep oranges and yellows, melting into the purples and blues of the early morning. Had Rose not been irritated with both herself and her wolf, she would have stopped and marveled at the beauty. Their sleeping rolls were still in the same spot, washed in the early morning dew, and deer roamed the clearing, poking their heads up from their breakfast grazing to watch.

"I didn't think it was a problem to bother you with, lass," Ollie replied as he stopped closely behind her. She could feel the heat radiate off his body, calling to her.

Rose whirled on her heel.

"Not a problem? Not a *problem*?" Her voice raised into a shout. "You could have been killed, Oliver!" Ollie's body tensed, flinching at her words. She'd used his first name. His *whole* first name. "What if I hadn't gotten there in time? What if they had killed you?"

"But they didn't, lassie. Besides, I'm fully capable of protecting myself." Sucking in another deep breath, Rose closed her eyes, fighting against nerves and anger. Fighting against the hold this damned wolf had on her world. Her lids peeled open and Rose closed the space between them, leaning into Ollie's bare form. She raised her hands to his cheeks and stared into his eyes for a long moment, eyes that stole her away.

"I can't—" she began, her voice trembling as she tore her gaze from his and looked into the distance. Ollie's warm finger grazed her chin, pulling her back to meet his gaze.

"That's not—" Rose pinched the bridge of her nose and closed her eyes.

"Can't what, lass?"

"I can't lose you," she whispered. Ollie's heart thudded in her ears, roaring like the beast he shielded within.

"And you won't, lassie," he whispered, his feral eyes boring into hers. His voice was weaker than it should be. Using his index finger, Ollie tilted her chin up toward his. The heiress's breath faltered as Dawson's lips met hers with a ferocity only his wolf could bring out.

Wild and hungry.

Rose pushed hers against his with equal hunger and something more. Longing? Desire? She didn't know nor did she care.

Ollie's hands caressed her face before deepening their kiss. He dipped his tongue into her mouth, dancing circles with her own. Her breath halted as his faltered, shattering Rose into a million tiny pieces. His teeth grazed at her bottom lip, beckoning for the primal sounds that grew within her body. Her hands roamed, studying the hardened muscles of his chest and abdomen. His heart thundered in her vampire ears as he pulled back. He studied her as though he was unsure he should continue, unsure of what exactly was happening.

Her hands slid to his side, becoming sticky with fresh blood. Ollie winced, gently grabbing her hand. His breathing was shallow now, his heart sluggish. The hand wrapped around her wrist trembled.

"Ollie?" Rose searched his face, frantic to find the cause of his distress.

"It's nothing, lass. Just a bit of silver, is all." His words came out forced, laced with pain. Why hadn't she seen it before? Tora had sliced him deeply with a silver dagger.

"Lass," Ollie grunted. "I need—" Ollie became unsteady, wobbling on his feet.

"Sit down! I have something to counteract the toxins coursing through your veins!" Rose snarled as she helped Ollie to sit. She had to make it back to camp, back to her supplies.

"Don't move," she warned before rushing back to their camp. Tossed in a heap to the side of where their bedrolls lay, sat her pouch of concoctions. Rose gritted her teeth and then began to rummage through the contents.

"Damn it! Where is it?" Rose dumped vial after vial of shimmering liquid onto the ground, praying to Dia that they didn't break. She wouldn't have time to replace everything. Not now. Not with ghouls after them.

It's got to be here someplace. Sucking in a breath, she scanned the ground, her eyes resting on the smallest vial. Thank the goddess! The vial was filled with shimmering gold and water lily nectar. A cure-all for silver-related ailments. Rose remembered finding the rarities on her venture through the snow-capped mountains of Caradar Hill on her way to the Bloodworth Manor.

Rose jumped to her feet; time was not on her side. The longer she fucked around, the more the silver would infect Ollie... and kill him. Moving faster than she'd ever ran before, Rose dashed back to the wounded wolf. Ollie had laid back on the wet grass, his long, tangled hair shone like honey in the sun's embrace. Rose moved, feeling a pull deep within her core like a moth to a flame. A very sexy flame. She kneeled down next to him, looking down into his paling face.

"Ollie, open up," she cooed, nudging him. A faint groan escaped his parted lips as Rose yanked the cork from the vial with her fang before offering the contents to him.

Ollie's eyes slipped open, finding her own. "You look like... an angel." Rose snorted a very unlady-like sound at the compliment.

"Oh, now I know you've lost it!" Yet, despite herself, she flushed at his words. "Take this, you big oaf."

Ollie obediently opened his mouth for her to drop her mixture into. The golden liquid pooled down his face as his throat worked on swallowing the magic. *Good boy.* Color rushed back into Ollie's pallor complexion, the effects quickly taking hold. Rose's lips quirked into a smile, radiating across her face, the pull within her strengthening, becoming an unbearable need.

"I want you," she whispered, pulling his mouth to hers, forcing him to prop on his elbows. Ollie pulled away and stared back into her hungry eyes. His eyes glinted a mischievous look. Oh, Rose's wolf was very much back to his normal antics.

"Want or need?" he asked, leaning in to trail kisses

136

down Rose's jaw to her neck. His fingers curled around the bottom of her shirt.

"Just... just shut up and fuck me."

A low groan resonated in Ollie's throat as Rose pulled her shirt over her head and unfastened the knives from her hip. Slowly, she lowered her leather pants from her legs, stepping out of them until she was in nothing at all. She kneeled down, closing the space between her and her wolf. His lips moved greedily against hers, probing her mouth wider with his tongue as the two danced in perfect harmony, coaxing the pull in her core closer to the edge. Rose pulled away, a moan tearing from her as her body relished the feel of Ollie's touch.

Ollie's mouth ravaged her body, sending bursts of unimaginable pleasure through her veins. Groaning, she begged for more, digging her nails into the wolf's shoulder as he kissed her hips. A primal growl answered her as he pulled back.

"Your moans are music to my ears, vampiress," his husky voice crooned, before his mouth slid between her thighs. Color flooded Rose's vision as Ollie's tongue played her body, flicking that sweet spot, tearing moan after moan from her before dipping in and out of her core. She tilted her head back, fingers scrunching in those luscious honey locks. Rose's back arched as ecstasy ripped through her. Surfacing, Ollie moved up her body and grasped her face between his hands, kissing her lips. She could taste herself on his tongue, taste his want, his need with every move of his lips.

"What do you want?" he asked, flicking his tongue out to lick at her lip.

"You," Rose panted. Ollie lowered her to the slick ground before moving himself to the spot beside her. His fingers wandered to places she'd longed for him to touch, squeezing and teasing her until that musical moan escaped her lips and she begged for him.

Nestling her hand between his thighs, Rose grasped at his hardened member and stroked. Ollie snarled, his wolf coming alive. He lurched forward, hand twining in her hair as he kissed her into oblivion. He positioned his newly healed body against hers, and then, he thrust into Rose over and over. Rose bit into her lip, nestling her face against the wolf's neck, stifling her cries of pleasure with each new thrust.

"Sing for me, lassie," he moaned. Skin against skin, mouth against mouth, Ollie and Rose clung to one another in a desperate attempt to fill a dark void within themselves. Each thrust brought them closer to the edge. A growl tore from Ollie's throat as he thrust deeper until release found them both.

❀

OLLIE

BLADES OF GRASS PRICKED AT OLLIE'S EXPOSED FLESH, irritating his taut tanned skin, as he pressed close to Rose's naked body, relishing the warmth of her skin next to his. She had fallen asleep quickly after finding her release for the second time, while he, on the other hand, was plagued with sleeplessness. His stomach knotted in on itself and Ollie swore it was because he knew what loomed ahead. He knew what danger it meant to follow his friend and the bloodbath the Prince of Blood would create.

Gently, he pushed his massive frame to a sitting position, careful as to not wake the sensual vampiress next to him. After an eventful dawn, he needed sustenance. They both would. Running his fingers through his sandy locks,

Ollie's jaw dropped as he spotted clothes folded neatly at the end of his bedroll. *Where had they come from?* He'd been stark naked when they fell asleep. Silently, the hulking wolf grabbed the clothes and pulled out a plain white tunic to cover Rose before ambling to his feet. He didn't treasure the thought of leaving her here lying naked alone.

Then, he pulled brown leather pants and grabbed one of Rose's discarded daggers and turned to take a look at Rose before setting out to hunt. She remained asleep, a halo of gold splayed around her head. Sunlight glistened off her bare body, shadowing the best parts of her. Ollie smiled as his mind played her moans over in his head. He'd made her sing and call his name as the sun rose. He'd staked his claim on the heiress. Ollie turned to face the Forest of Knowing and disappeared into the trees.

The underbrush was alive with movement, rodents running awry and birds close behind them, both unaware of the threat he posed. Just how Ollie liked his prey to be.

Unaware.

Bold.

Ollie crouched low and remained still, waiting for his breakfast to scamper by.

♠

CATCHING A FEW SQUIRRELS PROVED EASY, TAKING OLLIE no time at all. The further he ventured into the forest, the more he found, and soon, Ollie's wolf ears pricked at the sound of running water.

Shoving the carcasses into the waistband of his leathers, Ollie made for the pool. The mud sloshed beneath his feet as he approached. Wreathed in cattails, the body of water lay hidden within the trees. Ollie tightened his grip on the dagger's hilt and hacked at the vegetation until there was a clear path. He kneeled, splashing the spring water onto his dirty face, catching a glimpse of himself in the rippling pool. He raked his wet fingers through his tangled locks, an attempt at taming the curls running wild to his shoulders, but it was no use. His sandy curls tangled back together, hanging back into his face.

"Fuckin' aye," he said to no one. He cut a piece of leather from his pant leg away, securing back his hair. He'd need to get a fresh cut and shave when he reached Tatum. And maybe a visit to Madam Juniper's. A smile played on his wolfish lips. Gavin would be pleased. He'd always hated how unruly Ollie would let himself get.

"Aww, why so glum, puppy?" a female voice chirped. Ollie stiffened. He'd been so lost in his own thoughts that he'd let his guard down. His fingers tightened around the hilt of Rose's dagger, the cool tip resting along his forearm.

You fucking twit. Turning, Ollie stared into dark almond-shaped eyes and dark skin with dreaded hair.

"Come to kill me?" he asked, arching a brow. The bandit smirked as she sat down, kicking her booted feet into the water.

"Nay. If I wanted to do that, I'd have gutted you while you were deep in thought."

"So, what do you want then?" Ollie snapped. He didn't have time for trouble. Gavin had enough of it and Ollie was sure he'd be cleaning up the mess. His eyes flashed to the weapons fastened at the bandit's side. How quickly would she turn on him? Noting his lingering gaze, Tora's smile spread across her face.

"I'm not gonna kill you, mutt. Ease up, will you?"

"What? No posse with you today?"

"Well, granted that I'm alone, should be answer enough," she quipped. "Believe it or not, I can go off on my own, puppy."

"Stop calling me that, lassie."

Sticking out her bottom lip, Tora said, "Not a fan of pet names, I guess. So, I see you got my note."

"Um, what note, lass?" Ollie asked, truly confused.

The bandit leader simply rolled her eyes in response. Ollie knew he had to tell her something she'd want to hear, but would that get him killed?

"You set out the clothes?" Ollie asked, gesturing to his still naked chest and trousers.

"Ay, I did. I seek answers."

"Okay, let's begin with introductions. You know my name, but I seem to have missed yours," he grumbled.

"Tora. My name is Tora."

"And what are you doing in these parts, Tora?"

"Surviving," was all she said, tipping her head back and closing her eyes.

"We're just passing through," Ollie replied, hoping that his response would buy him enough time to get Rose and get the hell out of these woods.

"Ah, yes. You and your vampire enchantress. Tell her she has nice aim. But the next time she throws a knife my way, tell her not to miss, because when I throw one back, I won't." Ollie tensed. His jaw feathered as he gnashed his teeth together.

"Don't threaten her," he snarled as his wolf began to surface. Kicking her boots, Tora laughed as her eyes followed the ripples.

"I think the fangbanger can fend for herself, puppy," Tora replied in a matter-of-fact tone. Ollie's breaths came in short puffs as his heart thundered in his chest.

"Yes, she can, lass. But she doesn't have to do so with me around. And you're lucky I'm around."

"Is that so?" Tora asked, arching a brow at the wolf.

Ollie's heart beat faster in his chest as he watched the bandit slowly slide closer to him.

"It is."

"Why are you so nervous, pup?" Tora asked in a low, husky voice.

"I don't trust you."

Ollie stepped away from the girl. It was true, he didn't trust her, especially when she looked at him with a twinkle in her eye and a weapon strapped to her hip. The smell of Wolfsbane emanated from the bandit—the drug that was Ollie's undoing. He wasn't sure how she'd managed to get her hands on the substance.

"You dropped your squirrel," Tora said, picking up the kill and holding it out.

"Keep it," Ollie replied. "I-I'm- gonna go now. You're not gonna ambush me, are ya, lass?" A sly grin passed over Tora's lips.

"Not this time, puppy. Not this time."

❦

ROSE

A FEW HOURS PASSED AND THE SUN STREAMED DOWN, stirring Rose at the warmth of it. Smiling before even opening her eyes, Rose wriggled in the delightful sunshine, something that was not customary for her people, as creatures of the night.

"Ollie?" she whispered, cracking her eyelid open. Once again, she awoke to no sign of the wolf.

"Ollie!" she shouted, sitting upright.

"Calm ya'self, lass, I'm over here." Rose spun to the sound of his voice. She felt her heart return to a normal rhythm. He sat cross-legged on the ground, skinning squirrels, shirtless. Rose watched for a moment as the knife effortlessly slid through the creature's hide. Her eyes flickered to Ollie's arm, the way it flexed as it wielded the knife.

Goddess, what was she becoming? Her cheeks flushed as she recalled the events of the early morning. The way his body moved effortlessly with hers. The feel of him. *Oh goddess, yes.*

"I-uh, yeah, we should get going." Rose coughed, clearing her throat. She hopped to her feet, searching quickly for her trousers and tunic. When she came up empty, she looked to Ollie who was placing a bit of raw squirrel into his mouth from the blade. He nodded toward a low-hanging branch on the edge of the clearing. Rose scowled as she sauntered over to yank on her clothes, feeling eyes on her as she dressed.

"Okay, are you ready?" Rose asked, tossing him the linen shirt that had been draped over her. With a nod, Ollie stood, his mouth full of the tiny morsel and the remainder of the squirrel still in hand. He held out the second skinned squirrel and nodded.

"Eat. You need blood before you go into a rage."

"I'm not a Ripper," Rose huffed, pulling the dead animal from his hand.

"No, but you still need to eat," Ollie replied. He stood from his spot and bent down to sling their packs onto his shoulder. Rose sighed, knowing that he was right and lifted the squirrel to her lips and sank her fangs deep into its back. Cool blood rushed into her mouth, nearly gagging her as she drank. Her stomach churned, protesting, but Rose drank until the last drop was gone.

"Okay, let's go," she said, leading the way across the clearing toward Elirion's capital.

15

OLLIE

*H*ills of lush green greeted Ollie as his feet clambered up the loam-covered trail toward Northpass Village. He knew the place well, being so close to the stone quarry where his pack lived. Northpass was a small village on the outskirts of Tatum, where shops and fun could be found. Cleaner than The Pits, the townsfolk took pride in their quaint village. Humble and kind, they never once judged Ollie for his race. Never once looked down to him, unlike most places he ventured. But something told the wolf that the Northpass he remembered would remain only in his memory. A pain in his gut told him that whatever lay ahead was a product of a Ripper.

"Ollie," Rose said from his side, holding out her hand to stop him. "I smell blood. So much blood." Her muscles stiffened.

"I know, lass," he whispered, halting in place. Rose turned, her eyes widening. Elongated fangs poked past her cherry lips, dripping with venom strong enough to kill him with a nick.

"Ollie, that amount of blood... there's so much... I

don't know that I can..." she trailed off, unable to finish her thoughts.

"Aye, lassie, I know," he repeated.

"The amount of rage it would take to produce that—" Rose shook her head, her face twisting in pain. Lost in horror.

"Gavin's been here. They call him the Prince of Blood for a reason." Ollie's eyes flicked to Rose. He heard her heartbeat quicken, roaring in his ears.

"His Ripper is almost as bad as Celeste's," Rose replied. "Or so I've been told."

"Aye, lass. That it is. And with Gavin's emotions being his driving force, the demon within him easily latches hold of his pain, twisting and poisoning his mind. "He's told me time and time again, and I've watched firsthand as it nearly consumed him." What little color Rose had drained from her face as she turned to fully face Ollie.

"I don't think I can go up there, Dawson." She swallowed hard.

He knew how hard it was to fight against one's own nature. How hard it would be to fight the fiend within her. Rippers were born of tragedy. Would so much destruction trigger one in Rose? Reaching for her hand, Ollie entwined Rose's fingers within his own, giving them a reassuring squeeze. He swallowed back the fear creeping through him and met Rose's gaze with confidence. He would ground her, tether her to him and be her strength. Rose's pale blue irises begged for him to take the lead.

"You're not alone," he whispered. "I'll be right beside you, every step of the way, lassie." And with that, he walked forward, trudging up the hill with Rosalie Coston in tow.

BODIES. SO MANY BODIES LINED THE COBBLESTONED ROAD of Northpass Village, running a river of crimson through the narrow crevices. Ollie's stomach churned, twisting and knotting as his measly meal of squirrel threatened to reappear. Each human in a line of broken muscle and bone with their throats torn out. Bile lurched up the werewolf's throat as he emptied the contents of his stomach. He knew it would be bad. Rose stood at his side, pulling back fallen strands of his hair as vomit catapulted out of him.

The little town he'd fallen in love with, the place he wanted to make his home someday, lay in ruin. How many new ghosts would haunt his friend? How many demons would spawn from the life spilled?

Gavin had taken the time to lay them out respectfully. He had folded their arms over their chests and closed their eyes. There was a start of a grave at the beginning of the row to Ollie's left. He briefly wondered if Gavin had planned to bury all of these poor people.

Though the body count was high, Ollie's heart relaxed a fraction knowing Gavin had pulled himself out of his murderous reverie enough to show remorse and respect to these people.

"Ollie," Rose gritted out between clenched teeth. "We need to move. *I* need to move out of here. Please." He should have known by the tone of her voice. He should have moved. Should have followed the vampire's pleas to leave, but Ollie stood rooted in place.

"Dawson," Rose groaned. Ollie tore his attention away from his thoughts, turning to face the woman he had so much longing for. Her eyes shifted from lapis lazuli to dark purple as the bloodlust settled in. If they didn't move, he would be her only living prey. If they didn't move, Ollie would die.

Grabbing Rose's wrist, Ollie surged through the town.

Lanterns flickered in the windows of homes as they passed. Flames that should have been snuffed, roared with life. The pair pushed onward, stopping when Ollie's eyes fell suddenly on a little girl with her throat torn to shreds.

Gavin, what have you done?

"Daw-" Rose began, before the wolf cut her off with the flick of his wrist.

"Go, Rose. Get out of this town and wait for me on the other side. I need to check something out." Rose turned to look at Ollie, her gaze nearing the darkest shade of blue. Her eyes bore a craze to them that raised the hairs on the back of Ollie's neck. Was he too late? Rose's fangs oozed purple venom down her chin as they protruded from her lips, a feral look etched into her porcelain features.

"Rosalie," he snarled, watching her eyes flick to his. "*Go!*" Rose was gone in a flash, moving in a blur as she left Ollie alone in a town full of ghosts.

It was the right thing to do though. Without worrying if Rose would snap, Ollie could search for clues in the wake of Gavin's destruction. He'd known the Ripper would surface from Gavin's pain, but he never imagined this. Ollie looked up at the sky as if it would speak to him, feeling small pricks of rain as they fell to his face. The sky wept for the fallen, mixing with his own anguish. *Oh goddess.*

Taking a shuddering breath, Ollie kneeled beside the murdered child. The scent of copper and decay stuck in his nose. Ollie bowed his head and reached out to smooth her hair.

"Rest easy, little one," he whispered. "May you fly higher than the clouds. May your soul soar with the ancestors and Artemis's embrace. May the pain of this life leave you and treat you better in the next."

Ollie fought against the tears that pricked in his eyes.

He pushed to his feet and turned away. His chest heaved, ragged breaths tearing through his body. Tears fell down his olive cheeks in streams, dripping from his nose and face. Ollie wiped them away with his fingers and turned to face the vacant home before him and opened the door.

It was nothing spectacular, though nicer than his living quarters back in the Underground. Ollie stood in the living room, sparsely furnished with natural wooden chairs and a kitchen table. The wolf's brows furrowed, finding it peculiar to have kitchen furniture in the living room.

Giving his head a quick shake, he closed the door. Natural light was scarce in the home, lighting only through the one window that sat next to the front door. The pitter-patter of rain fell harder in the streets, washing away the gore that befell Northpass.

Ollie scanned the home, noting a bed big enough for a family, a wood stove, and brick flooring that stepped up to the living room and kitchen. His eyes fell back on the kitchen table, on the letters that appeared strewn about and the ink pen that sat dry upon the page. Walking to the table, Ollie withdrew the letter scanning the contents.

The sympathizers are dead.
For it is far time a new coven sits upon the throne.
Northpass is gone.
Conquered by the night in the name of Chaos.
We take Tatum at dawn.
The rebellion has begun.

The rebellion has begun? What in the—what? Ollie pinched the bridge of his nose trying to make sense of the words. *Were the covens rebelling against Gavin? Were the humans rebelling against the vampires?* Nothing made sense. Crushing the note, Ollie thrust it into his trouser pocket and opened the door.

Water splashed from the cobblestones onto his pant legs. His hair clung to his face, drenched. Ollie's tunic was soaked in seconds as the rain poured from the heavens. His skin pebbled against the cool air, but Ollie didn't seem to notice. His mind whirled over the note and its contents.

Whatever evil lay ahead was coming for Tatum and he sure as hell wasn't going to have Rose be a part of it. Tilting his head up, Ollie sniffed the air, catching Rose's scent and ran.

GAVIN

*R*ose.
      He had chosen Rose? Why hadn't he fought to hold the ceremony off until Dahlia was found? Sure, it left the kingdom without a technical ruler, but Gavin knew that between him and Declan, they could handle the day-to-day decisions.

Rose. That sly little minx had lost him his coin, guaranteeing his fight in the Underground that led to Ollie's death. Gavin gnashed his teeth together, flexing his jaw. He didn't know if he could ever face her. There was so much history between them. So much that he'd buried in the past, now trudging up. He knew he'd hurt her when he'd chosen Lorelei. Would Rose forgive him or condemn him? She knew what he'd done, after all. Would she be able to chain the Prince of Blood? Raking his hands through his hair, Gavin stood in the Council room long after the meeting ended.

He supposed the council meeting could have been worse. The covens could have demanded that he marry Lorelei. Hell, they'd tried that, and thankfully, Lord Bloodworth had been shot down. But now his past was staring him straight in the face. Every kiss, every whispered word, every tear shed, haunting him like the Ripper's victims. A shudder ran down his spine. *Fuck.*

Gavin closed his eyes and pinched the bridge of his nose between his forefinger and thumb, sucking in a breath. He needed a goddessdamned cigarillo. Racing through his mind was a golden halo bobbing through the Underground crowds. Rose had been cunning enough to survive the Pits, running bets in the Underground, and dealing with the likes of ghouls. But would she be enchanting enough to win the hearts in Tatum?

Gavin opened his eyes and fished in his pocket for his matchbook and smokes. Pulling them free, he lifted a clove cigarillo to his lips, lit the end, and took a deep drag. He closed his eyes, relishing the taste in his mouth, the burn in his lungs as he released a puff of grey smoke from his parted lips. He peeled his eyelids open and walked from the Council room, up the staircase toward his room.

Gavin felt the guilt of Ollie's ghost closing in on him as his legs moved faster toward his chamber. He couldn't let anyone see him vulnerable, most of all, Lorelei. His door was in sight as pain shot through his chest, making it hard to breathe.

Ollie…

Gavin's legs moved faster, halting in front of his chamber door. His fingers curled around the cool knob, twisting as he hurled the door open and flew inside.

He had gladly and unforgivingly destroyed his best friend; the memory of it seared in his brain.

He reached out, his fingers curling around Ollie's neck, forcing the air from his windpipe. The vampire pushed to his feet, lifting the beast with him, his arm screamed beneath the wolf's weight. The Ripper within Gavin didn't seem to mind the strain as Ollie's yellow eyes widened. Fear gripped his features as he feverishly dug at Gavin's unyielding hand.

"I'm sorry, brother, I win."

He won. He won... nothing! He'd won a lifetime of guilt and damnation. Oh goddess, what had he done? What had he become? Gavin clutched at the tightness in his chest, feeling dread course through his veins. His breath hitched; his eyes widened. He needed his vices; needed to drown out the pain, numb it with everything and anything he had. His eyes flickered to the whiskey decanter on his nightstand. He quickly moved; the nightstand was before him in the blink of an eye. Gavin reached for the decanter. Pulling the stopper free, he lifted it to his lips and took a swig. The whiskey burned in his mouth as he sloshed it around before swallowing. The smokey taste singed his throat and did little to soothe the ache in his chest.

Ollie was his voice of reason in the storm. The lighthouse in the dark. Without his best friend, his lifeline to humanity, who would he become? What other monstrosities would his Ripper cause without a ground? Surely, Rose couldn't quail his inner demon. Such a woman would probably balk at the idea of blood and murder. Assumptions tended to doom him as of late though.

Before his thoughts could take him to very dark places, the wooden doors to his chamber flew open with a *bang* and a very wet, very irritable sentry walked in.

"What?" Gavin snapped, twirling the crystal decanter in his fingers.

"S-sorry, my lord." Water dripped from the sentry onto the dark wooden floors. Gavin grimaced, flicking his eyes to the drops staining the precious wood.

"Were-w-wolf," the sentry stuttered. Gavin's eyes shot up toward the door. Looking past the sentry, he dropped the whiskey from his fingers, hearing it smash as he bolted for the grand foyer. Air couldn't come fast enough as he lunged down the winding staircases.

It couldn't be.

Two steps at a time, he bounded down until he was in the stone and marble hall that led to the grand entrance. Gavin paused, trying to even his haggard breaths. His chest heaved and his lungs burned. He took a tentative step forward and could hear the steady hum of Declan's voice from around the corner.

"What are you doing here, mutt? Don't you know where you stand?" A hushed male voice answered him back, too low for even Gavin's ears to interpret. Whatever was said, however, had steel releasing from sheaths. Squaring his shoulders, Gavin strode around the corner.

"What is the meaning of this, Declan?" he asked as cordially as possible. He could feel Declan's animosity from where he stood across the room.

"This street dog wants to barge in here and—" Gavin held up a hand, cutting the words from Declan's tongue.

"Dog?" he asked. Declan nodded, stepping aside as Rosalie Coston emerged from the rainy doorway with Ollie in tow. Her blonde hair clung in wavy strands to her face. Rose brushed the strands away and stepped in front of the wolf, using her small frame as a shield.

Silence fell.

Gavin's heart stopped as he placed his hand over it. Pain stabbed through Gavin's knees as he fell to the floor. His vision blurred before bright red lips, piercing lapis lazuli eyes, and that ungodly golden halo of hair met him all over again.

"My lord!" the sentry yelled, rushing to his side, pulling Gavin to his feet. Gavin's eyes locked with Rose's. Heat radiated through his cold body as Gavin took a step forward.

"H-hello, Heiress. Welcome home." Gavin's voice was rough as he bit back the emotion that threatened to poke through and Rose's eyes fluttered to the side.

"This," she gestured around the castle foyer, "is not my home. And I am none too happy about being left in the rain while being berated by a princeling with his ass on his shoulders." Her voice took on a matter-of-fact tone that Gavin hardly had the gusto to challenge. It had been a long day. A trying day. A gust of stormy wind caught Rose's hair, wafting her scent his way as Gavin sucked in a deep breath. His eyes widened, his brows arched. And then Gavin, the Prince of Blood, saw nothing but red.

His gaze flicked past Rose to the wolf behind her. All the hatred, self-loathing and sadness were replaced with a possessive anger he'd never known.

"Gavin... Now, please... Listen to reason, mate," Ollie said, raising his hands out before him in submission. Gavin's fingers curled into a fist. Red flashed in his vision, tunneling as he pushed past Declan and Rose, facing Oliver Dawson. Gavin raised his fist and with blinding speed collided it with the wolf's face, sending blood spurting across the floor.

"Ah fer fuck's sake, aye!" Ollie cursed, his hands flying to his bleeding nose.

Rose's face became hard steel. "What in the actual hell is wrong with you?" Gavin simply stalked off, bloody knuckles and all, leaving the rest of them to sort it out. Bristling with energy, Gavin stopped short of the stairs leading back to his chamber hall.

"Gavin, look at me." An all too familiar voice drew his gaze ever so slowly. Gavin thundered down the hall and slammed his fist into the man's gut and then his nose again. Gavin's chest rose and fell rapidly. Tears filled his eyes as he looked down at the man hunched over before him.

Kill him!

"O-Ollie?" he stammered out.

"Yea-yeah, mate." He grunted out in pain as his palm cupped his nose, oozing with blood.

Kill him, you fool!

A sob erupted from Gavin's throat as Ollie straightened, tossing sandy-colored hair over his shoulder, blood leaking from his nose. "Did ya have to hit the schnoz? That's the moneymaker, ya know?"

Gavin sucked in a ragged breath, pushing the Ripper down. His eyes crossed, his vision blurring as the reddened tunnel disappeared. Gavin rubbed his eyes with the base of his palms before gazing upon his *dead* friend, alive, in front of him. His first reaction was pure rage. Smelling another male's scent on Rose threw him off-kilter. Then, he recognized the scent, flooding him with relief and shame. Staring at him now, Gavin couldn't bring himself to be angry. That would come later, much later.

"Um, what the actual fuck, you guys?" Rose's voice cut through his thoughts. The Prince of Blood ebbed in his vision again, beckoning Gavin to set him free.

Kill him! Make them pay!

Gavin gritted his teeth and kicked out, side swiping Ollie's legs from under him. The hulking form of his friend crashed to the floor.

"What was that fer?" Ollie spouted.

"You know damn well what! You fucking prick," Gavin sneered. "I need a damn drink. You?" He nodded to Rose. She shook her head.

"Well I need whiskey," Gavin muttered. Pushing past Rose for yet the second time, Gavin left, trudging up the staircase.

"What was that all about?" he heard Rose ask Ollie.

"Nothing I didn't deserve, lassie."

155

Gavin smiled despite himself. He could feel the heat of her blue eyes on his back as he retreated up the stairs. Blood had stained his cuffs, and he wanted nothing more than to strip it off and drink himself into a stupor. He paid no mind to the sound of footsteps behind him. Ollie's presence worked its magic on his mind, lulling the beast to sleep for a bit longer. Reaching his chamber, Gavin unbuttoned his linen shirt and tossed it to the floor. He crossed his chamber to the small private bar he'd had installed to entertain his female guests and poured himself a drink.

The crystalline decanter he'd dropped was cleaned up. Watching the amber liquid slosh around the sides of the glass, the smokey smell welcomed him like that of an old friend. He lifted the brim to his lips, feeling the familiar burn trickle down his throat, swallowing the contents before pouring himself another. Glass in hand, he sank into an armchair before the fireplace and stared into the dark. Soon, footsteps echoed down the hall, ending at his open door. Gavin didn't need to turn to see who it was. He already knew they'd both followed him, whispering as though he couldn't hear them. Ollie stepped into the room, followed by the alluring Rose, his bride-to-be, who turned to shut the door.

"Change your mind about the drink?" Gavin asked, setting his aside as he fished in his pants pocket for a cigarillo and his matchbook. Raising the smoke to his lips, he flicked the match to life, relishing the taste of cloves on his tongue.

"Since when do you smoke those, mate?" Ollie asked, his voice low as he rounded the chair and sank onto the sofa.

"Since you died. I'm going insane right now, aren't I? You're not really here."

"I'm as much here as that cigarillo you're sucking on."

Gavin sucked a long drag before passing the smoke to his friend.

"Why her, mate?"

"Huh?"

"Rose," Gavin clarified. "Why'd you fuck her?"

"I had to stake my claim on her. I had to try."

"Why, though?" Gavin gritted out, releasing tendrils of wispy smoke between his parted lips.

"Perhaps, I should leave," Rose replied from behind the two.

"Perhaps, you should," Gavin snarled.

"No, love, please stay," Ollie intervened, shooting his friend an irritated look.

"I'd rather not be part of the ego bath that is about to unfurl." Rose crossed her arms under her breasts that Gavin couldn't help but to notice were peeking out from the top of her shirt.

"Oh, it could be a party alright," Gavin slurred, raking his gaze up and down her body, drinking in her every curve before turning his gaze back to Ollie. "Answer the fucking question, Dawson."

"I can't, mate. I can't explain it to you," Ollie replied.

"I'm still here, you pompous asses!" Gavin saw Rose's fingers curl around the crystal ashtray sitting on his night-stand. She pulled her arm back and launched it toward Gavin's head. Gavin effortlessly lifted his hand and let it spin around his index finger before setting it on the side table and dumped his ashes into it. "Thanks, dollface. I needed that."

"Listen here you self-righteous ass! If you hadn't gambled and whored all your coin away, none of that shit back there would have happened!"

Gavin sprang to his feet, rippling with anger. Ollie

followed suit, stepping between Gavin and Rose. "Gav," Ollie cautioned, pressing his palm to Gavin's chest.

"What?" he snapped, momentarily glancing down at his friend's hand and back to his face. "What the fuck, Ollie. Like I haven't thought of that! I don't need *Mistress Obvious* over there to tell me I'm the reason my best fucking friend is dead!" Ollie looked taken aback. "I don't need more people to tell me I messed up, no matter how goddessdamn sexy they are. I kick myself in the ass enough! I fight with this demon every single second of the day! I don't need a reminder." Heaving a sigh, Gavin fell back into his chair to hold his temples, cigarillo perched in his mouth. "You know, it's really fucking frustrating to see your best friend die by your own hand while you smile about it, all the fucking while, all you can picture is a blonde head of hair and sappy blue eyes." His voice was heavy, the whiskey and cloves taking hold.

"But, Gavin, I'm not dead, mate." Ollie's brow was furrowed as Gavin studied his face.

"I saw you die. I crushed your windpipe. And now, somehow, you're here before me and you fucked my bride," Gavin snarled, closing his eyes as the room around him went still.

"But—"

"Just leave me to my insanity."

PART II

LIGHT

*S*he felt the magic ripple, breaking its hold on them before cracking, spider-webbing all around them. Darkness streamed through the fissures and the bars of light that separated good from evil shattered.

Her eyes widened, watching as he stepped forward, rubbing his hands together as a wicked grin spread across his face.

"I told you, Sorceress. I have won."

GAVIN

*G*hosts haunted Gavin. Ghosts his Ripper had created. Ghosts that could laugh and drink and smoke and bed his girl. Ghosts that knew his secrets. He was losing his damn mind. No matter how many times Ollie had told him he wasn't going crazy, Gavin knew otherwise. He'd watched the fear cross his friend's face before crushing his windpipe. But the Ollie that sat with him, just moments before, insisted he was *alive*.

Impossible.

Gavin pinched the bridge of his nose, taking steadying breaths as he sorted out his thoughts. He sure as hell didn't know what or who to believe.

"Ay, mate. I did screw the lass." Gavin opened his eyes as Ollie shot Rose an apologetic look. "But you have no claim on her."

"Actually, I do."

"Excuse me?" Rose asked, arching a brow as she rounded the sofa and took a seat next to the wolf, draping her legs over his. Gavin's eyes lingered on the intimacy of their touch. The fact that they were even touching was driving him insane. Groaning, Gavin began to tell Rose all about the meeting that had happened earlier that day. How the covens had chosen her sister as his betrothed, but in wake of her absence, Rose was chosen. His eyes flicked to the feathering muscle in Rose's jaw.

"They can't do that!" she snapped.

"They can and they have. It was either you or Lorelei Bloodworth."

"And I was the better choice? Actually," she huffed a breath, "I will take a drink right about now."

"Bloodwhore or alcohol?" Gavin asked.

"Brandy." Pushing from his seat, Gavin crossed the room to the bar and uncorked a bottle he had saved for the exceptionally rough days, pouring the contents into two small rock glasses. He settled the cork back into place and returned to his phantom company, handing the drink to his little minx.

"Gavin?" Rose asked.

"Hmm?" he replied, sinking back into his chair as he lifted the glass to his lips.

"I know you think you're going crazy and that we aren't real, but I assure you, we are very real and we have some very important things to talk about."

"Well, by all means, talk." Gavin took a swig of his drink wishing it were something more hearty. Wishing it were whiskey…

Rose looked uncomfortable as she pulled a crumpled piece of parchment from the bag at her side. Ollie wrung his hands impatiently when Gavin took the outstretched note and read its contents.

The sympathizers are dead.

For it is far time a new coven sits upon the throne.
Northpass is gone.
Conquered by the night in the name of Chaos.
We take Tatum at dawn.
The rebellion has begun.

THE WORDS SANK IN HIS STOMACH, TWISTING AND TAKING root, sending shivers spider-walking down Gavin's spine. His eyes snapped up from the note, searching for an explanation.

"What the damn hell did I just read?"

"That's what we're trying to figure out," Rose replied. "It obviously is speaking about your parents in the first line."

"Stop," Gavin seethed. "It's speaking about me. They died because of me."

"They died because some asshats killed 'em, mate. Not because of you," Ollie interjected.

Gavin stood and began pacing before the fireplace, reading the note over and over again. *The sympathizers are dead.* Okay, his parents had been murdered. *For it is far time a new coven sits upon the throne.* A threat. Someone wanted him and his family off the throne, and to take Tatum for themselves. *Northpass is gone, Conquered by the night in the name of Chaos.* He knew that much. His Ripper had torn through the village destroying it and as a result, he'd spent his first few days in Tatum trying to drown out the pain he'd caused with whores and booze. *We take Tatum at dawn.* We. Take. Tatum. At. Dawn.

Who the fuck is the "*we*" the note referred to? That much he needed to figure out. If Gavin could nail that down, then he knew he could find out who led the rebel-

164

lion and end it before it got much, much worse for his family.

Hours passed as the sun peeked above the horizon, streaking rays against the dark wooden floorboards as Gavin paced. The rock glass in his hand sloshed with what little bit of brandy he had left, swirling like the information in his brain. He'd spent the rest of the evening walking in circles only to be left empty-handed. Ollie and Rose had grown weary of him reciting the note over and over and retired to the guest wing of the castle, leaving him entirely alone with his thoughts. Gavin's eyelids burned as he scanned the contents of the note once again, halting when a small knock sounded at his door.

"Yes?" he called out, watching the door crack open and a sleepy Aurora poked her head in. Her hair was a mess of knots as she rubbed at her eyes with the back of her hand. Dried drool stained her chin and the hem of her baby pink nightgown skimmed the floor. Gavin set his glass down on the nearest table and strode to his baby sister, pulling the door open as he kneeled down and scooped her into his arms; a sliver of peace to ease his heart.

"What are you doing up so late, little one?" he asked, pecking a kiss to Aurora's cheek.

"The shadow men are back. They woke me up, like they did when Momma and Papa joined the stars." A chill ran down Gavin's spine. His baby sister's words woke something sinister within him. *Shadow men?*

"Tell me about these *shadow men*," Gavin said gently, kicking the door shut before walking the both of them over to the couch. He set Aurora down and began tending to the hearth, watching as flames roared to life around the logs. Reds and oranges and hints of angry blues licked at the charred wood, emanating heat.

"They only come when the castle is asleep."

"And what do they do?" Gavin asked, his brows knitting together.

"They search."

"Aurora, does Declan know about this? Does anyone else know about this?"

"No." Aurora shook her head, yawning. "Declan doesn't like to listen to me."

Gavin's heart ached again for his sister. "What do they search for?" Gavin pushed.

"They told me it was a secret. "

"Then why are you telling me?" he mused, taking a seat next to his youngest sibling. Aurora lifted her eyes to meet his.

"Because I don't want you to become a star too," her little voice replied. Gavin's lips perked up, betraying the ice that filled his veins. His expression softened.

"Come here, my sweet girl," he said, pulling her into his lap as he wrapped her in a warm embrace. Aurora's head rested against his chest. "You don't have to ever worry about that. No one is going to take me away from you. Not Declan, not the covens, and definitely not some shadow men." Gavin closed his eyes, inhaling the sweet smell of his baby sister's hair as the two of them sat there in the quiet, relishing one another's company until the sun was high in the sky.

1 8

ZACHARY COSTON

"*I* told you! I wanted the girl *dead*!" Coston hissed into the hearth, pacing his guest chambers. The entire plan was becoming an outright mess and if it grew any nastier, he'd have to get his own impeccably clean hands, dirty.

"I-I'm sorry, sir," the voice on the other end sputtered. Coston sucked in a breath, feeling his anger grow within him. His jaw tensed as he licked at his fang. Fire roared with life before him with the high sun, heating the room to an uncomfortable degree. Sweat beaded his brow, dripping salty liquid into his eyes. Zachary grabbed at the handkerchief in the breast pocket of his blazer and dabbed his face. He'd spent the entire night howling into the flames, sorting out business, and soon, he would need to leave his chamber and attend meetings. Despite it being the 'middle of the night' for his kind, Zachary knew that humans operated during the day. His absence would bring unwanted attention to his unsavory plans and he couldn't allow that.

"Get your ghouls on the same page. If there are any more mishaps, I will steal a Bloodworth Pegasus, fly back

167

to the Pits and gut you myself." Silence rang through on the other end.

"Understoo—"

"Oh, Daddy," a female voice rang through, cutting off the ghoul kingpin's words from Zachary's ears. "Must you always be so vivid with your threats?"

"Dahlia," he huffed, exasperated. "I placed you in charge of all of this."

"Yes, but you also sold away *my* throne to Rose." Dahlia's wispy form pouted, crossing her arms over her chest within the fire.

"I did it to teach you a lesson. If the Sinclairs had been killed properly, *all* of them, then there would've been no reason for me to give away your rightful place."

"But, you did," Dahlia sneered from the other end. Coston dabbed at his face once more. He walked to his window and cracked it ajar, allowing a midday's breeze to chill his skin before he returned to the fire.

"I saved you from a loveless marriage. I thought that was what you wanted, so that you and—"

"Do *not* say his name," Dahlia warned.

"Dahlia, kill the Sinclairs at all cost or I will punish you and Palmer, myself. Am I clear?" Reaching for the poker, Coston snuffed the fire, ending the conversation. His blood boiled beneath his skin. How dare Dahlia question him after everything he'd done for her? After even allowing her to hole up with that *'pet'* of hers.

Walking to the wardrobe, Coston pulled out fresh clothing. He stripped, discarding his used ones and dressed. He was late. The covens ran meetings at all times, something that would change once the Costons took the throne and freed Limos from his prison. Everything would change then. Reaching for the door handle, he yanked it open before entering the hall, not bothering to close it behind him.

If his daughter failed him… things in Tatum would get bloody.

✸

Dahlia

Dahlia rapped her fingers along the smooth wooden chair of her office, listening to the crackle of the fire. The hearth near her desk roared with life, glowing as the magic dust burned away the remnants of her conversation. Shelves of alchemy books lined the dark interior, keeping her office quiet and otherwise, dark. Echoing thuds outside her door piqued Dahlia's interest as she crooked a brow but remained seated. Palmer's office was located directly across from hers in the dungeon and she suspected he had gotten rough with some of his men after the tongue-lashing she and her father had given him.

Her blood-red lips curled into a sneer as she stared at the wolfsbane strewn along her desk. Every color and variety the realm had to offer, twisted with magic, sat glittering in the low light before her. She had always been fond of purple bane, known in Elirion as the Kiss of Death for its potency. The Wolfsbane trade was her and her father's exclusive work, a network of illegal substances that rendered the werewolves useless but gave them an incredible high. Purple was of her own making, a concoction so vile that it rendered the wolf, nearly dead. Not many tried it, but those that did, were instantly hooked. Dahlia had networked her way into the grimiest corners of the realm and acquired some nasty enemies with other races including the Hunters. But she never feared them. Once her wolves were hooked, they protected her; ate right out of the palm of her hand. Wolves such as the lustrous Conan. *Her* Conan.

Dahlia sighed, relishing in her lovely memories. She hadn't expected to fall for a wolf, hadn't expected to employ one either, but Conan had *mated* with her, an imprint bond that deemed her untouchable within the Wolven communities. She was his, and his alone. And though Dahlia had over time grown to love their bond, she knew that upon her arrival in the Underground, Conan could be nothing more to her than a fighter. It was the way things had to be... for now. At least until she took the throne.

Dahlia's father had been adamant about killing the Sinclairs, which of course she had. She'd sent Palmer's ghouls in to take out the king, but to leave the children alone. Premeditated murder, she could handle, but cold-blooded child slaying, was another. She wasn't going to harm children, regardless of their social standing, but she also knew that the death of the king and his soul-tethered wife would bring the Prince of Blood home. And then her real plans could commence.

Dahlia knew she would be no match for the prince. She didn't care enough about fighting to get strong. She had magic, thanks to Dia. All she'd had to give up was that which she loved most. Dahlia knew that if she waited and played her cards right, she could have both, and Gavin would fall right into her hands.

Staring down at the purple petals, Dahlia's black nails pinched the stem of one and brought it to her face. She inhaled a deep breath, allowing the fragrance to calm her energy. The bane wouldn't hurt her, couldn't touch her due to magic. The price she paid for *potential...* Her lips curled into a wicked grin as she inspected the petals.

Such money could be found in but a small flower. Money and power. She cared more about the substance business that rendered wolves to her beck and call. To hell with her father's agenda, if she could get the Pits and Tatum's wolves hooked on the stuff, then she could take Gavin's throne by force, with a werewolf army.

"Gavin Sinclair," she purred, twisting the stem between her thumb and forefinger. "Wait until I get my claws in you. Perhaps, I ought to poison you with a bit of Monkshood. Maybe a Kiss of Death? Perhaps, you're immune?" She took a pause, to contemplate. "But, the puppy at your side has a weakness to exploit, and I know just how to do it," she sneered. Pushing from her chair, Dahlia strode to the door and yanked it open.

"Sven," she crooned, looking past the guards that sat in a crumpled heap next to her office door. Palmer stood, rolling the sleeves of his white tunic down, blood dripping from his hands as he shot her a glare before shaking his head.

"Eh, boss?"

"Send some of your men to fetch Conan. Tell him I need to see him immediately. I have a job offer that I think he will fancy."

"We could send more ghouls," he countered.

"No, no, I think they've failed enough. I need Conan. Get him for me."

"Of course, m'lady," Palmer replied.

Satisfied with herself, Dahlia turned on her black stiletto heel and retreated back to her desk, leaving the door open.

"Oh, and Palmer?" she called.

"Eh?"

"Send him in as soon as he arrives. The throne cannot

wait and neither can I." She winked, making Palmer's colorless face flush.

＊

Palmer

PALMER MEANDERED THROUGH THE UNDERGROUND, listening to the sounds of cheers, fights and moans echo through the air. Coins glistened in the low light, passing from hand to hand as he walked under cream-colored arches filled with gamblers. Smoke hung in the air, dancing from lit cigarillos, giving the pits a smoggy look. Turning the corner, Palmer nodded, with a smile spread across his lips, to vagabonds as he descended a flight of stairs leading to the holding cells. The biting scent of sweat and excrement wafted to Palmer's nose, churning his stomach. For a ghoul, he never could stomach the unsavory smells of the ring.

Wolves in different transformation phases snarled and shouted at him, their eyes glowing in the low lit dungeon. The tang of copper filtered into the stench as Sven waddled up to the last cage on his right.

Darkness shrouded the cell, hiding the wolf contained within. Palmer smirked and pulled a baton from his trouser loop, clinking it against the bars, further agitating the deadly creatures. Dark curls cascaded over the wolf's face, hiding it from view, but Palmer knew who he was and how to goad him. Blood seeped from long gashes in the wolf's chest as the clanging on the bars grew deafening. Wolves screeched and howled at Palmer, spitting curses in dual tongues, but he ignored them.

"Get up, dog!" Sven snarled. "Your master awaits."

One blue piercing eye glared at him through dark strands, sending a shiver down the kingpin's spine.

"An Alpha has no master. He listens to no man."

"Ah, I think our mistress would think differently, don't you?" The pungent man laughed. Claws grew at the tips of the wolves' fingers, his back hunched as he rose to full height, towering over Palmer.

"Leave her out of it," the male snarled back.

"Tsk, tsk." Palmer wagged a portly finger back and forth. "I don't think so, Conan." Palmer turned, calling for two guards to go in and shackle the wolf in silver, nullifying his ability to transition. Two ghoul guards, both in different stages of decay, quietly obliged and the one closest to Palmer fumbled with his keys before the cell door slid open and they both entered. Palmer's fingers slid around the cool bars, pulling the door shut.

Conan lunged at the ghouls, teeth bared, pinning one to the wall with one hand around the guard's neck as the other fought to get him off. Palmer stood silent. He loved watching mayhem ensue, even if it was at his guard's expense.

"Quit dicking around, you sons of bitches!" he hollered. "Fucking cuff the dog and get out!" The free guard fumbled with his belt, alas grappling a silver stake between his gloved hands and fashioned it at the wolf's spine.

"Drop the guard," his slimy voice slithered. The wolf eyed up the guard and his eyes widened as realization set in. Do as he was told or be staked. The wolf let out a growl and dropped the guard who grabbed at his own neck as if to fight off phantom fingers. "Kneel on the ground, dog, splay your hands on the back of your head. And if you fucking move, you worthless piece of shit, I'll fucking stake you." Palmer smiled. This was delicious, more than he'd anticipated. He knew shit would hit the proverbial fan when he addressed his boss's dog, but he wasn't sure how far the wolf would go before getting 'put down'. The guard with the stake walked to Conan's side, handing the stake over to the weaker guard and grabbed his silver handcuffs slinging them around the were-wolf's wrists. The wolf's skin sizzled and turned red where the silver had touched, slowly burning the wolf down to the bone. He cuffed the other hand and helped Conan to his feet.

"Open the door," the ghoul commanded, and though Palmer could have reprimanded him for his demanding tone, he let the mishap slide and opened the door. They ushered Conan out, grasping a hold of his elbows.

"Clean him up," Palmer ordered. "Then take him to Mistress Dahlia." Palmer walked two paces past the wolf before turning and hitting the backside of his legs with his baton. Conan's knees buckled beneath him, hitting the concrete floors with a crack. The wolf behind Palmer howled out in pain, rearing against his captors as he snapped at the ghoul. "And if you let on to her that I've been holding you, that you've been with me, I'll make sure you never speak again," he hissed before walking back down the hall of cells.

ROSE

*H*eat blossomed on her cheeks and along her neck as Rose paced the hall, trying to calm her mind after spending so many hours in Gavin's room with Ollie. Her mind whirled, trying to process the news of her recent engagement and she found that her eyes wouldn't close for a wink of sleep. She stopped, rubbing at her stinging eyes; her body tired as she let out a yawn.

Ollie had offered to stay with her, a bold statement as he'd just been decked hours before. Rose knew that if he'd stayed in her chambers, she wouldn't be able to help herself. They'd shared a moment in the forest. A moment that was burned into her memory. Rose bit at her lip, her body reacting to the memory of Ollie on her, inside of her. She shook her head and stared at the ruby carpet beneath her bare feet. Her ears rang in the eerie silence the castle wing had taken on, humming loud enough to distract her sultry thoughts.

A creak from behind snapped Rose's attention away from Ollie, away from the news, just... *away.* She turned on her heel, catching a glimpse of a shadowy being emerging from the low lit hall.

"Rosalie Coston," a cool female voice slithered from the shadows.

"Lorelei Bloodworth," she sneered between clenched teeth, watching as the Bloodworth heir slinked from a doorway toward her. Lorelei's hips swayed in her fitted black riding leathers in that entrancing way of hers. She wore, what Rose only imagined was a glorified corset for a top, clad in black leather and silver spikes. The top pushed Lorelei's assets to threatening levels.

"Don't you have somewhere better to be than here watching me like a ghoul?"

"Well, well, well," Lorelei purred; her lips spread into a grin. "You've found out about your title as queen and have grown a pair of lady-balls in the process."

"Go run your mouth off to someone else," Rose spat. Lorelei barked out a laugh.

"I used to be like you. Thinking the world revolved around me."

"You still do," Rose cut in. Lorelei released a huff and continued on.

"But I was never enough for his Ripper. He's called the Prince of Blood for a reason, you know. I couldn't rein in his darkness, and I sure as hell doubt you'll be able to either." Every muscle in Rose's body tensed. Lorelei was right, and, *goddess* did it pain her to think about it. But, Gavin had a past that superseded him. A Ripper could only be grounded by one person. And to hell if she was its master...

"So, what did you do? How did you handle Gavin's darkness when you were with him?" she asked.

Lorelei smirked and shook her head, taking a step closer.

"Oh, poppet," she crooned, placing her hand suggestively on Rose's cheek. "Sweet, little Coston, there's only one person who can tame Gavin's beast. It was never me, and it will never be you."

"Then, who?"

"It will *always* be that damn puppy at his flank," Lorelei replied, walking past Rose toward the descending stairwell. Rose turned, watching her retreat.

"What should I do then?" she called. Lorelei stopped and looked back. She cocked a brow before flashing her pearly fangs.

"Get a leash?" She shrugged and continued on her way.

✢

GAVIN

"GAV, WAKE UP, MATE!" OLLIE'S VOICE RANG IN HIS EAR.

Gavin stirred, blinking back the blurred figure clouding his vision. He rubbed at his face, noting the empty spot on his lap where Aurora had been and sat upright. A chill ran down his spine as his nerves shifted into overdrive. She'd spoken of shadow men lurking the corridors and rooms at night. What if they had taken her? What if they had found whatever it was they were searching for? What if she was what they wanted all along?

"Where's my sister?" Gavin croaked, staring into Ollie's amber eyes.

"She's been with her maids all afternoon, mate. Why?" Pushing to his feet, Gavin crossed the room toward his door without a word before turning back.

"I need to see Declan. The castle's been breached."

✿

AN ICY CHILL RAN THROUGH GAVIN'S VEINS AS HE STORMED the castle halls. Anger rolled off him in waves as he rounded corner after corner with Ollie on his tail. *The castle had been breached.* Placing the *covens* at risk. Placing *everyone* at risk. His parents' murderer had made it in right under his very nose, and now, Aurora was seeing creatures. *Shadow men.*

"Ya have to talk to me, mate," Ollie blew out between breaths. Gavin knew he was moving faster than the wolf, but this was important. "Or at least, slow the fuck down." Gavin stopped momentarily and looked at his best friend.

"I'll explain everything when we find Declan, but we have to move quickly and we have to go now." The pair reached the end of one corridor, rounding on the next, as Gavin ran straight into Zachary Coston. The lord appeared disheveled, his hair in a mess atop of his head. He bore bags under his eyes and a tie around his neck that sat off-kilter.

"Watch where you're going, you... Sire! I did not see you there. My apologies." Coston bowed his head, averting his eyes.

"Ya know, Zachary, I hear that vampire hides are very valuable in other parts of this realm. Shall we try our luck?" Ollie sneered.

"Perhaps we'll see how much a lone wolf hide can get us. I hear a wolf without a pack is better off dead, anyway," Coston spat. Ollie took a step forward, his muscles flexing beneath his linen shirt as he closed the space between himself and the vampire lord.

"Are you fuckin' threatening me, fangbanger?" he hissed.

"If you don't stand down, it will be a goddessdamned promise, dog!"

"Enough!" Gavin snarled, flicking his tongue against his fang, the urge for a cigarillo tingling on his lips. "Lord Coston, please excuse us. We have..." Gavin trailed off. Zachary's brows knit together. He took a step to the side, away from the werewolf.

"Is everything alright, sire?" he asked, bringing his gaze up to meet Gavin's. He squinted, as though trying to read the prince and smiled.

"It's none of your business," Ollie snapped. Gavin whirled, shooting a glare at his friend.

"Everything is fine. But, truly, we must be going, please excuse us." Trying his best to remain neutral and polite, Gavin grasped his wolf by the elbow and pulled his friend along, sidestepping the lord. They walked in silence until they were well out of earshot. Gavin stopped and turned on his friend.

"Really? You just had to go and shoot your mouth off to my future father-in-law?"

"The fuck if I care, mate. That bloke can sod off." Ollie rolled his eyes.

"I fucking care!" he snarled, raking his hands through his chocolate locks, exasperated. "Let's just... Let's just get to Declan's chamber without fighting anyone else."

It didn't take Gavin and Ollie much longer to reach Declan's chambers. The hallways remained clear the rest of the way. Gavin raised his fist to his brother's closed door and knocked, listening to the muffled sounds behind.

Moments later, the door creaked open and Declan stuck his head out.

"What the bloody hell do you want?" he hissed. Sweat

peppered his brows and his usually neat hair was ruffled. Gavin's nostril flared, picking up a lusty scent creeping from the room.

"We need to talk," Gavin replied, arching a brow.

"Can't we talk later? I'm a bit preoccupied at the moment."

"No, mate," Ollie said, jabbing his elbow into Gavin's side. "You're getting it in, eh?" he asked, wagging his eyebrows up and down as a wolfish grin spread across his features. Declan's eyes shot to the werewolf, looking him up and down. His face crinkled with disgust.

"No, it can't wait, Dec," Gavin cut in. Stifling a sigh, Declan opened the door and fastened the tie on his plush white robe.

"Fine, come in. But by the goddess, go sit by the hearth. I'll be with you shortly."

Opening the door, Gavin and Ollie stepped in and down three steps until their feet rested on a red crushed velvet carpet runner. To their left, sat the hearth, unlit and draped in white stone. There was no mantle—much different from Gavin's chamber—instead above the sterile fireplace hung a painting of Old Tatum, the city Gavin knew from his childhood.

Discreetly, Gavin scanned the room. To his right was a four-poster bed, with a snazzy little redhead tied to the posts, leaving her womanhood on full display. Gavin's lips curled.

"Kail," he murmured, nodding to the bloodwhore as he moved to take a seat on a white loveseat that faced the fireplace.

"You know that saucy, little minx?" Ollie asked and plopped down next to the prince.

"I think everyone in Tatum knows her," Gavin replied.

Moments later, moans of ecstasy and the creaking of

the bed frame filled the room like a song Gavin was very familiar with. Every now and then, an occasional grunt would sneak in followed by a giggle, but overall, this was by far, the most awkward experience of Gavin's life. He shifted in his seat, swallowing hard as he tried to think of anything but what was going on behind him.

Ollie huffed a laugh and flashed the prince a look.

"Dec's really givin' it to her, eh?" he asked, throwing his elbow in the vampire's ribs. Gavin gritted his teeth against the jabbing pain that erupted through his side and rolled his eyes.

Fixing his gaze on the charred logs, Gavin barked, "Shut up, Dawson," and crossed his arms over his chest. The wolf at his side let out a sigh and took up the same pose. They listened for about ten minutes until the racket died and Declan joined them, sinking into a white chair to Gavin's right.

"Sorry about that," Declan said, grinning in a way that told Gavin that he was far from being sorry.

"Aren't ya gonna untie the lass?" Ollie asked, motioning back to the tied-up human.

"No," Declan replied matter-of-factly. "I'm gearing up for another round when you two leave."

"You couldn't have waited to finish round one until we left?"

"No, you interrupted. Hope it was awkward for you," Declan replied, flashing his fangs in a grin. Gavin ignored his brother's comment and leaned forward, resting his arms against his knees.

"You might rethink round two after we talk. Besides, Kail is going to need time to heal. Mortals aren't as strong as we are." Declan perked a brow, silently pushing Gavin to continue. "Has Aurora told you about shadows haunting her while she sleeps?"

"Yeah and she told me about the fucking boogeyman too. Didn't you know that he has teatime with Limos and the Fae? Goddess, Gav, the fuck?" Gavin gnashed his teeth together, grinding them against one another as the muscles in his jaw tensed. He felt his demon awaken to the fire coursing through his veins.

Let me out to play, princeling. Let us show the brat why we are called the Prince of Blood. Flicking his tongue over his fang, he took in a long breath, trying to stifle the beast.

You can't silence me. You can't quench my thirst. Sooner or later, I'll come out and I'll teach you a lesson.

"Aurora said she's seeing shadows. They're searching the castle while we sleep," Gavin gritted out between clenched teeth.

"Are you really going to take the word of a babe?" Declan asked.

"I am. It's clear that we aren't liked, that the people of Tatum want to see another coven on the throne. I think these shadows are very real and I think they're behind our parents' murders." Declan's eyes widened at the mention of their parents. His eyebrows rose as he sat a little straighter.

"You think the castle has truly been breached?"

Sucking in another long breath, Gavin replied, "Yes, and I think we're housing the devil."

ROSE

*O*llie was the Ripper's master...
Ollie...
How?
Why?
Lorelei's words swam through Rose's thoughts as she walked through the halls searching for the meeting room she knew the covens would be convened in. Any time spent in Tatum was in meetings or balls. But, since the announcement of her betrothal to the Prince of Blood, Rose bet on the first. The ceremony would need to be planned, after all, it wasn't every day that a new ruler took the throne. *And* to Rose's dismay, she would be the next queen. Rose stopped, closed her eyes and groaned.

Tatum had strict laws on the practice of alchemy, something she was free to dabble in back in the Pits. Something that made her family standout amongst the rest. She'd had to give up something dear to her, the price for using magic and alchemy, the price Dia, herself, had to pay. But Rose knew that if she practiced her magic here, things wouldn't end well for her. A thought occurred to her, stiffening her muscles. If she even dabbled with wolfsbane, things would be worse than bad. *I have to get the decision revoked!* There was absolutely no way she was marrying Gavin Sinclair. She opened her eyes and continued to search for the meeting as her booted footsteps echoed in the quiet corridor.

Tapestries of the covens lineage hung from the dark stone walls in each house's colors. Her own hung proud in emerald green and gold next to the Sinclair's ruby and white. Rose's eyes lingered on the Bloodworth's in purple and black and the Barclay's in teal and silver.

The covens should have chosen Lorelei in Dahlia's place. Not me.

Exasperated, Rose rounded the corner, stopping before the stairwell. She leaned on the railing, crossing her forearms and looked at the ambient light below. Her breaths came in slow, shallow huffs and her heart hammered against her chest. Voices rose up in the adjacent hallway, growing louder as they approached.

"What the bloody hell do you want done?" Declan shouted, throwing his hands in the air. He had a wild, disheveled look about him. His face twisted with anger. Gavin and Oliver followed closely behind him. The young prince halted as he spotted Rose standing next to the railing. His body language shifted, anger fleeing from his features. Declan's lips curled into a grin, exposing his pearly white fangs. The smell of lust and blood emanated from the princeling as his eyes narrowed to her.

"Hello there," the young prince crooned, taking a step toward Rose. He turned back to his brother and said, "If you don't want her, I'll certainly have a go." Anger bubbled within Rose. He was talking about her like a goddess-damned cut of meat! Rose's heart beat a little faster as the blood in her veins ran red-hot. Magic tingled at her fingertips, bidding to be set free.

"You disgusting little twat!" Rose snarled, whirling to face Declan. "You think that being a prince has granted you the right to speak to me that way? Didn't your parents teach you respect? Didn't they teach you the proper way to speak to a lady or at least in the presence of one?" Ollie shifted in the corner of Rose's vision, moving to stand between the pair. Gavin cleared his throat from the other side of Declan, trying hard to hide his smile.

"Rose," Ollie's voice warned, but she ignored him.

"Get out of my way, Oliver! This is between me and the brat!" she snapped.

"I don't think that's such a good idea, lassie."

"I said *move!*" Rose snarled. Ollie stepped aside, flashing an apologetic glance to Gavin, who stood silent, watching, stone faced.

"And *you*," Rose hissed between clenched teeth, pushing Declan aside as she stepped toward Gavin. "Did you just think that I would be okay with an arranged marriage? That I wouldn't want a say in my future? You Sinclairs think the world will bend to your will. But it won't. And I sure as hell am not marrying you."

"The covens have decided," Gavin replied matter-of-factly, thrusting his hands into his trouser pockets and pulling out a cigarillo and matchbook. He lifted the smoke to his lips and flicked a match to life, lighting the end.

"No, Gavin Sinclair, *you've* decided. I had no say in the matter!"

"Rosalie," Ollie tried again, his animalistic side growling her name.

"Can it, Dawson."

"Look," Gavin said, pinching the smoke between his index and middle finger as he puffed out a grey plume. "I was presented with a decision and I made one. I'm sorry if

185

you don't agree, but it's done. The ceremony is being planned."

"I will not!" Rose shouted, throwing her hands into the air. She had half a mind to grab a dagger and hurl it toward the prince. Gavin let out a breath.

"Gentlemen, please excuse Miss Coston and I while we chat. See to it that the castle is locked down." Turning his attention back on Rose, Gavin held out his elbow, silently issuing for her to take it.

Ollie looked sheepishly at Rose as she begrudgingly took hold of Gavin's extended elbow and released an irritated sigh. He at the very least remembered his manners training. Flicking her tongue over her fangs, Rose looked back over her shoulder to Ollie who stood like a statue next to Declan, his eyes studying her features as Gavin led her away.

"Just breathe," Gavin whispered when the two of them were out of earshot. Rose's eyes snapped to his stony face. He was like cut marble; his emotions undetectable beneath his arrogant mask. They trailed in silence, arm in arm down corridor after corridor, stopping at a sturdy wooden door, carved to look like roots and vines tangled within it. Releasing Rose from his arm, Gavin moved forward, moving iron etchings in a spiral motion before the door snapped open.

"After you," Gavin said, gesturing for Rose to enter.

The scent of bitter alcohol permeated the air, stinging Rose's nostril as she entered the dimly lit room. A bedchamber, with a king-size sleigh bed to her right pushed against the wall. Beside it sat two night tables with lit candelabras. To Rose's left was a fireplace, flickering with life as the flames licked at charred wood and crushed red velvet furniture. Rose turned to the sizable bar that was to the right of the hearth, noting the different shades of

186

amber that glistened in their bottles from the firelight. The sight was magnificent and the smell of booze, abhorrent. Rose whirled to face the prince.

"How can you be okay with this? What is wrong with you?" she growled.

"What makes you think I am okay with it?" Gavin bit back. Pinching the bridge of his nose between his thumb and forefinger, Rose watched his chest rise and fall as he took a long drag on his cigarillo and exhaled. Pain etched his features, lowering the wall he had put into place. Lowering a wall that was clearly built after he left her all those years ago.

"I see how you and Ollie look at one another," he began. Rose stood still, waiting for him to continue. Part of her wanted to ease his pain, something that she had unknowingly caused, but she did nothing. Gavin's mask returned, his face growing hard once again. His Adam's apple bobbed as his voice choked out words she knew were eating at him.

"I can smell the connection between you two. The subtle differences in your body when you're around him. The way his heartbeat quickens at the sight of you. Do you really think that I want to take something from someone who has already lost so much?" His voice wavered. "He's my best friend. I may be a monster but I'm not heartless."

I may be a monster, but I'm not heartless. Gavin's words rang through her brain, swirling and consuming her. Rose didn't feel her legs move as she stood before the hearth, the prince's words echoing through her like the stab of a blade. She collapsed into a velvet armchair, feeling the warmth of the fire wash over her skin as if trying to comfort her.

"I just..." she began. "I just don't see why they chose me instead of Lorelei. You two already have history, why didn't they choose her?"

Gavin stifled a laugh.

"What's so funny?" Rose demanded, flashing her fangs.

"Do you really want Lorelei as the Queen of Tatum?" he asked. It was a serious question. Did she want that bitch as the Queen of Tatum? Of the realm? Rose thought for a moment while Gavin continued, "She'd kill and maim as many innocent people as she could. Humans would never stand a chance. Rippers would emerge from every corner. Our own race would extinguish itself. I can't let that happen. I can't stand to let it happen."

"But aren't you a Ripper, Gavin 'Jagger' Sinclair?" The room fell silent before Gavin answered.

"The Prince of Blood is, yes, but me, no." His voice was quiet as he rounded the sofa and sat down next to her. Rose looked up, watching a hue of pink creep along Gavin's milky cheeks.

"Aren't you one and the same?" she pressed.

"In essence, yes. We share the same flesh suit. In mindset, no. We're very different. Why are you asking me this? We're talking about Lorelei."

"I know. But... but don't I have a right to know these things?" Gavin rose from his seat and crossed the room toward the bar that had an assortment of bottles neatly lined on clear crystal shelves, in silence. He grabbed two crystal rock glasses and poured amber liquid into both before crossing back toward the fireplace, sinking back into the spot next to Rose. He offered her a glass, which she graciously accepted.

"A Ripper feeds on negative energy. It thrives on it and is something that you're born with—an inner demon that takes control when your emotions are out of check. It thrives on destruction. Mine awoke during the war when I witnessed all those deaths and felt the hatred in the air..." He paused, taking a spit of his drink before continuing,

"Something like that changes you. That's all Lorelei would create if she were queen. Yes, we have a past, a complicated one at that, but I don't want to feel the hate that runs through her veins, the deception she masks and her cruel agenda. She is many things, but queen material is not one of them."

The room fell silent again as Gavin's words sank into Rose. She lifted the glass to her lips, immediately recognizing the smell of strawberry infused brandy, *her favorite*, and tilted the glass back, relishing in the bite as the liquid drained down her throat. She felt an unwanted flutter in her stomach when the prince looked up at her from his glass. Those chocolate, haunted eyes peered through her, all the way to her crumbling heart.

"I-thank you," she sputtered, taking another sip.

"Rose, I don't want to do this either. I told them no. They told me I had no choice. That the bylaws stated that a queen must be chosen and a Rose Bound ceremony must commence. They said that failure to do so would leave the realm at risk." Gavin shook his head, draining the last of his glass. "I don't believe any of that though. Tatum could go without a queen for a while. Especially after losing my mother." His voice trailed off and Rose remembered just what the Sinclair children had lost, what *Gavin* had lost. "But if anyone can fill her shoes, it would be you. I, on the other hand, do not want to sully my father's memory by fucking this up. Pardon my language, m'lady."

A traitorous tear slipped down Rose's cheek. "This is just so unfair." Her voice broke and she inwardly cursed herself. Gavin's eyes shot to her face. Instead of ridicule and judgment, she saw nothing but empathy. His hardened expression melted away leaving an unearthly beautiful man in its wake.

"I know, and I am sorry to drag you down with me. If I

could choose to be alone, I would. I wouldn't want anyone to be bound to me for eternity, especially not with what's coming to Tatum." He flashed her a weak smile and all the tears she had fought to choke back streamed down her cheeks, marking her skin in black eye makeup smudges but she didn't care. In that moment, she was not a warrior noble, she was not the heiress she had practiced so hard to be. She was just a girl, in an arranged marriage that neither of them wanted.

"Rose," Gavin whispered, pushing from his seat so that he crouched before her. He reached out to cup her face with his palm, wiping away the tears with his thumb. "You can try to have the marriage revoked. I won't stop you and I won't be mad. This," he gestured around the room as though it was the entire kingdom, itself, "is a lot to handle. It's a lot to ask. I'm a lot to ask." Rose gripped Gavin's fingers within her own, her silent sobs still wracking her body as she lowered his fingers to her lips and planted a kiss before raising her eyes to meet his.

"Thank you," she whispered before another bout of emotion took hold.

✿

BLACK STREAKS STAINED ROSE'S MILKY CHEEKS, SMEARING onto the backs of her hands as she attempted to wipe away her tears. She was a mess. A goddessdamned mess. And she'd let the prince see her that way.

But Gavin had been kind, gentle, even as he offered her his hands and pulled her to her feet. Rose stared as he walked into the next room and started a bath for her.

"No princess should be seen with tear-stained cheeks. Take all the time you need. I'll send for some clothes and be out of your hair," Gavin said when he returned from

the bathing chamber. He moved faster than she'd anticipated, pulled the chamber door open without another
word and disappeared into the hall.

Rose moved slowly, her body tired, her muscles numb
as she entered the bathing chamber and undressed. Steam
billowed from the black porcelain tub as scents of sandal-
wood and lavender whisked her away. Slowly, she crept
into the water and sank down. Warmth enveloped her,
easing the tension she'd been carrying. Rose scanned the
dark stone walls and noticed the absence of sconces or
candelabras. The only light filtering in was from the arch-
shaped window that sat before her, giving her a view of the
grounds below—stables for the Bloodworth's Pegasi and
the meadow that spread behind them. It was gorgeous. It
was a sight she could definitely get used to. Rose sighed
before she tilted back her head and allowed her mind to
wander.

Gavin had given her an out. He'd given permission for
her to go to the Council and try to get the decision for the
marriage to be overturned, and she wanted nothing more
than to do just that. But a part of Rose wondered if she
did get it revoked, what her life would look like after? She
had no other options for marriage, no other prospects
besides the Pits. Although she felt something for Ollie—
whether it was lust or the beginnings of something more—
she knew that in the long run, their relationship would
never work out. Wolves and vampires just didn't mix.

Rose didn't know how long she'd sat with her head
tilted back and her eyes shut, thinking about everything,
but when her eyes peeled back open, her body became
alert. Her skin pruned, having soaked far too long in the
chilled bathwater. Rose gripped the sides of the tub and
stood up, grabbing for a white linen towel situated on the
sink for her. She toweled dry and wrapped herself in the

damp linen before opening the door to see if the coast was clear. Gavin had left, but he'd also said that he would have clothes delivered to her.

Light breathing sounded from the chamber as Rose nudged the door open a bit more with her foot. She stepped out of the washroom into the darkened bedroom. Gavin laid on the four-poster bed, atop the white duvet with his back to her. Rose could briefly make out the rise and fall of his breathing before discarding her sodden towel to the floor. Cool air wafting in from the opened windows bit at her exposed skin, pebbling it. Rose crossed the room to the red velvet couch where a servant had laid out one of the late queen's dresses for her. The dress was completely black with lace that covered her neck and chest. A sweetheart neckline made of the finest silk started where the lace ended. Rose gasped. It was *stunning*. Rose pinched the silk skirts between her thumb and middle finger, rubbing the soft fabric, admiring the handiwork that had gone into making such an exquisite garment. She dropped the silk and picked up the dress and slid it up over her head. The gown caressed her every curve.

"You look beautiful," Gavin said from behind her, his voice breaking the silence. Rose whirled, eyeing his lazy expression. Gavin laid upon his back, having turned while she was dressing. He peered from one peeled eye, and his head rested on his arm, which extended behind his head. Rose wasn't worried about him seeing her naked. She had nothing to be ashamed of.

"Thank you," she replied, but the slow breathing commenced as Gavin drifted back to sleep. Rose let out a sigh. *Just as well.* She had a Rose Bound ceremony to dismantle. Rose returned to the washroom long enough to pin up her hair and left the chamber in search of the Council.

✦

THE COUNCIL WAS SEATED RIGHT WHERE THEY HAD BEEN since arriving in Tatum, their attention on Rose as they sat around the elongated table. Rose stood to the right of her father and took a deep breath.

"Do not waste our time," Linden Barclay snarled from his seat.

"As if we had anything better to do, Linden," Zachary Coston snapped before turning his attention to his daughter. "She is to be our next queen."

"Not until a Rose Bound ceremony takes place," Tobias Bloodworth corrected. He was seated down the table next to Gavin's empty chair. "And still, she isn't the best option."

"Yes, yes, I know the damn bylaws, you twit. Like your trollop of a daughter would be any better!" Coston barked.

"Enough!" Linden exclaimed. "Let's hear what Rose has to say. It must be important if she is interrupting." Rose took another deep breath. It was important. It was her whole damn future at stake!

"Gentlemen," she began, addressing the coven leaders, "as you've stated, a Rose Bound ceremony must commence in order for a new king and queen to take the throne. But customarily the queen is chosen as the next eldest heiress in line from one of the four covens. That title does not fall upon me. *Dahlia* should be taking a seat with Gavin. *She* is the one who should be blood bound, the one who's soul and life should be tethered to Gavin, not I."

"As much as I would like to agree with you," Lord Coston began, "Gavin chose you. His choice overrules the bylaws."

"Nothing, overrules the bylaws!" Linden snarled. "We have them in place for a reason."

"Yes, I understand the bylaws," Rose said, respectfully.

"But, in these circumstances, Rose, Gavin is king by proxy. Therefore, he does have a say. And seeing as your sister is missing, you are the next eldest heiress available."

"But, Lorelei and I are the same age."

"Yes, but you were born six months before her. Hence, Gavin's choice has not violated the bylaws."

"But—" Rose began. She wanted to tell them that Gavin had given her an out, but the Council didn't want to hear it. He'd warned her of this as well. Rose's heart sank at her father's next words.

"Enough! This meeting is done. You will be bound. You will be queen, Rosalie," Zachary said. "The Council's decision is final."

DAHLIA

*D*ahlia's office door opened with a creak, two hours after she'd given Palmer the order to bring Conan to her. Her heart paced faster in her chest as she awaited the sight of her wolf. The door nudged opened some more before giving her a view of dark hair and olive skin. Piercing dark eyes dragged over her as Dahlia rose to her feet. Conan moved, closing the door behind him and walked with purpose to where she stood. He was a great deal taller than Dahlia, despite the height her black heels gave to her.

Excitement coursed through the heiress as she took him in. She could feel the tension growing between their bodies when he leaned forward to inhale the scent of her neck, placing a quick kiss on her cheek.

"I've waited so long to see you, darling." His deep voice purred, rattling Dahlia to her core. Her feral instincts writhed within her, begging for release. She bit her full bottom lip, eyeing him longingly. Conan slowly brought his hand to her mouth, gently prying her lip from the vice of her teeth. He said, "Now, you know I want to do that."

That was all she could take. The animalistic need in his eyes swept her up into a stupor only he could give her. Conan trailed his index finger from her lips, along her jaw, making his way down her chest to hook her blouse. "This is in my way, milady." His breath was molten fire on her otherwise cool skin.

"Well, by all means tear the thing from me," she pleaded. Conan's breath hitched. Grabbing her shoulders, he roughly tore the fragile fabric, exposing her completely to him. Her nipples hardened as Conan leaned back appreciating his view. A coy smile played at the corners of Dahlia's lips. She hadn't only summoned him for business, but for pleasure as well. Something they had grown masterful at.

Seconds later, Dahlia crashed her lips into his, unable to wait any longer. She pressed herself against his hard frame, running her hands up the front of his tunic. How she loved the plains of his body. The heat from his skin sunk into her, fueling her need and driving her wild with desire. This would surely be a destructive encounter for her office, but she didn't care. The only thing in her mind was Conan. Conan with eyes the color of the sun at harvest. The same wolf that was scarred because of her, scars that told a story, one that she traced with her fingers every time she could touch him. She knew every mark on him, just as he knew hers. The *only* one that marred her marble body.

Conan's hands roamed her body, coming to rest on her thighs. Slouching over, he pulled her up so she could wrap her legs around his waist. She greedily kissed him, running her own hands up into his hair. Knotting her right hand there, she guided him to her throat, exposing it for him to kiss. Placing her on the desk, Conan made his way to her breasts lavishing them with his tongue.

A sound at the door snapped Dahlia's eyes open.

Palmer stood in her doorway, red-faced and wide-eyed. Dahlia smirked as Conan continued his relentless assault. Palmer trailed his eyes over her exposed form to land on the man between her legs. Soft moans escaped her lips despite the unwanted audience.

Conan's hand slipped from her thigh to her ankle sheath. Fingering a blade, he flung it backward, narrowly missing Palmer's left ear to lodge into the wall. Without taking his attention from Dahlia, Conan said out of breath, "If you wish to keep your eyes, I suggest you take them off of what is mine."

Palmer quickly scuttled backward nearly smashing through the wall behind him. Dahlia laughed. "You know," she purred, "I love it when you get possessive."

"I wouldn't have it any other way, Heiress." Conan lowered his head again, lining her abdomen with gentle nibbles that sent shivers down her spine as he lowered to his knees. She opened her thighs a bit wider, flashing a stunned Palmer a grin over her shoulder as her wolf descended. His tongue lapped at her sweet spot, sending bursts of ecstasy through the vampiress. A moan tore from her lips as she tangled her fingers in Conan's dark mane.

"Oh fuck," she cried, another moan tore from her core. He felt so good. So goddessdamned good. Conan continued his assault with his tongue, bringing his mistress right to the edge. Dahlia leaned her head back, feeling her wolf dip in and out of her. She rocked into his mouth, her body begging for release and peeled an eye open. She flashed a grin over her shoulder to the shell-shocked ghoul that stood in the doorway and let out another moan. Conan stopped and rose from between her thighs, knotting his hands in her plum locks. His mouth crashed to hers with fervor, asking for more. And she would give him more. She needed him inside of her. She needed to feel his claim.

Pulling from his kiss, Dahlia looked into Conan's sunset eyes, seeing the love and need that matched her own.

"Take off your pants," she breathed, eyeing up the hardened bulge that strained against his trousers. Conan complied, unsheathing himself fully. His hands fumbled to hoist up her skirts before he closed the space between them, claiming Dahlia's mouth once more with his own. Their kiss deepened and without hesitation, Conan squared his hips with Dahlia's as she lowered herself onto him, rising and falling as he plunged into her completely.

Sweat glistened the werewolf's skin as Dahlia rode him closer to oblivion. His hands clasped her backside, holding her close to him, though she wasn't sure there was any closer she could get. Conan quickened his pace and lowered his face into the crook of her neck. His breath was hot against her skin and claws threatened to break her milky flesh as a guttural moan roared through the wolf. The desk beneath Dahlia groaned, feigning to collapse beneath their weight, but neither of them paid it any mind, refusing to stop until a leg beneath them gave way. Instead, Dahlia tipped her head back, allowing her wolf to claim her and rose into pure bliss.

❀

DAHLIA PICKED UP THE REMNANTS OF HER TORN CLOTHING and tossed it to Conan. "You owe me silk," she chided, inspecting her destroyed blouse. "And not that cheap garb from the other end of the realm. Tatum silk, the highest quality."

"Anything you desire, my sweet," Conan replied; a lazy grin spread across his lips. His eyes drooped, watching Dahlia as she dressed. His satisfied expression was payment enough, for the moment. Pulling the wolf's tunic from the floor, Dahlia's lips pulled into a frown as she inspected the cheap thread.

"We really have to dress you better," she muttered before pulling the rough fabric over her head.

"You want to dress me?"

"More like undress. But I want you to be dressed well while I tear your clothing off," she replied, perching on the corner of her wrecked desk. Conan watched her. A primal, protective, gleam shone in his eye, one that she used to hate. Dahlia caught his stare, her lips perking up into a smirk. There was a time she used to think he assumed her weak, in need of protection, despite her vampiric nature, but now she understood it was not only for her, but for him as well. Protecting his heart's investment—in *her*.

"My wolf," she crooned. "My love, I need something from you."

"You mean more than what I just gave you?" Conan winked at her before breaking eye contact to button his trousers.

"*Yes*, my love. I need you to kill—a *wolf*," Dahlia said matter-of-factly.

"And what pray tell, did my kin do to dissatisfy you, m'lady?" Conan's face fell only slightly, his brows furrowed, wrinkling a crease in his otherwise smooth forehead.

"He's in my way." Dahlia pouted, as if she needed a reason for him to do as she asked. She knew pouting was childish, but Dahlia also knew that Conan couldn't resist her requests. This would drive it home. Oliver Dawson was the closest thing to a weakness the Prince of Blood had, and she would exploit it. "He's Sinclair's puppy and I need him put down."

"Ah." Conan pursed his lips. "So suicide missions are on my resume now, are they?"

"I know you're more than capable."

"You're asking more than you think. My love, what is my last name?" Conan asked, changing the subject. Dahlia thought for a moment, rapping her fingernail on the wood. What was his last name? Why the damn hell did it matter?

"And just what does that have to do with anything?" Dahlia snapped.

"Just humor me," Conan said. Had she ever learned it? Ever bothered? Her forehead creased as she sifted through her memories. He must have told her at some point, right?

"Dawson," Conan said, taking her silence as an answer. "My last name is Dawson. And what you're asking is for me to kill my brother." A chill ran down the heiress's spine. She hadn't anticipated her meeting to take such an unexpected turn.

"I see," she replied. Her heart hammered against her ribcage. Brothers.

Brothers? Oh, goddess, how had she not put two and two together? She'd seen Oliver countless times in the Underground, had even bet on him. And here before her, holding her heart in the palm of his hand, was his brother! Dahlia released a sigh. Her mind was whirling, trying to comprehend everything.

"Despite your familial ties, can you do as I've requested?" she asked. She knew it was a long shot. A dead request if there ever was one. Hell, if the roles were reversed and he was requesting this of her, would she be able to kill Rose? No, probably not.

Conan's eyes dropped to the floor and Dahlia knew that he didn't want to answer her. This hesitation, however, was something she knew well. A dark swirl of emotion fluttered in her gut. It was *almost* enough to make her nauseous.

His eyes lifted back to her and he said, "Command it and it shall be so, Heiress." There was a sadness that hung on his features, in his voice; a chill to his demeanor and a bite to his words. Dahlia bit at her lip and hated herself for what came next.

"Do it," she snarled. She had just signed Oliver Dawson's death warrant.

❦

PALMER

A DEEP-SEATED HATRED REVERBERATED THROUGH PALMER'S pudgy frame. Shaking with fury and jealousy, he scuttled down the dark stony hall as quickly as he could. He knew Dahlia had taunted him on purpose, enjoying the look of embarrassment it brought him.

These past few weeks with the disgruntled vampiress had been hell for the Ghoul Boss. He would much rather deal with the undead than a pampered, spoiled daughter of an aristocrat. But alas, here he was, neck deep in coven bullshit. Palmer admitted only to himself that he lusted after Dahlia Coston. Fantasies flitted through his mind, picturing himself as the one pleasuring her, imagining that it was his name she cried.

A shadow swirled on the wall in front of him, pulling him from his sordid thoughts. Walking closer, the shadow darted down the hall, bouncing back and forth for him to follow. "I'm coming, dammit. My legs are short, you impatient bastard." Waddling on after the elusive creature, Palmer finally opened the door to a large cell. It smelled of filth and moldy decay.

The shadow danced in the air before him, disappearing for a moment only to reappear in a burst of purple light. As the light dissipated, a ghoulish man stood naked before Palmer. The shadows never had bothered with

201

clothes, why would they? Transformations into physical form were rare.

"What news have you? Out with it." Palmer waved his hand impatiently.

"Yes, Boss. Jagger has been made aware of our presence. He has barricaded the castle to prevent our scouts from entering or leaving. We have recruits still inside." Palmer's eyebrows shot up as he continued to listen.

"But we are still able to travel through wherever air can." The ghoul glimmered in and out of focus. Physical projection was straining without a host to provide energy to the shadow.

Palmer stroked his double chin, thoughtfully. "The Mistress will want to know about this *immediately*. How in fuck's sake did he discover you?"

"The child, Boss."

"The ramblings of a child caused a full-blown coven lockdown? You *fools!*" he seethed. "Jagger is seizing more power than we had anticipated. Fuck!" The ghoul before him flickered quickly now. "You'd better rectify this situation or there will be hell to pay! Kill the girl! I don't give two flying fucks what happens! Fix it!" Palmer snarled.

"Y-yes, Boss!" With a wave of his hand, the ghoul dissipated back into nothing, leaving Palmer fuming and alone.

"Idiots!" he yelled into the empty room, throwing his fist into the wall. The wall remained unscathed by his anger. Palmer's hand was a bloody mangled mess, but it relented to releasing his rage.

"I hope you are not speaking of me?" Dahlia's sultry voice sounded behind him. Palmer turned, shaking his bloodied knuckles, clutching them with his good hand. He faced a disheveled-looking mistress. Though her hair was tangled and lipstick smeared, she was still a goddess. Palmer's lips pulled into a smile as his stomach twisted.

"Of course not, m'lady! I trust your, erm, meeting went well?" he asked, his tone insinuating what they both already knew.

Dahlia rolled her eyes, clucking her tongue on a fang. "So, what was it that had you yelling into nothing? Or do you enjoy the sound of your own voice?"

"I-uh-a shadow appeared and gave a most disturbing report."

Dahlia's jaw set. Her eyes slit, waiting for him to continue. Palmer opened his mouth to do just that, wanting to please his mistress, but just as he was about to speak, Conan appeared behind Dahlia. He smirked at the ghoul, enjoying the discomfort his presence brought. Conan wrapped his arms around Dahlia's waist, nuzzling his lips to her neck. A riptide of anger washed over Palmer, making him wish it were his lips. He shifted away from the pair and narrowed his gaze on Conan. He'd make him pay. Oh, how he'd wish he'd never set foot in the Pits.

"Perhaps, it would be best if we spoke in private," Palmer said, trying to muster up the smooth, powerful voice his cronies were accustomed to. Dahlia waved off his request with a flick of her hand.

"There's no need. Say what you must before I have to go for," she flashed a come-hither grin at Palmer, "another meeting."

Heat swept over the ghoul, coursing through his veins, peppering his cheeks and neck. He ground his teeth against one another.

"The castle is under lockdown. Gavin has won the council over and the covens have taken provisions to ensure that the fall of Tatum does not happen."

"Is that so?" Dahlia mused, paying no mind to the kingpin as she ran her fingers through the wolf's dark locks. "Well played, Sinclair. Well played." Flicking her tongue out, Palmer watched as Dahlia licked Conan's cheek before pulling away from his embrace. She whirled on her black heels and faced the wolf.

"I want you to ready the packs. Gather the villagers and tell them that the Rebellion is coming to the castle's front door."

"Do you still want me to—"

"Kill Oliver Dawson? Yes."

"And how do you suppose we'll breach the castle?" Conan asked. A valid point, but his mistress's lips curled into a sneer as Palmer stood silent.

"Shadows can always slip through the cracks," she replied. "Lucky for us that Dia has been generous with her magic. We'll walk right through the front door."

"And what should I do, m'lady?" Palmer asked, still cradling his bloodied hand.

"Sit here and take care of my establishment. And for the goddess' sake, you better not fuck this up."

GAVIN

The castle was in full swing, every servant and coven member running about as orders were given to the council members. No one was to be let in or out. Not until the murderer was found. Gavin felt the pang in his gut, one that told him that he was onto something. Growing up in this goddessforsaken place, one would think a prince would get used to having people obey him, but that wasn't the case for the Prince of Blood.

Rounding the corner on the ground floor, Gavin swiftly ducked into an alcove just off the main foyer to evade yet another council member's daughter. The questions, the worry etched into each of their immortally beautiful faces was enough to drive him mad. And with a murderer in their midst, Gavin had no time for their vying attention.

"Hiding from another beautiful lass, are ya?" Ollie's low drawl drew Gavin's attention to the large entry doors.

"Get in here and be quiet," he hissed. "There's no fucking escape from them! What do those old fuckers do, procreate every damn second of every day?" Gavin snarled as he ducked behind the door to hide from a Barclay heiress.

"Doesn't sound like a bad gig to me, mate." Ollie winked "Besides, did you expect anything less from the covens?"

"No, but goddessdamnit, they should keep a leash on their offspring!" Gavin looked at his best friend. Ollie looked at ease today, almost too much so. He was casually dressed in a sleeveless white linen shirt and dark pants with his trademark leather boots and a smug gleam to his eye.

"What're you so damned happy about?" Gavin raised a brow, anticipating some sarcastic reply about being tied down to one woman forever.

Instead Ollie replied, "Rose will make a great queen." Gavin looked past his friend at the covens as they rounded everyone up. Voices quieted down as the past surged within Gavin's mind.

"Shush, Gav!" Rose snapped from behind the double doors of the castle foyer. "Your songs will give us away!" Gavin grinned a toothy smile as he pulled her to his chest. She was soft against his body.

"But you always love it when I sing for you," he whispered. Wind rustled through the open windows, playing with her golden locks. A young Rose pushed her lips into his, stealing a kiss, stealing his breath yet again, before Lorelei Bloodworth rounded a corner.

"What are you two doing?" she asked, eyeing up the pair. "We said no pair hiding and you two are breaking the rules!"

"Some rules are meant to be broken, Lor," Gavin replied. Lorelei crossed her arms and squinted. At sixteen, Gavin had his hands full with the coven's daughters.

"Well," she huffed, "you two look like you're up to something and I don't like it!" Taking a step forward, Lorelei grabbed for Rose's

wrist, pulling her away from Gavin. "Come on, Rose," she whined some more. "We have to get ready for a junior council meeting!"

Rose turned, mouthing 'I'm sorry' to Gavin as she was pulled away, leaving a love-sick teenager in her wake.

THOUGH GAVIN HAD A HISTORY WITH ROSE FIRST, HE couldn't help feeling like he was stealing something from his best friend. Tatum needed to be unified. Hell, Elirion needed to be unified and Gavin knew the best way to do that was to ensure the line of succession and have the Rose Bound ceremony. But everything was on Rose now. If she wanted to be with Ollie, then he wouldn't stop her.

"I know," was all Gavin could come up with to say. *Pathetic.* "Ollie, I—"

"You don't have to say anything, mate, I'm a grown wolf." Gavin's stony face fell. He was usually so composed, so stoic, but now all he wanted was a smoke, a drink and to fuck.

"Gavvvvv!" a young shrill voice yelled, echoing off the walls. Aurora came bounding around the corner and smacked right into Ollie's side, nearly toppling over. Ollie reached out to steady her but she jerked away. A wounded look spread across the wolf's face.

"Aurora. Why'd you do that?" Gavin asked as she reached for her brother to pick her up. He quickly obliged.

Whispering in his ear she said, "Lollie looks like the bad man." Her voice quivered.

Gavin leaned back to look in her face. "Ollie is not a bad man. He has saved my life countless times. You should thank him. You still have Gavie here with you." Gavin booped her nose with his index finger, sending her into a fit of giggles. "Are you ready to be a princess for all to see?" Gavin asked, hoping to lift her tired spirits. She had bluish circles under her eyes like she hadn't slept in days.

Aurora rubbed at her eyes with the base of her palms, a yawn tearing from her tired lips. She nodded sleepily.

"All right, youngin'," Gavin said. "Time for you to get some sleep!" Sunlight poured through the open doors, the middle of the night for vampires, and Gavin huffed a sigh. They should all be getting some rest. With Aurora asleep, perhaps he could lure out the shadows. And then, he could get to the bottom of this once and for all.

"No!" Aurora screamed. "No sleep. That's when the shadows come..." her voice trailed off.

"Aurora," he said gently. "No one will ever hurt you when I am with you, okay?" Gavin felt her body relax into his. Aurora yawned again, her eyes flitting shut as she rested her head on his shoulder. Gavin shot Ollie a silent plea to take over. Ollie stood with his muscled arms across his chest and a curt nod, a silent confirmation as Gavin started for the stairs.

"Your highness?" a rough familiar voice came from behind him. Gavin cursed under his breath.

"Counsellor, if you wake my sister, we will be having an execution instead of a Rose Bound ceremony." An audible gulp from Tobias Barclay indicated that the threat was well received.

"But—"

"Sod off, Barclay. I'm putting my sister to bed. Ollie, would you please deal with Tobias?" Gavin's voice was cool and clipped as he hastily made his way up the stairs, leaving a sheepish Tobias to deal with Oliver.

He would find out what was plaguing his home.

And he would destroy it.

🌹

ROSE

LOUNGING ON A VELVET CHAISE IN HER GUEST CHAMBER, Rose thought of Ollie.

Then Gavin.

Then Ollie *again*.

Whoever the fuck wrote the bylaws deserved to be mauled by dogs. The thought brought a smile to her lips and a blistering heat between her legs. She wanted to be manhandled by her wolf. Rose snorted softly. When would that happen now?

Before being roped into returning to Tatum, a place she loathed, Rose had one goal. *Find Dahlia*. Now, everything was on hold and her future was going to be forever tied to the Prince of Blood. On top of everything else on her plate, Rose knew Gavin would find out about her bargain with Dia.

Magic comes with a price. And goddess, she'd paid it dearly.

Footsteps down the hall pulled Rose from her vivid reverie. She heard a quiet melodic voice that pricked at her memories. She knew that voice all too well as it sang to her once upon a time.

Gavin was singing a lullaby. One he used to sing when they were children. One that he'd sang when Lorelei made her cry. He'd sang to her as he wiped away her tears and calmed her. Before the Ripper rooted within him. Before he'd turned to vices like drinking and gambling and blood-whores. He'd been decent once. Perhaps, there was still a part of the old Gavin she'd loved in there. *Perhaps*. Rose stood and stretched before heading to her open door.

"Gavin?" she called, looking up and down the hallway.

"Shh," he responded as he reached the landing. Rose's breath hitched. He was carrying Aurora cradled against his chest. "She won't sleep if I put her down," he replied and continued on to the next verse. Rose's lips pulled upward into a smile. She felt her heart quake, making way for the dam of emotions that swelled up within her. She'd placed up wall after wall when Gavin had run off with Lorelei, choosing her over Rose. She vowed never to let anyone cause her that sort of pain again, but now, those walls were screaming against the flood. Against old feelings.

"She looked exhausted earlier too. Are these shadows still bothering her?" Rose asked, stepping into the hall. Gavin nodded, never faltering. His eyes glinted with the darkness that had stolen this gentle prince away from Tatum.

Gavin finished the end of the song, listening to the soft breaths of his sleeping sister before whispering, "The council is up my ass today and all I can do is hold her and walk the halls."

"Here, let me see her." Rose opened her arms for him to pass Aurora.

"No!" Aurora cried, struggling to keep hold of Gavin's neck.

"Shh, baby girl. Gavie has to go for a bit. Would you stay with Rosalie? I promise, you'll like her more." Aurora wrapped her arms tighter around Gavin's neck.

"I promise to be back soon. Rose will protect you just like I would, Rory." *Rory*. He had a special name for her.

"Aurora?" Rose peeked around Gavin's broad shoulder to peer into the child's tear-stained face. "I can show you how I get rid of my shadows. Do you want to take a nap with me?" Rose started to hum. It was the same melody that Gavin was singing earlier, though hers wasn't as beautiful.

"You know the magic song too?" Aurora asked, her brilliant blue eyes snapping to Rose.

"I do, now can we let Gavie go to work for a bit?" Rose smiled up at Gavin who looked shell-shocked, which was saying something for the man of few emotions. She had seen glimpses though, especially around his siblings. His heart beat for them and them alone. Aurora was sweet and innocent while Declan was challenging and honest. Aurora reached for Rose, who welcomed her into her arms.

"All right, Princess, let's fight those shadows, shall we?" Rose wrinkled her nose at the girl playfully, earning her a grin and a sleepy yawn.

"Thank you, Rosie," Gavin breathed. Hearing her name on his lips was like strawberry brandy, sweet, burning, and familiar.

She turned back to him, expecting the same mask of indifference he always wore, but it was replaced with grateful eyes and a weary smile. "You're welcome, Gavin," she replied. "She'll be well watched after."

"There's very few I would believe, but with you, I have no doubt." The confidence in his voice sent shivers down her spine—a trust that had long since been forgotten by the heiress. Aurora was already dozing against her and Rose thanked the goddess that she had the child in her arms to ground her. Gavin touched his hand over his heart with a subtle bow and turned, retreating back down the stairs.

LIGHT

*S*he took a step back, raising her hands in front of her, her eyes widening. She called for the light, watching it crumble around them like ash. A smile spread across his lips.

"Five hundred years you kept me prisoner. Do you know just how long I've waited to see you? How long I've waited for your magic to run out?" he asked.

"You haven't won!" she cried.

"Take a look around you, Dia!" Dia turned, watching the darkness seep in around them like smokey tendrils. She blinked, tears stinging her eyes as the Forest of Knowing sprang up around them. It looked the same, but there was another that owned these woods. Dia turned her attention back to Limos.

"Do you feel it?" he asked, arching a brow at her. "Do you feel the chaos? Let it sink into you. Let it consume you, Dia."

"No."

"No?"

"No," she said, matter-of-factly. "Because no matter

what, light will always triumph over darkness." Limos stepped closer, closing the space between them. He reached a gloved hand out and tilted her face up toward his and laughed.

"*We* are the light and the dark. For if there is no you, then there is no me."

"But my magic failed! You just said it."

"Yes, well, blood magic does that when there isn't any blood shared."

GAVIN

*A*urora was safe with Rose. The same girl he'd once loved, once trusted. There was still a gnawing feeling in Gavin's gut. Could he trust her with the Sinclair princess? She did work in the illustrious Underground, after all. But, even as the prince had those thoughts and feelings another took over. There was a gentleness about Rose when she held Aurora in her arms, one that melted Gavin's icy heart. One that eased that ache in his belly that told him to grab his sister and run. Rose's lapis lazuli eyes softened, her face turned motherly, and she'd sang, really sang, for his sister.

Aurora was safe. She. Was. Safe. Letting his mind play those words over, Gavin switched his attention over to the matter at hand. The halls were empty as he raced down the stairs toward the main foyer, skipping steps, jumping over the railing, and landing next to Ollie and Declan. Ollie's lips curled into a smirk, one that he usually held before giving some snarky comment, but the hulking wolf remained silent. Declan narrowed his eyes on his brother and huffed a sigh.

"The covens are all packed away in their respectable chambers, but the Council is calling for a meeting," Declan said. Gavin closed his eyes and took a deep breath. Of course they'd want to call a meeting. He'd expected it. But they needed to find the shadows, find out what they were and who commanded them.

Releasing a sigh, Gavin opened his eyes and looked between his best friend and his brother.

"Okay, you two search the castle. I want to know what these shadows are and what the fuck they want with Aurora. I'll," he huffed, "I'll go deal with the council."

"I'm part of that council," Declan hissed. "I should be there when we all convene."

"He needs us out here, mate. If you want to help, then help me search," Ollie replied, placing his hand on Declan's shoulder.

"Don't fucking touch me, dog!"

"Call me dog, one more time, you little—"

"Enough. It's settled." Gavin cut in before Ollie or Declan could retort. "Go find the shadows and I'll come find you. And for the sake of the three goddesses, stay the fuck away from each other!" Gavin turned on his heels and retreated down a side hall, toward the meeting room.

IT DIDN'T TAKE LONG FOR THE COUNCIL TO GATHER THERE. Gavin had personally notified each leader and waited for them all to arrive. His fingers thrummed against the cool mahogany table as he leaned forward in his chair. He'd taken the seat at the head of the table, one that his father had used once upon a time, as each member took a seat, the heavy feeling in Gavin's heart increasing. Gavin rolled his eyes, annoyed, waiting for Lord Coston, the last coven leader to take his seat before he began.

215

"We need to postpone tomorrow's ceremony. The castle has been breached, as you all know, and a very real threat is lurking within these walls. It's not safe for any of us to be out. We must neutralize the demons lurking within before anything else occurs."

"You keep saying that there is a threat within these walls, Sinclair, but what proof have you got besides the dribblings of a wee babe?" Lord Coston chimed, leaning forward to Gavin's right. He steepled his fingers to his chin and flashed the prince a glare.

"Aurora is the princess!" Linden Barclay snarled from across the table, flashing his fangs at the Coston lord. "You won't speak disrespectfully about her!"

"Agreed," Tobias Bloodworth said, coolly. "If the Sinclair princess saw the threat, then we should be exploring every option to find it."

"I have Declan and Ollie out searching as we speak," Gavin replied.

"Oh great! Let's send the prince and your pet to look around, shall we? Goddess, I feel so much safer! What about you, gentlemen?" Lord Coston growled, pushing up from his seat.

"Sit down, Coston," Gavin gritted out between clenched teeth.

"Gavin. Gentlemen," Zachary said, lowering his voice to a smooth, controlled tone. "Any other time, I'd agree with you. Yes, the ceremony should be postponed, however, tomorrow is the full moon. There is no more time. The ceremony cannot be postponed, not unless you want to put Elirion even further at risk," Lord Coston said, turning his attention over to Gavin. "And don't get me started on your manhunt efforts, Sinclair."

Gavin flicked his tongue against his fang, his teeth grinding against one another, sending a sharp pain up through his feathering jaw. "Of course, I don't want Elirion to be at risk, but we have three High Lords here to help oversee it. Tatum can wait on a king."

"Tatum cannot wait, sire," Linden Barclay replied. "The bylaws——"

"To fucking hell with the bylaws!" Gavin yelled, throwing his hands in the air as he took to his feet. His mind whirled as he paced before the council. Hushed whispers sounded through the room as the three lords deliberated between one another. Finally, they stopped and it was Lord Barclay that spoke, his tone low.

"I'm sorry, Gavin, but we cannot postpone the ceremony on the imaginations of a child, regardless of her title. The Rose Bound ceremony will commence at dusk tomorrow."

Anger boiled beneath the surface, but Gavin remained quiet, sitting back down in his seat. He looked between the three council leaders, noting Zachary. His eyes narrowed as he watched his soon-to-be father-in-law, a smirk of triumph curling around his lips as he leaned back in his chair.

Snide bastard.

❦

THE AIR WAS BRISK WITH THE OVERCAST SKY, SHADING JUST enough sun for the vampires to operate during daylight hours. Soon the sun would set and if they waited any longer, the kingdom would not see souls tethering above the ceremonial basin, bound together for eternity. Gavin took a deep breath as he held the enchanted white rose that never wilted or stained from all the blood it drew in. Encased in glass, the plush, ancient petals remained unscathed. Five hundred years it remained. The very rose that Dia, herself, had used to trap Limos with. It truly amazed Gavin that something so small could be so withstanding. He carried the rose to an altar in the courtyard where every Rose Bound ceremony was held, overlooking the city below. Every nerve in his body screamed that this was wrong. That he should be searching every crack within the castle, sniffing out the enemy, closing in on his parents' murderer.

Soon, there would be droves of people clamoring to see the ceremony take place, but with the castle on lockdown, things would be very different from previous bindings. Guards were stationed along the castle's perimeter, allowing just enough space for spectators to see, but not to get through.

Gavin had called upon the only Alchemist in Tatum, the one that had been approved by the late king, to perform the ceremony and use his magics of love to tether his soul. Gavin knew that Rose would join him soon, so he set the white rose down upon the ceremonial altar before hurrying off to his chamber.

It was customary in the Sinclair coven to wear white upon a Rose Bound ceremony, a symbol of light against the darkness, but Gavin had chosen a suit of black, instead. This was no joyous occasion for him, but a life sentence, bound to a woman who loved his best friend. Albeit they had history, he and Rose, it was nothing compared to the claim Ollie had bestowed upon her. Rose was his... well, he didn't quite know what she was exactly. If Ollie had a mated bond with her, he was sure his friend would tell him, but what he did have, was something else entirely.

Gavin quickly dressed and crossed his room to the bar and poured himself a drink. He knew that later he would feast on bloodwhores, and *Rosalie*. Amber liquid poured smoothly over cubes of ice, the faint crack of the freeze breaking, as Gavin lifted a crystal glass to his lips, downing the drink in one gulp. It burned as it raced down his throat, spreading a warmth through the vampire's body. Gavin reached to uncork the decanter again when a knock sounded at his door.

"Come in," he grunted. The door creaked open and Declan crept in. He wore the customary white garb; his suit free of any wrinkles, and a sword strapped at his hip. With an intruder lurking among them, Gavin didn't blame him for such precautions.

"The entire kingdom is waiting for you, Gav," he said, slowly turning to shut the chamber door behind him. "Are you ready?" Gavin knew the answer to that, that he would never be ready. But, politics won out when it came to royalty. There was no love in politics.

"As I'll ever be," he responded, before crossing the room to his brother, pulling him into a hug. "Thank you," he whispered into Declan's ear before pulling away. Declan's body stiffened in his arms, but before his brother had a chance to react, Gavin released him and opened the door to his chamber.

Then he walked to his destiny.

GAVIN

$\mathcal{T}$he chanting began, spoken in a language long since forgotten as Gavin walked the corridors toward the courtyard. Old hymns of the covens rang through the air, creating an electricity that rose the hair on Gavin's arms. It was as though everything was on edge. Gavin fished in his trouser pocket for his matchbook and smokes. His fingers fumbled around the loose cigarettes, pulling one out and lifting it to his lips. He opened his matchbook and struck the match to life, lighting the end of the smoke. The sweet taste of cloves eased his troubled mind and the chanting grew louder. Gavin took a few more drags from his cigarette and dropped it to the marble floor, crushing it beneath his shiny black dress shoe.

A set of French double doors sat open before him, leading the way into the courtyard Gavin used to play in as a child, the place where he and Rose had stolen kisses and long talks, a place where he and Lorelei had fallen in love and the same place he'd found out she's sold him out to the coven leaders and his parents. So many memories swirled in his head as Gavin headed out the doors into the yard.

A large, grey stone fountain sat in the middle with statues of the first rulers in an embrace, forever bound together. Water poured from the man's outstretched hand, over top of the pair into a basin below. The same basin that the Alchemist would drop the enchanted rose into. The woman was known as Celeste. No one truly knew which house she came from, but she had enthralled Tiberius Sinclair long ago and the rest was ancient history. She was a grandmother he'd never known, but the love that forever etched her features was something Gavin hoped he could find one day with Rose.

The crowd cheered as Gavin approached and there, beside the Alchemist, stood Rose. She wore a teacup ruby gown that cinched at the waist and hung low on her shoulders, exposing her unmarred alabaster skin to the world. Her blonde hair cascaded down her shoulders in curls and a white daisy crown sat upon her fair head.

She was stunning.

Absolutely *breathtaking*. Gavin's hand reached up to cover his heart. He felt it thundering beneath his fingers. How had he gotten so lucky, with a bride so strikingly beautiful and headstrong? His steps faltered as he looked at her—strong willed, shoulders squared, defiant until the end. He admired her strength.

When her eyes met his, she quickly looked away again as a blush crept into her fair cheeks. Gavin couldn't help but smirk. She was nervous. Because of him, he realized.

When Gavin reached them, the Alchemist turned, the gleam of lowlight shining off his bald, leathery head, and began speaking.

"Gentlefolk of Elirion, today at this most sacred hour on Hallows Day, we gather for a most momentous occasion. A Rose Bound ceremony to tether the souls of our new King and Queen. The magic binding of souls has been a sacred part of our conventry since the dawn of vampires. Such magic has been scarcely witnessed in our life spans, as Kings and Queens live momentous lives. In truth, I have only born witness to two ceremonies. Your mother and father," a nod to Gavin had him gulping down fresh pain at the mention of his parents, "and that of Tiberius and Celeste. They stood before me, five hundred years ago, taking the same oath that Gavin from house Sinclair and Rosalie from house Coston pledge today. I ask that during the Blood Oath that you remain silent in order for our unified pair to pledge their vows to one another."

Gavin's heart raced, thumping wildly in his chest, threatening to break through his ribcage. He wasn't aware of any vows. He hadn't written any and to ask him to speak from his bloodthirsty heart was… *dangerous*. He took in a breath in order to steady his nerves and tuned back into the Alchemist who walked behind the altar and picked up the enchanted Rose.

"Rosalie," he called. "I call you before me to recite the words of Tiberius and Celeste, the binding oath they took to ensure the sanctity and safety of their counterpart. For Gavin will be an extension of you and you of him. What-ever befalls you, is to be done unto him. You must ground him. Cherish him and honor his plans for our nation. Do you accept these responsibilities without reservation?"

"And if I don't?" Rose pondered aloud drawing the ire of her father.

"Rosalie," Zachary snarled from the sidelines. "The Council has spoken." But Rose ignored him.

"But, I do have a choice here, don't I?" she asked the Alchemist. Gavin stood silent; he knew this was a possibil-ity. He knew Rose didn't want this. Hell, he'd given her an out. He hated to admit the tinge of pain he felt at her words.

"You do." The Alchemist hesitated. "But the magic will know your true intentions. It knows all. For your true feelings will be branded onto each of you for all to see. If the foundation is not there, then magic will not take effect."

"Branded?" Gavin asked, slipping from his silent demeanor. No one ever mentioned being branded.

"Every king and queen are physically marked with the symbol of their counterpart. It is not painful but will simply remind you to guard your heart. A sigil of your promise." Rose took several moments in silence. Off in the distance, Gavin heard wind chimes ringing despite the lack of wind.

How peculiar.

"I agree," she responded. Relief flooded Gavin's gut.

"Excellent. Come forth," the Alchemist said. Rose rounded the altar as the Alchemist raised the glass dome that protected the enchanted rose and set it aside, carefully picking up the stem. He whispered something into Rose's ear, quiet enough so that Gavin's vampire ears couldn't decipher the words. He watched as Rose nodded and drew her wrist to her lips, sinking her fangs in. Shakily, Rose positioned her wounded wrist over the rose. Blood poured from where her fangs penetrated her skin, soaking the white petals until they were stained. Liquid oozed down the stem, painting the Alchemist's own pallid tone.

"Repeat after me, *'From the blood of the queen, I give myself over to the great unknown, pledging my life, my loyalty and my soul to my partner. I offer my blood as a sacrifice to you. Soul Bound forever, I tether myself unto thee until the darkness of death calls upon us and together we perish.'*"

"Gavin," Rose said, turning her attention toward him. "Could you please join me?" she asked. Gavin felt his legs move, but it was as if time itself stood still. Then, all too soon, he stood before her, drinking in her beauty as she took his sweaty palms within her own gentle fingers. Blood coagulated at her wrists, the skin closing slowly before Gavin's eyes.

"Gavin," she said again, her voice trembling. "From the blood of the queen, I give myself over to the great unknown, pledging my life, my loyalty and my soul to you, my partner. I offer my blood as a sacrifice to you. Soul Bound forever, I tether myself unto thee until the darkness calls upon us and together we perish." Golden light flooded from Rose as she finished speaking her oath, floating above her in a mist.

"What is that?" Gavin asked, looking from the mist to the Alchemist, who smiled broadly. The magic had worked.

"Her soul," he replied. "Gavin." Rose smiled and looked above her, a look of pure joy overtaking her. She stepped to the side to allow Gavin access to the Alchemist. "I call you before me to recite the words of Tiberius and Celeste, the binding oath they took to ensure the sanctity and safety of their counterpart. For Rosalie will be an extension of you and you of her. Whatever befalls you, is to be done unto her. You must guard her. Cherish her and honor her place at your side. Do you accept these responsibilities without reservation?"

"I accept," Gavin grunted throatily.

The Alchemist leaned in and whispered into his ear, "I'm going to need your blood. Draw enough to soak the rose but not even to induce fainting." Gavin pulled back and looked at the timeless man.

"Vampires don't faint," he stated matter-of-factly. The Alchemist smiled again.

"I've seen many things, Gavin Sinclair, and I can assure you, vampires do, in fact, faint."

Gavin unbuttoned his black sleeve and rolled it up to

expose his wrist without tarnishing the shirt. He lifted his wrist to his lips, grazing his fangs along his skin and clamped down. Pain seared momentarily where his fangs had punctured, filling his own mouth with blood, before easing. The Ripper within him sang. *Sick fucker.* Blood pooled down his chin as he lifted his wrist toward the Alchemist. The enchanted rose was white, unmarred by Rose's offering as if it drank it all in. The Alchemist took his wrist and poured the liquid over the rose, staining it.

"Gavin," his voice boomed, loud enough for the kingdom to hear, "repeat after me, *'From the blood of the king, I give myself over to the great unknown, pledging my life, my loyalty and my soul to my partner and my kingdom. I offer my blood as a sacrifice to you. Soul Bound forever, I tether myself unto thee until the darkness calls upon us and together we perish.'*"

"Rose, Gentlefolk of Elirion and all of Tatum, from the blood of the king, I give myself over to the great unknown, pledging my *life*, my *loyalty* and my *soul* to my partner and my kingdom. I offer my blood as a sacrifice to *you*. Soul Bound forever, I tether myself unto thee until the darkness calls upon me - *us*- and together we perish." Black mist rose above Gavin like a shadow, singing to the Blood Prince within him, calling him to surface. Gavin couldn't see a thing, shrouded by darkness, blinding him.

"Why is it black?" he heard Rose ask.

"All Rippers have a dark soul, my dear. This will be your burden to bear now as well," the Alchemist replied. Gavin looked to him with pure rage.

"Calm yourself, child. Your soulbound mate shall diminish your thirst and steady your heart."

The Alchemist whispered beneath his breath in a language Gavin didn't know and raised his hands, lifting the shadow from the prince's eyes. One hand remained in the air while the other held the enchanted rose, white and pure, once more. He walked toward the fountain and the words he whispered grew louder. Voices swirled within the Alchemist's like an entire clan funneled through him. Male and female, all speaking tongues that Gavin couldn't understand. Gavin's eyes shot to Rose, whose eyes were wide as she mouthed something indiscernible. Then, the Alchemist dropped the rose into the fountain. The water bubbled red, flowing like blood over top of his ancestors and the black and gold mist swirled together above them. Gavin felt the skin on his chest prickle and tore his gaze away from the magic.

His skin was white and hot but did not hurt as a symbol formed above his heart. A rose branded into his skin, its stem forming an infinity symbol. The voices of the Alchemist grew louder still, deafening until the water ran clear and the mist above the prince and Rose fell down around them. Gavin's magical soul prodded at Rose's lips. When she parted them, it soaked into her as she inhaled air. Gavin watched intently. Rose closed her eyes as if the sensation was pleasurable, an expression he would want to draw out of her *later*, if she allowed him.

Before another thought could muddle his mind, Rose's golden pure soul appeared before him beckoning for entry. He followed Rose's lead and inhaled. Bliss filled his senses as her essence absorbed into him. Purity, lighting the darkness within. He fought the urge to moan at the tingling feeling sweeping through his body. A closeness, a bond, he had never felt before. She was as much a part of him as he was hers. Gavin opened his eyes to meet Rose's startling blue gaze. She was studying him. It was as though she was seeing him for the first time. *Truly* seeing him.

Gavin did the same, feeling as if he was just bestowed with the most beautiful queen this kingdom had ever seen. Her hair was luminous, eyes bright, and her pale skin rivaled that of the moon. He felt her intentions, knew her dreams. He knew her heart and most of all, felt an overwhelming love for it. She was—*Perfection.*

Gavin raised his hand to touch Rose, an overwhelming need to feel her energy pulsed through him, but before his fingers met her skin, the Alchemist slouched and fell to his knees. He was drained of energy and looked as if five hundred years had stolen what was left of his soul.

"Kiss her," he croaked. "For the kingdom has its new king and queen." Gavin leaned into Rose, pulling her close to him, feeling as though he'd never let her go. He needed her. Electricity pulsed through him as Rose's soft fingers caressed his face between her palms, looking into his eyes and then darting past him.

"Gavin!" she cried as something sharp pricked at his back. A tiny scream he knew all too well erupted from behind him.

Aurora.

✿

DAHLIA

RED-HOT ANGER LANCED THROUGH DAHLIA AS SHE MOVED swiftly through the Underground dungeons, calling ghouls and shadows alike to her side. Her black stiletto heels clicked and clacked in time with her thoughts.

She was pissed.

No, scratch that, she was *beyond* pissed. Things were not going as she'd planned. She closed her eyes, trying to steady the thrum of dark energy that coursed through her with every beat of her heart. There should not have been a breach, not *yet.* Syphoning magic in glossy black tendrils that streamed from the ghouls and shadows at her side,

Dahlia rounded the corner, heading down the passage that led to her office. It wouldn't take her long to concoct a potion to allow her full shadow-like abilities, something only Limos's truly devoted were able to wield. And god, was she devoted. Dahlia's blood-red lips curled into a snarled grin.

"Be gone," she said without turning around as she headed into her open office and closed the door. She turned, thumbing through the books on her shelves until she found exactly what she was looking for and pulled its spine from her shelf. Dahlia moved to her ruined desk, placing the book down as she searched for the exact spell she'd need until at last, she found it. Dahlia's eyes widened. Magic like this would cost her dearly. Would cost her that which she loved most. Her heart hammered in her chest as a lump formed in her throat. She tried to swallow, nearly choking on saliva. Could she risk it?

Could she risk *him*? Dahlia shook her head, snapping her eyes shut as she sucked in a breath. What other choice did she have? Slowly, she opened her lids and started pulling the nastiest bits of magic she'd collected over the years from jars hidden behind her books. She uncorked one, labelled *Death* and called to the shadow magic she'd pulled from the ghouls, twisting and curling the dark magic between her thumb and forefinger as though she were forming a ball. And then, ever so slowly, she lowered the shadow magic into *Death*.

At first, nothing happened. Black liquid remained unfazed within the jar, but seconds later, it began to fizz. Bile stung at the back of the vampire's throat, stinging, as she forced it back down. Then, Dahlia brought the dank liquid to her parted lips.

I'm so sorry.

Tilting her head back, the liquid moved down her

throat in a gulp, nearly gagging her. Death tasted just as its name stated. Her insides twisted, knotting and curling in on itself. Dahlia bit her lip, stifling the cry on her tongue, but then, her hands began to fade and soon, she was nothing but darkness. There was no pain as a shadow. There was only darkness.

"Interesting," she murmured beneath her breath before bolting for the door. Her legs moved faster than her solid form ever had. And despite not being able to see herself, she noted that she could see the forms of other shadows.

"Misssstresss," a female shadow hissed. "Come with us. Together we will travel under the coat of darknesssss."

"Yes. Let's go."

The shadows showed her the fastest way to move and Dahlia, to her surprise, *enjoyed* moving in this form. She was faster than a vampire, darting in and out of trees, even moving through The Forest of Knowing faster than she ever had before, evading the vagabonds and unsavory characters on her path. A trip that should have taken her days to complete took her merely a few hours.

Soon, Dahlia found herself with Tatum's castle in her view. She could see the Rose Bound ceremony beginning and she knew it had to end there. She hoped Conan had been able to rally his pack and the rebellious humans. She would tell him what was on her mind. She'd say her goodbyes.

Together, they could break Gavin Sinclair, one bone at a time. But magic was tricky, and she didn't know how much time she'd have with Conan before it came to reap its offering. Had Dahlia been in her physical form, she knew she'd be wrecked with sobs. But as a shadow, there was nothing.

She would break Gavin Sinclair, and then, she'd take what was hers. *Elirion.* Dahlia refused to let family ties dissuade her from her goal. If Rose got her in way, she'd destroy her.

Sweeping closer to the edge of the trees, Dahlia saw her shining sister standing at the altar alone. Gavin had not emerged yet. Bells rang announcing the hour and simultaneously, the prince appeared, clad in all black, untraditional to say the least. Leave it to the princeling to shit on tradition. But what did she really expect from a Ripper?

With a thrill of excitement, Dahlia flitted through the remaining trees and ducked in and out of corners along the streets leading up to the fountain. Her path was empty, as presumably everyone was in attendance up ahead. No one would suspect her. In shadow form, she could be anywhere she pleased. Dahlia's red lips curled into a smirk.

They won't know what hit them. She pushed herself faster up the winding roads. Appearing at the edge of the congregation was no great feat, everyone was enamored by the magic the Alchemist spoke of. The sight was awe-inspiring, indeed. The council stood around the altar in glistening white robes, a king and queen at their center. The Alchemist, an immortal being who appeared to be no older than forty, appeared in a red cloak. The light of dusk glistened off of his bald head as he spoke high and fast. Then, he lifted the enchanted rose. The one that should be coated with her blood, *not* her sister's.

She was fit to be a queen. She was ruthless and organized, while her sister was weak and soft-hearted. Dahlia scoffed, watching Rose bite into her wrist. Pain etched her young features. *Weak.* She was so goddessdamned weak. Then, she pulled her fangs away and smothered the rose in her blood. Anger gnawed at Dahlia the longer she watched. Then Gavin did the same. Something shifted within Dahlia. The magic left her exhilarated. Being in the presence of such power was *intoxicating*, and while everyone was feeling the effects, that's when Dahlia knew she would strike. Her own concocted magic was wavering. She could see her form again, flickering in and out. Dahlia kneeled down, pulling the dagger strapped to her ankle and stood, watching the ceremony unfold.

Plan be damned.

She couldn't wait for Conan and his crew. Not when the binding was nearly complete.

She would handle this.

At last, the Alchemist said, "Kiss her. For the kingdom has its new king and queen."

The man had aged significantly and Dahlia knew no more magic would leave the mage tonight. A cool dread laced itself into a tight knot within her belly as Dahlia swallowed. She could do this. She had to do this—for herself... for Limos. Plastering a grin on her face, she swept forward, issuing for the shadows around her to do their assigned jobs. Without a moment of hesitation, they dispersed, fanning out to cover the grounds. Dahlia moved toward the first guard, slipping her blade into his neck. The unknowing guard slipped from her grasp, crumpling to the ground in a bleeding heap. Dahlia nodded to her crew and quietly, they disarmed the guards, moving closer to the ceremony.

Next, was the princess, Dahlia knew this. And when she screamed, Dahlia watched the trance on Gavin break as she moved in behind him and shoved her knife between his shoulder blades, right into the sweet spot of his spine.

"Not so fast, princeling," she snarled into his ear, leaning forward, sucking a tender lobe into her mouth. Her tongue flicked against the soft bit of cartilage and Gavin's body went rigid beneath her blade. "We don't want the little princess to stop breathing now, do we?"

Her form flickered again. She could see the dagger in

her hands. Dahlia's gaze flitted to her sister as Rose's stunned eyes found her own, and in that moment, Dahlia knew chaos was coming. Screams enveloped them all as the shadows all began forming around the courtyard. Ghouls surrounded the covens and human onlookers, brandishing knives, and then, they began taking lives.

Blood pooled around them, running through stony grooves, soaking the plaza. Rose stared, frozen to the spot. Bodies fell one by one. And still, she simply stared into Dahlia's cooling expression.

"Rose," Gavin ground out, his voice rough and sexy to Dahlia's ears, igniting things that only Conan could make her feel. Maybe it was the heady mix of fear in the air, maybe it was the stench of blood, invigorating her primal needs, but in that moment, Dahlia was taken with the prince.

"No wonder you like this one, sister," Dahlia crooned. "Sexy little thing, isn't he?" Rage flashed across the new queen's face, yet, she remained rooted to the spot. A fierce growl penetrated the air around them.

"What's this dark magic you've used on the queen?" Oliver Dawson snapped, fighting his way through the chaos to Rose's side.

"And the mongrel appears, ladies and gentlemen! Oh, I have a surprise for you, dog boy." Dahlia smirked, her red lips solidifying as the potion wore off.

"D-Dahlia," Rose stammered. Dahlia sucked in a deep breath and let out a heady laugh.

"Oh, she does speak!"

"What?" Rose shook her head. "What are you doing here? What are you doing to him? Let Gavin go!"

"What does it look like?" Dahlia snarled, motioning with her gaze to the fights around them. Each council member lunged into action, fighting their way to the shadow ghoul holding Aurora, the last Sinclair princess. But as one member closed in, the ghouls played a game of cat and mouse with the girl, shuffling her around. Each ghoul that held her, wielded a silver dagger to her neck, just as Dahlia had instructed, and the little girl whimpered beneath their hold. If she squirmed any harder, the ghoul would cut her throat. The girl cried out again.

"Leave my sister out of this," Gavin hissed, but Dahlia answered by pushing the dagger harder against Gavin's spine. She leaned in, grazing her lips against his neck, placing small kisses right near his ear and jawline. "You're mine, Sinclair," she purred. "Besides, it seems as though your pet has fucked your wife." This time it was Rose that let out a cry. Gavin tensed before the heiress, snapping his attention from his new bride to his best friend.

"I can smell wolf on you too, Dahlia," he sneered.

"Such a pity," Dahlia whispered. "You would have been a great king, with the proper queen at your side." She pulled away and straightened, as she called out to her sister, "You could have been such a great sorceress, Rose, if only you didn't take that which is mine."

"Fight me, you bitch," Rose snarled. Dahlia's lips curled.

"Fine," she said before clenching her free hand. She felt the darkness around her whirl, tendrils of it pouring into Rose, dropping her to one knee as her fingers closed into a fist.

"Rose," Gavin's low voice said, giving a warning Dahlia knew was much needed. She could see her sister fighting against the black magic and Dahlia knew that it would kill her and end Gavin as well, which was her plan, after all. She wanted the throne with or without Gavin Sinclair. And she would have it. The Prince of Blood's

233

voice was dangerous and gravelly and Dahlia knew if she punished him any more, the Ripper would emerge.

"Let him go and fight me, you coward!" her sister yelled. "You want to fight? Fight magic with magic! Only the true queen will win!" Dahlia's head cocked to the side, taking her sister's words into consideration. She liked those odds. She was, after all, the stronger of the two.

"Game on," she replied, pushing the Prince of Blood away. Her dagger was gone with the flick of her wrist and in its place was darkness.

Complete and utter destruction.

DARKNESS

*L*imos could taste the tang of magic on his tongue. Could smell the ginger of desperation and bloodshed in the air. There was a darkness that sang to him. Electricity pulsed through his veins, filling him with a feeling he hadn't felt since that ill-fated night five hundred years ago.

He should have known falling in love with a human would bring his demise, but, there was a darkness about Celeste that had called to his soul.

The same darkness that called to him now.

Twigs snapped beneath his black shoes as whispers filled the air. So many secrets the trees were filling him in on. Limos stopped and outstretched an arm, rooting Dia in place.

"Wha-" she began, only to silence her tongue with a mere look from him.

"Do you hear that?" he asked, the sing of metal against metal ringing in his ears.

"Hear what?" Dia asked.

"Chaos."

GAVIN

*G*avin stumbled forward, his Ripper tearing to the surface. Red glinted in his vision as the overwhelming need for blood pulled on him. His eyes narrowed on the shadows that swirled around Dahlia's hands, calling to the darkness within him. The demon surged as Gavin bit into his lip and fought. He couldn't let him out. Not yet.

Not.

Yet.

Gavin bit down harder on his lip, splitting the skin, willing the Ripper to the darkest parts of him, but it was no use. The need to kill was too strong. The taste of blood saturated his tongue, clouding any hope he had left of being decent. So many would die tonight. So many innocents. Gavin sucked in a breath, his shoulders slumping in defeat.

There was no more fighting the Ripper... and just when his mind was about to give up, something happened that renewed the spark within him. The spark to hold on. To fight. Golden light burst forth from Rose. And in that instant, he could feel her anger and excitement course through his veins. It was a balance of good and bad all muddled into one being. Rose was amazing. Gavin's heart hammered in his chest as he watched her wield something outlawed in the Tatum, and use it as a weapon.

Move.

He wanted to stand and watch the sisters. Wanted to watch a battle of enchantments as they raced toward one another throwing spelled fists, but he knew the Ripper was right. He needed to move and save his sister. Light burst from Rose's hands forming fireballs which she hurdled toward the eldest Coston daughter. But Dahlia deflected and shot streams of shadows at her sister.

"Gavin, go!" Rose shouted over the ring of death, pushing more light from her hands. Screams echoed through the air as death took from all around him. There was no time to waste. Yes, he was shocked, so incredibly stunned by his newfound bride, but she was right. This was no time to freeze. As the new king, he needed to protect his kingdom. He needed to get Aurora as far away from here as possible.

Gavin glanced around for a brief moment, searching for Declan, finding him fighting off ghouls of his own. Blood coated his brother from head to toe, his sword slick with black blood. His gaze caught Gavin's in a worried panic that was quickly replaced with determination.

Gavin moved toward his brother when six ghouls moved into his path, each one bigger and nastier than the one before. Black, rotten skin hung from their bones, their clothing in tatters, each carrying an array of weaponry meant for his assassination. He took a deep breath and gave in to the Ripper.

Rage, so much built-up rage coursed through Gavin, slamming into him all at once. His vision burned red as the lust for death surged through him. He felt his fangs drip with venom, felt his nails become daggers before he surged forward and tore into ghoul after ghoul. Gore, black as his soul, coated Gavin's hands and painted his already black suit, soaking him to the core. But he wasn't done with just the six. Oh no, he would tear apart each and every ghoul that invaded the palace, until they were destroyed, and then, he'd go after their kingpin.

Palmer.

He'd paid his debt to the ghoul—technically. But Ollie had survived. Was that why the ghouls were after him? And why was Dahlia, heiress to the Underground, teamed up with the ghoul king? If she'd shown up in time, he'd have tethered himself to her. But she's been gone. Was this all his fault?

Gavin launched himself further into the chaos as humans began to break through the barriers and set the courtyard ablaze.

❦

OLLIE

OLLIE DIDN'T NEED TO HEAR GAVIN'S COMMAND—A FLICK of his gaze and a nod was enough to get him moving into action. He rushed into the gore, knowing full well what was rising within the prince. He'd fought for a moment, knowing that the aftermath the Prince of Blood would create would be substantial, but Gavin had given a look to him and that look was all he needed. So, Ollie decided to let the Ripper out to play as he raced toward the ghoul that held Aurora. Her blonde curls were matted in black blood and a silver dagger pressed against her neck. Although the covens had moved into action, fighting against other ghouls, racing to get to the Sinclair princess, Ollie knew he would get there first, until the brigade of humans and wolves burst through the guard barrier into the courtyard. Vampires fought against wolves and humans and ghouls. Blood hurled through the air. The singing of metal against metal rang mixing in time with screams. Ollie knew these wolves, hell, he was supposed to be their alpha, fighting against the people he'd grown to love as a dysfunctional family.

A bob of ruby ran through the crowd causing Ollie's stomach to drop.

No.

No.

No!

Ollie knew that hair, could pick it out from a crowd a thousand times, just as he'd done now. His heart beat fiercely in his chest. Ollie fought against the bubbling emotions rising up within him. His back began to arch and Ollie knew what was coming next. Tears pricked at the corners of his eyes, threatening to spill. Scarlett, his sister, was among the rebels. Why? How? But before Ollie was able to process, another wolf stepped into his path. Dark hair and olive skin, a wolf he'd grown up with and looked up to for the longest time. A wolf he'd called, *brother.*

Conan.

"Moon juice," Conan sneered, throwing the insult at Ollie to get a rise out of him, just as he'd done when they were pups. "What a pleasant surprise."

"Aye, but is it?" Ollie knew his brother had stepped in as the pack alpha in his absence. He knew the stigma that was placed on him for being a deserter, a lone wolf, the repercussions of his actions unfolding before him.

"What the fuck do you want, traitor?" Ollie growled.

"Traitor, aye? I'm not the one who abandoned his pack

in their time of need. Seems to me as though you're the traitor." Anger rippled through Oliver like a riptide in the sea. Conan was right. But to have it thrown in his face...

Ollie's nails pushed into claws as the change began. Bones crunched, forcing him to all fours. He snarled and allowed the transformation to consume him fully until he stood in his true form. His animalistic instincts kicked in and Oliver Dawson, sweet and loveable, became a monster. He lunged for his brother.

Teeth bared and maw dripping with saliva, the urge to spill Conan's blood was strong.

"Fuck you," Conan hissed, rolling to the left. Ollie was on him again, but Conan was faster and bigger. He pushed to his feet and roared into the air as he transformed. Fur blacker than night and striking eyes met Ollie's, filled with hate and bloodlust.

Ollie launched himself again. His teeth sank into fur, drawing blood as Conan let out a yelp. Flesh tore. Blood poured from the wound, soaking Conan's fur as Ollie shook his massive wolf head. Conan snapped at Ollie's throat causing Ollie to leap back and release his brother. Mangled black fur hung from Conan's left flank. There was a reason Oliver was chosen for alpha. Strength was not the only trait deemed worthy of a pack leader. Mercy was as well. Something Conan had never possessed.

I don't want this Conan, Ollie sent his brother, before he dodged Conan's angry snarl. Fangs grazed Ollie's face, leaving behind a nasty red line in his tawny coat. Ollie's maw stung as he opened to retaliate.

You think I give two fucks about what you want, brother? Conan shot back with an audible roar.

Ollie jumped out of the way before Conan could smash into him. They were a sight to behold. Two massive alphas paired off, drawing the notice of those around them, and forcing those nearby to scatter. Teeth clacked against one another, claws shredding through flesh and fur. And then, Conan took his massive paw and knocked Ollie to the ground. The air left Ollie's lungs, leaving him panting. Ollie's heart thundered in his ears, in his chest, trying to break free from his wolf form.

Get on your feet, boy, and fight me, Conan shot at him telepathically. Ollie cringed. He was hurt, blood pooling in his fur, and out of breath. He needed to stall. Just for a moment, just enough to regain himself.

I will fucking end you, he hissed back. *And make you wish you never found me. I will show no mercy. Not anymore.*

I'd like to see you try, pup. Ollie slowly pushed himself to his feet, stumbling as pain lanced through his body. His injuries were taking a toll on him and he still needed to get Aurora to safety. A growl tore from his throat as the two brothers circled one another. Ollie's gaze faltered from his brother. His ears perked with another heartbreaking scream from Aurora, and Ollie knew that he had to end the fight—one way or another. When he turned to look for the princess, he was met with shining hazel eyes and stiffened. She was screaming for *him*. His eyes darted back, but Conan was gone. Ollie crouched, looking in every direction only to see more gore and blood and ghouls around him.

"Lollie!" Aurora screamed again. Ollie turned just as Conan plunged down upon him.

ROSE

Fire rose up on both sides of Rose, licking the skin on the back of her calves, charring them black. She wanted to scream between the burning pain and the magic, but that would exude too much energy, so instead, she bit down on her lip, and kept throwing streams of light at her sister. Sweat slicked her skin and glistened her brow, salty tears streaming down her forehead into the heiress's eyes.

She knew the magic was taking a toll on her. How much longer could she keep it up? For every minute she used it, it took twice as much from her in return. Soon, she would become nothing but a heap of bones on the ground, nothing more than a puppet ready for a puppeteer, but who would pull her strings? Magic was never free, and she'd learned that the hard way, more than once.

Rose summoned more energy, forming white and gold lightning in the center of her palms before hurling them at her sister with all the strength she could muster. "Is-is that all you've got, *your highness?*" Dahlia panted, spitting out the last words as though they had been rotting in her mouth. Her shoulders slumped, showing Rose that she too, was exhausted. But Dahlia had syphoned shadows and dark magic and despite Rose's lightning, the darkness consumed her power, saving Dahlia from utter destruction. Ghouls and wolves and vampires alike all battled around the fiery ring that surrounded the Coston sisters. Gore painted the stones both black and red.

"Stop this!" Rose thundered. "Just stop, Dee! We can talk this out!"

"We have nothing to talk about," Dahlia snarled before unleashing tendrils of darkness at Rose. Rose rolled to the right, narrowly missing the attack aimed at her skull. Stone cracked from where she'd stood moments before, crumbling and sizzling.

"Then why in the goddess' name are you trying to end me?" Rose huffed, pushing to a knee as she hurled another lightning ball.

"Shut up!" Dahlia hissed, flicking her wrist. Rose watched as a shield of darkness enveloped her sister, swallowing the light. How was she supposed to win if Dahlia deflected everything she threw at her? Every attack she issued did nothing but chip away at what remained of her energy before disappearing right before her eyes.

"Give up, Rosalie," Dahlia's singsong voice rang, sailing through the space between them. "Light will never win against the dark, just like you will never win against me."

"She might not win against you alone," a voice chimed from behind Rose as a caramel-skinned bandit clad in tanned leathers stepped to Rose's side. "But perhaps with an entire tribe, she can!"

Rose's eyes widened. "Tora?"

Tora plastered a grin to her beautiful face that told Rose this was no dream or stress-induced hallucination.

"Hey there, fangbanger. Let's kick some ass!" Without any further explanation, Tora pulled the twin daggers from her hips and thrust them in Dahlia's direction. It allowed Rose a second to recoup, enough time for her to catch a breath before summoning lightning to her.

"Remind me to thank you later, bandit," Rose rasped before unleashing all of her power at Dahlia.

"You'll owe me," Tora replied before reaching for her bow and quiver. She knocked a quiver into place. "Widows!" she called, her voice strong and stoic. "Unleash your fury and strike!" She released her arrow.

※

Lorelei

Lorelei had never seen so much blood and chaos in her entire existence. It was true, that for the most part, she'd caused most of the chaos that enveloped her daily life, relishing in the little rumors and lies she spread, but this, this was otherworldly. This was pure terror. Heart thumping and breath hitching in her throat, she raced through the throng of gore and ghouls toward the castle and stables when a shadow emerged into her path, halting the heiress in place.

"G-g-g-going somewhere?" it hissed, materializing before her. A boy, approximately twenty years of age, appeared before Lorelei. His grey skin was taut, his cheeks gaunt as he looked at her with blank dark pupils. Tattered clothing hung from his skeletal figure, the smell of rot suffocating Lorelei where she stood. Bile churned in her stomach, threatening to make an appearance, but Lorelei would not give this boy, this rotting sack of flesh and bones, the satisfaction of making her sick. Instead, she placed a hand on her leather clad hip and raised the other up as if to inspect her black nails.

"That depends," she replied.

"Depp-pp-pendssss on whatt-t?" the shadow ghoul inquired, reaching for a weapon that the heiress couldn't see.

"It depends on if you live another worthless second, maggot!" Declan roared from her side, wielding knives between his fingers. She hadn't heard him emerge. Hadn't even known he'd been flanking her. The last Lorelei knew was that Declan was knee-deep in ghouls. His blades danced from knuckle to knuckle in a show meant to intimidate the shadow.

"Two-ooo against onn-nne is not a fair fightt-tt," the ghoul snarled, exposing his rotten mouth. Her stomach twisted in on itself. Lorelei bit her lip and shot a glance at Declan. A smile brimmed on his lips from ear to ear, flashing pearly white fangs at the ghoul. His eyes were cold, calculating, every bit predatorial as his brother's.

"Do you like to pick on women?" Declan asked' The knife dancing across his knuckles came to a halt and he took a step forward. Shadows covered half of his face, sending a chill down Lorelei's spine. She'd never seen him in this light. Never so... *dangerous*.

"Do you like picking on someone who can't defend themselves?" he pushed, taking another step forward, catching his knife by the hilt. Flicking his wrist back, Declan hurled the knife at the ghoul. Metal hissed through the air. The boy let out a howl as the blade lodged itself in between his ribs, a mark that would have killed a mortal, but not a ghoul. Lorelei steadied herself, preparing for blood to spill, watching as Declan pulled the sword sheathed at his side. "You want to talk about being fair? Then fight me!" he snarled, driving his blade at the ghoul's mangled chest. The ghoul melted into a shadow on the ground, springing up behind Declan. Declan whirled, striking out as the ghoul wielded a sword of his own.

"Go get my sister!" Declan shouted, a note of panic in his voice, fighting off the attack. Lorelei whirled on her heel. If she could get to Demetrius, her noble Pegasus, then she could get out of Tatum and back home where it was safe. But that wasn't going to be the case for Lor.

Declan wanted her of all people to rescue his sister, making something within her chest break. The pleading in his voice echoed in her sensitive ears. She would do what was needed to save the last Sinclair princess. Because Declan had asked. Heat rushed into Lorelei's cheeks at the request, at the thought of doing something for the prince simply because *he'd* asked. But, she couldn't dwell on that now.

Screams echoed down the castle hallway, through the open French doors Gavin had emerged from before the ceremony. It was bloodcurdling and scared and... Lorelei knew that scream.

Aurora. Fuck...

All of her plans fled from her thoughts as the Blood-worth heiress pushed her legs into overdrive and raced down the hall. She would save the last Sinclair princess, even if it meant giving up her own life.

✤

GAVIN

THE RIPPER TORE INTO THE JUGULARS OF GHOUL AFTER ghoul. Bones snapped as necks came free from undead bodies. The stench of burning death filled the Ripper's nostrils, edging him further into oblivion. He watched the bodies perish into ash. Flames licked at his clothing, charring the black suit. Blood painted his pants, his shirt, his face, dripping down his chin. Screams and metal drowned in his ears and for a moment, Gavin, the Ripper, felt nothing.

But the moment quickly faded and with it, Gavin's bloodlust. His body grew heavy and tired, a side effect from the brand etched on his chest. Gavin knew it wasn't he who was tired. No, he was just getting started. But Rose... Her magic nearly gone, her body trying hard as it may, to replenish. But it wasn't enough.

Bandits fought beside vampires, hurling knives and wielding blades better than any swordsman Gavin had met. Better than him. A rain of arrows plummeted from the sky, hitting body after body. Gavin watched, dodging until the last arrow met its target. Bodies dropped to the stones beneath their feet, left and right, ghouls, humans, vampires and wolves. The dead burned around them.

From the corner of his eye, Gavin saw Rose's shoulders slump and from the other, he saw two massive wolves fighting to the death. One, he knew, was Ollie. But the other? He had no idea. All he did know was that the black wolf had ambushed his mate and was going in for the kill.

He had to choose.

Rose or Ollie?

His heart told him Ollie, but his soul told him Rose. Gavin shook his head. He didn't have *time* to think. Death could be dealt in a single second. So who to choose? Gavin saw the bandit leader step in front of Rose, pulling more arrows from her back, knocking them back into her bow. Squaring her shoulders, Tora took up a fighting stance against Dahlia. Gavin turned his attention to Ollie.

Ollie dropped to the ground, a snarl on his maw as the black wolf loomed overhead. Teeth bared, the wolf reeled for the kill. Gavin moved faster than he ever had before, pushing back into his Ripper. Fangs dripped with venom. Bloodlust in his eyes, Gavin barreled into the wolf, driving his shoulder into its side. Pain radiated up his neck, a sickening crack sounded from his socket, but the Ripper within him kept the hurt at bay. The wolf beneath him snarled and turned his neck to snap at Gavin, but the Ripper merely smiled before plunging his deadly fangs deep into the wolf's neck.

⁂

LORELEI

LORELEI KNEW SHE WAS ON HER OWN AS SHE QUIETLY raced through the castle halls, listening for any sign of Aurora, but everything around her was silent. An uneasy feeling crept into her gut as she pushed onward. The princess could be anywhere in the massive fortress. Lorelei moved stealthily through the halls, placing one booted foot in front of the other. A snap here, a crack there, had her whirling on her heels perched for a fight.

The double doors behind her slammed shut, freezing the Bloodworth heiress in place. She whipped toward the door that faced the end of the grand foyer, only to find the space empty. A shiver wracked down her spine, hot breath at her neck, her ears...

"Come to die?" it asked. The voice was neither male nor female. It was simply there, breathing hot plumes of moisture down her neck. Lorelei gulped. She had no weapons, nothing to fight with but her hands. Her knuckles curled into fists.

"Where's the princess?" she asked, rooted in place, voice strong though nerves wreaked havoc within her body.

"Dead," the voice slithered out.

"I don't believe you," Lorelei whispered. Her breath hitched in her throat, chest heaving, burning. The words couldn't be true.

"Such a pretty thing you are," the voice hissed. "Master would be pleased to have you." Wisps of fingers caressed Lorelei's cheek, her hair, moving strands aside.

"Where is the princess?" she asked again, digging her nails into her palms. The sting was enough to keep her in check. She wouldn't let the phantom have the satisfaction of seeing her break. Not now.

"Dead!" it snarled.

"You lie!" Lorelei snapped, turning to face her phantom. But nothing was behind her. "Quit hiding from me you son of a bitch!"

"Help!" Aurora screamed. Her voice echoed around the heiress as she ran, pushing her body to its limits. Chest thundering, blood racing, Lorelei ran with conviction in her heart and fire in her veins, leaving the assailant before her in the shadows.

Aurora was seated in a small wooden chair, her hands and feet bound to the legs when Lorelei found her. Tears smeared down her face, joining the blood that painted the young princess's dress black and red. She didn't know where the shadow ghoul was, if it was watching her or out gathering friends for its sick, twisted games, but Lorelei wasn't ready to find out. She snapped the half-assed tethers within seconds and pulled the young girl into her arms, caressing her head as she held her close. Sobs rocked the young princess, pulling on Lor's heartstrings.

"Shhh," she cooed. "It's going to be okay. I've got you and we're going someplace where the bad guys can't reach us," she said. She lifted the girl up and bound for the stables. They made their way to the door as the shadows consumed the path they had just taken.

DEMETRIUS STOOD IN HIS STABLE, WHITE WINGS TUCKED TO his back as the two approached. A whinny on his lips let Lorelei know he was unharmed and unfazed by the commotion all around. The heiress stole inside and kneeled down in the hay that covered the floor.

"I'm going to put you down, little duckie. Have you ever flown before?" she asked the princess. Aurora shook her head, throwing her hands over her ears as another scream penetrated the air. Lorelei pulled her hand away and looked the girl straight in the eye.

"Just focus on me. You and me. We're getting out of here and going someplace safe. Don't listen to what's going on out there, you hear me?" Aurora nodded and Lorelei pushed herself up and began readying the Pegasus for travel.

"Lor." Aurora's voice shook. "They're coming." Her hazel eyes widened in horror as the shadows crept in around the stables. Lorelei moved quickly, pulling the Pegasus from his stall into the open. Aurora *oohed* and *ahhed* at him, patting him gently on the snout before Lorelei hoisted her onto the creature's bare back. Her eyes darted to the door, seeing the darkness increase around them. Quickly, Lorelei bit into her finger and wrote a message on the stable door.

I have her. We're safe. -Lor

Then she moved back to the steed and pulled herself up behind the princess.

"Just you and me, little duckie," Lorelei whispered before she took hold of the reins and kicked Demetrius into overdrive. He plowed forward through the stable doors, taking to the sky.

"Take us home, boy," Lorelei said, patting the beast as they rose in the air. "Take us away."

ROSE

*D*arkness tunneled Rose's vision as she fell to her knees. Her magic was gone and her strength, soon to follow. Rose wasn't typically one to give up, roll over and die, but in that moment, she wondered if it would just solve everything. Dahlia wanted the throne. She wanted Gavin, despite having Conan. She wanted power and greed and all things that would make her the worst ruler Elirion would know. But those reasons were exactly why Rose couldn't give up. Why she couldn't just roll over and die. And then, Tora had stepped in front of her. Battered and bloodied, she stood wielding her arrows against her sister.

The bandit leader's chest heaved, sucking in smoke and rot in the air, choking her lungs. And Dahlia, cloaked in shadows, only snickered.

"Your toothpicks will do nothing against the darkness," she sneered. "Give up. Defeat is already on your doorstep. Do you hear the bells ringing for you?"

"Fuck you, vamp bitch," Tora snarled, charging with the Widows from all sides toward the dark heiress. Arrows flew through the air, raining down on Dahlia. Rose's vision blurred, she was fading fast, the darkness taking her. Her head swam as her body grew heavier by the second. She felt hands on her back, strong hands hoisting her up over a shoulder.

"You're going to die, bitch," the male voice snarled, but Rose had no strength to fight back. "I'm going to watch the light fade from your pretty eyes before the goddess takes me." Rose opened her mouth to scream for Gavin, for Ollie. Fuck, for anyone. But no sound came out. Something hot and sticky soaked through her dress, the familiar and delicious tang of copper filling her nostrils.

Blood.

※

GAVIN

"PUT. HER. DOWN," THE RIPPER SEETHED. SEEING ROSE slumped over the wolf's shoulder fueled the hatred pumping through Gavin's veins. There was so much darkness and bloodshed and hate. Oh goddess, did he relish the hate that hung heavy in the air. His nostrils flared, smelling the tang of death. Gavin's vision was a red haze.

"Or what fanger?"

"Or I'll kill you before the venom does," The Ripper replied. The wolf before him curled his lip on his maw, half-beast, half-man the creature stood holding that which was his. Its claws curled, tearing into his queen's dress, breaking skin on her milky thighs. The smell permeated the air, smothering Gavin's senses. His body went rigid, eyes narrowing on the wolf, ready to strike. Ready to kill...

"Oh, I'm quaking in my boots," the wolf retorted. The

Ripper's brows flashed, his muscles screaming to end the beast when—

"Gavin," Rose rasped, her throat raw and burning. "Let them take me."

"No," he said.

"They have Aurora. They'll kill her. Let them take me, please..." Rose said again, mustering whatever energy she had left. Her voice still trailed off weakly.

"No," Gavin repeated. "I won't let them take you or her."

"Time's up," the wolf sneered, shooting a look at Dahlia Coston. Gavin's gaze flicked to her as well.

"Fine," Dahlia snarled from her position amongst the bandit women, curling her fingers as she held them frozen in dark webs of power. One hand remained raised as the other began weaving through the air. Tendrils of darkness curled forming balls of abysmal black. They hovered, vibrating with power before barreling toward the Prince of Blood. The Ripper moved, barely dodging the dark magic. Bones snapped, stones cracked and blood pooled in rivers at their feet. There was so much blood... so much death. Dahlia would kill every last one of them. Gavin knew it and so did Rose. Fear gripped at his insides, raw and primal, clawing its way up. The Ripper paused, feeling Rose's terror well up within him, the bond between them ever present.

A scream, guttural in nature erupted behind Gavin. He whirled, eyes widening in horror as another ball of shadows pummeled into Tora. There was nowhere for her to escape. The darkness plowed through her, dropping the bandit leader like a sack of potatoes to the ground. Scarlett liquid ran from parted lips as the life faded slowly from the woman's eyes.

Gavin gulped back the lump forming in his throat, the

demon within him giving way to his queen's emotions. A cry to Gavin's left captured his attention. He whirled, watching as his best friend, mangled, beaten and bloodied race forward, dropping himself before the girl, shielding her body with what was left of his. Tora's dark eyes were wide, staring into nothing. Had death taken her quickly? Or was it here to play some cruel sick joke on them all?

"Give up the throne, Gavin," Dahlia called, forming another sphere with her fingers. Gavin had never witnessed such sorcery. There was a reason it was outlawed and this was why. His eyes shifted from Dahlia to Rose still hunched over the dying wolf's shoulder and back to the bandit lying in a pool of ruby blood. Ollie pushed the girl onto her back and placed an ear to her chest.

"She's alive," Ollie murmured. "Barely."

"After everything that you've done, do you really think I'd hand the kingdom over?"

"Yes."

"Then let me clarify this for you, Dahlia. I won't give you the throne," Gavin growled.

"Then that sweet little sister of yours, dies," Dahlia stated nonchalantly. Gavin knew he couldn't give up the throne, despite finding himself in the stickiest of situations. He needed time, which was far from being on his side.

He needed to think.

❦

Ollie

Life.

Ollie saw life flash before his eyes. Not his own, of course, but Tora's and Rose's. His body trembled, fear pooling in his gut, twisting and curling in on himself as he looked from one woman to the other, both dying. Rose was slumped over his brother's shoulder like a sack of potatoes, her body weak and her spirit quickly fading. He knew Gavin could feel it in the brand and had to do something unless he wanted to die. Gavin had stepped up to the plate, facing off with Conan and Dahlia.

But Tora, the girl who had spared his life more than once, laid before him, with death at her doorstep. The wolf knew he had a choice to make. Let sweet death pull her from this world or save her with a bite. Though it was true that Ollie had never imprinted on someone before, he knew that if he bit Tora and saved her life that he would forever be hers. The change didn't come without a price, leaving no room in his heart for Rosalie Elena Coston.

Ollie reached out to whatever goddess was listening and sent up a silent prayer for guidance and forgiveness before he pulled Tora's wrist to his mouth. He peppered a kiss to her supple skin before curling back his lips and biting down. He knew she would likely skin him alive when she woke, yet, he couldn't find it in himself to let her die. Not when there was something he could do about it.

Her blood sang to him, burning his eyes a brilliant blue and casting his life force into her. Tora lay unmoving before him. Her full lips cut and bleeding still looked so enticing, so full of smart remarks and life. Tora was the embodiment of what life meant for the wolf. Wild and free. Untamable by society.

When the fire within her was snuffed, the only thing Ollie could think to do was rekindle it. And if that meant an eternity of her animosity, that was something he could live with. As long as she was breathing and snarky, he could deal with the consequences. He'd only lament her anguish at being the thing she seemed to hate.

Pulling back from her to fully look her in the face, Ollie

felt the connection growing within him. Something primal and protective. A bond to be molded however one saw fit. She'd unleash hell upon him and he wanted her to have a safe place to slice him into tiny pieces. Her chest began rising and falling once again, giving Ollie the sign he needed to move her.

Scooping the wounded leader into his arms, Ollie looked to Gavin, whose eyes had not left his bride. Rose looked so small, thrown over Conan's arms, growing heavier with each passing second. Ollie knew that Gavin's venom was slowing the alpha. Taking Conan's strength from him, searing his life force away bit by bit. Gavin turned his attention over to Ollie.

"Get her to safety, Oliver. Take her and her clan to Auntie Mo. She'll know what to do. She'll keep her safe. Just get everyone as far away from here as you can, brother." Gavin spoke with resolve. Ollie's eyes widened. Gavin never used his full first name.

That could only mean one thing.

"Gavin, think about this," he warned.

"Go. Now," Gavin snarled. Ollie knew that voice. That sinister, authoritative voice that would not be argued with. So he cradled Tora to his chest and with one last look at Rose and Gavin, the wolf bolted for the castle, trusting the Widows would follow and with them, any sane person left alive.

＊

Gavin

HER HEART WAS SLOWING, BEATING LESS EACH MINUTE THAT passed. Seeing her helplessly in the enemy's arms drove him mad in a way he never knew he could experience.

Loathing his inability to relieve her suffering, Gavin stood there coated in gore and stared at his bride in the arms of a dying werewolf; Dahlia flanking its side.

"Well, wasn't that sweet," Dahlia drawled, studying her nails.

"Give her to me, Dahlia." Gavin's voice bordered on manic.

"I think not, little princeling." Dahlia strode forward and grabbed a handful of Rose's tangled blonde curls. The prince wasn't sure when the wolf had moved away from him, but he stood close to Dahlia and her protective shadows. "I always did hate these curls," she hissed. Rose whimpered, not able to resist when Dahlia pulled her head to stare Gavin in the face. Dahlia dropped her grip sending Rose's head lulling to the side with a painful bounce.

Only longing colored her eyes. He feared if she closed them, they would never reopen. His one reprieve was that Rose was not afraid. Fear, along the bond, had shifted to acceptance and a steely resolve that rivaled his own. Gavin pushed as much strength as he could to his bride, his love, to his life, hoping it would be enough to sustain her. He'd afford her every ounce of his being if it meant her suffering would end. He felt the ache in his bones, as if they had been snapped and shattered into a million shards. Magic had drained her so completely that her body had begun to deteriorate.

He felt the pull, the unending need to be with her. So this is what the Alchemist meant by soul bound, forever anchored to one another. His heart beat within her. And if he was being honest with himself, it always had.

Whores and gambling filled a void when he'd cast himself out and left behind the only woman to truly know him. She'd have helped him, had he only asked. She would have helped him defy the world.

But he'd given up.

Thought he loved another.

He would *not* give up now.

"Dahlia, release her."

"Oh, I think Daddy and I have better and bigger plans for our little sorceress."

Daddy? Realization swept through Gavin like a tidal wave. *Fucking Coston.* That skeevy motherfucker had orchestrated the entire thing, from Dahlia's disappearance to his parents' murder to having Rose on the throne. His parents murder...

A tingling numbness crept through Gavin, slinking into his bones as he sucked in a deep breath. He swallowed, his mouth dry, his tongue suddenly parched. A single tear pricked his eye, spilling over and down his cheek as his fingers curled into fists.

Mother...

Father... I'm so sorry.

Dahlia patted a sickly looking Conan on the back. "Let us depart, my sweet. We have what we came for."

"Dahlia!" Gavin screamed, lurching forward as shadows and ghouls rose to cover the trio.

"G-Gavin..." Rose reached for him as he tore into decaying flesh, fighting his way toward her, extending his own hand.

"Ah ah ah! Can't have you following us now, can we?" Dahlia swirled her pointer finger, sending him flailing in circles with stone encasing his feet.

"Dahlia!" Gavin wailed again. She smirked over her shoulder at him, satisfied.

Too satisfied.

"Gavin, it's alright..." Rose's voice was weak, so low only his vampire hearing could pick up her words. "I-I love you..."

"Rose!" Gavin roared, fighting with all his might to reach her, to touch her. She smiled sadly, silver tears lining her eyes, before vanishing along with her sister. "Rose! No! Goddess be damned!" Gavin screamed, bending to yank at the stone cementing him in place. It wouldn't budge. "Rosalie! I will come for you!" he choked as his emotions flooded up toward the surface. Power erupted around Gavin Sinclair. Pure, raw, inexhaustible power. It ripped the earth apart, allowing Gavin free rein of his legs. And with his freedom, Gavin rained bloody hell down upon the ghouls and all those who crossed his path.

GAVIN

S moke billowed from the carnage in the courtyard. Bodies burned and the smell of charred flesh hung heavily in the air. The Rose Bound ceremony was certainly something that would go down in infamy with Gavin. Sharp stabbing pain radiated through Gavin's chest, the reminder that he'd failed Rose.

Standing alone in the plaza, having been left the ruins to clean up, Gavin sank to his knees. Tears sprang to his tired eyes, staining red down his alabaster cheeks. He sat alone for what seemed like an eternity. Darkness swept across the sky melding with early morning rays. The fight had lasted the entire night. Gavin pounded the stone beneath him with his fists, the tears and the failure flowing from him as footsteps echoed behind him.

"Gav," Declan gasped, clutching at his knees as though to catch a breath before sizing up his destroyed older brother. "The Rebellion doesn't have Aurora. She and Lorelei made it to the Bloodworth Manor safely." Gavin looked to his brother.

"The Rebellion has Rose. They have my life in their

fucking hands, Dec." Declan nodded, swallowing as he righted himself. Silently, he held out his hand to Gavin. Gavin took it and was pulled to his feet.

"Then we'll just have to give them a reason to keep her alive."

To be continued...

ABOUT J.R. WALDEN

 Wolves, fae, vampires and witches are only a few of J.R.'s favorite things. She also enjoys riding horses, beach trips, and spending time with her husband and fur babies.

ABOUT J.J. MARSHALL

When J.J. isn't slumming with outcasted princes, hunting down sea witches or saving mankind from a zombie invasion, you can usually find her nose deep into a book or on adventures with her husband, friends, and furbabies.

Printed in Great Britain
by Amazon